Stories of Crime & Detection

Volume Two

Murder in the Family

James Ronald

Edited by Chris Verner

 Moonstone Press

This edition published in 2023 by Moonstone Press
www.moonstonepress.co.uk

Introduction and About the Author © 2023 Chris Verner

Murder in the Family originally published in 1936 by John Lane.
The Monocled Man originally published in 1931 by The Age.
The Second Bottle originally published in 1945 by Liberty Magazine.

ISBN 978-1-899000-68-5
eISBN 978-1-899000-69-2

A CIP catalogue record for this book is available from the British Library
Text designed and typeset by Moonstone Press
Cover illustration by Jason Anscomb

Royalties from the sale of this book will be donated to MND Scotland, who fund ground-breaking MND (motor neurone disease) research and world-class clinical trials to combat an uncommon condition that affects the brain and nerves, and causes weakness that gets worse over time, eventually resulting in death.

Contents

INTRODUCTION

This second volume of *James Ronald, Stories of Crime and Detection* contains a novel, a novelette, and a short story.

Murder in the Family is considered to be one of the finest detective novels you are likely to read, first published by John Lane in 1936. There was a U.S. hard cover edition published by J. B. Lippincott Company, Philadelphia, in 1940. The story was published by Hodder & Stoughton in July 1949. The novel is dedicated to the Aleys, Ronald's literary agents.

The same story is also titled *The Murder in Gay Ladies*—an abridged paperback edition, Mercury Mystery No.172, Mercury Press 1939. Another abridged paperback was published by Belmont Books in 1964. An earlier serialised version, by King Features Syndicate, appeared under the title *Trial Without Jury*.

The story concerns the murder of a wealthy woman:

Stephen Osborne has just lost his job, not a good one and not one he particularly enjoyed. But at 50-some years of age in the Depression era and with no savings, he doesn't know how he's going to provide for his large family except by asking his sister, a wealthy woman, to help him financially. Unfortunately, Octavia Osborne is a most unpleasant person. During her annual visit to Stephen's home, she not only refuses to help but tells the family that she is writing all of them out of her will. Bad timing on her part, for while she is sitting in a room with her niece, who is engrossed in a book, someone comes in and chokes her, causing death by heart failure.

Murder in the Family was made into a film, released in February 1938 for 20th Century Fox Productions. Directed by Albert Parker, it starred Barry Jones, Jessica Tandy and Evelyn Ankers.

The second story is a novelette, *The Monocled Man*. One of James Ronald's earliest works, the story is a fast-moving, tongue in cheek mystery with American 'pulp fiction' overtones. Chicago gangster Pete Carponi and his associates, 'Shorty', 'Squiffy' and the alluring 'Cincinnati Sadie', are transported to London in pursuit of 'The Dude' and a stolen diamond: "A harsh voice came to him from the other end of the wire. "Is that 'The Dude'?" it demanded. "This is Carponi. Say, you poor fish, don't kid yourself. You're fooling with dynamite and you're liable to get hurt any minute now. If you don't 'come across' right now, you'll be sorry. You got 'Squiffy' but we'll get you and get you good."

The Monocled Man was published by Gramol in 1933 (Mystery Novels No.10). However, the story is mentioned as previously written in *The Age*, Melbourne, Australia 1931, and *The Irish Independent,* Dublin, Republic of Ireland, January 1932, and so was written before 1931 and most likely serialised. This is the exact same story as *The Gentleman Crook* published in 1935 by Arthur Gray (Books) Ltd and Gramol Mystery Novels No.42, under Ronald's pseudonym, Michael Crombie.

The final piece in this volume is a short story, *The Second Bottle*. Tense and suspenseful, the story takes place in a diner in the US during a cold hard winter. It was first published in *Liberty Magazine*, 18 August 1945, and then in *Murder for the Millions: A Harvest of Horror and Homicide* (anthology of eight stories) ed. Frank Owen, Frederick Fell, New York, 1946. It is also to be found in *Horror and Homicide*, No. 5 (another anthology of eight stories) published by Checkerbooks, New York 1949, and *Famous Short Stories* (stories from *Liberty Magazine*) ed. Frank Cheney Platt, Signet, 1966.

ABOUT THE AUTHOR

James Jack Ronald, to give his full name, was born 11 May 1905, in North Kelvinside, Glasgow, Scotland. He was the son of James Jack Ronald, a Chartered Public Accountant, and Katherine Hamilton Ronald. He was educated at Hillhead High School, Glasgow, established in 1885.

Until he was five, James Ronald says he was chubby, happy, and irresponsible; but in 1911, his sixth year, he was run over by an automobile causing a very real morbidity to creep in. For ten years following the accident he suffered recurrent dreams about a wheel that became larger and larger as it turned faster and faster. He was invalided over a long period during which, with his mother Catherine's encouragement, he enjoyed a prodigious amount of reading. He later claimed he owed his literary gift and resultant career to this near-fatal automobile accident, which caused him to change from a sunny little extrovert to a cloudy introvert.

When he was fourteen he wrote an account of the accident, setting down all the details in a somewhat light vein, not forgetting to note that the candy he had purchased with such delight on that foggy morning was found sticking to the wheels of the car as he was being carried off. The piece won him first prize for composition and congratulations from the masters at the school and even the headmaster wished him well, but that did not prevent corporal punishment for his appalling handwriting. He was called into the headmaster's office, but kept waiting so that everybody knew that he, James Ronald, was going to receive a beating from the headmaster. This injustice obviously affected him very deeply, because it remained with him all his life, and crops up in interview after interview:

> After all, I taught myself to read before going to school and could see no reason for accepting a beating because they failed to teach me how to write, so I bolted.

In a spirit of rebellion against repeated punishments for bad handwriting for compositions for which he invariably got an 'A', Ronald came home from school one day announcing he would never return. It was time to leave. His mother Catherine was understandably distressed, concerned her elder son leaving school at such a young age would diminish his career prospects. Aware of the scarcity of jobs just then in Glasgow, she told him he could only stay away from school if he remained active in some useful employment, making it clear she would not condone an idler in the family.

Within three days James Ronald was an errand boy for the *Glasgow Evening News*, a paper into which he had smuggled a poem some months earlier. But there was 'no writing, nothing editorial' in his set up and he thoroughly disliked it and lost the job. He found another post immediately with the *Glasgow Sunday Mail* and kept this one until he printed his own rival paper on the office mimeograph. He broke the machine and, failing to cover his tracks by leaving a sheet in the copier, he was fired. Then came a dozen jobs, including one with an art dealer for whom he gilded statues and washed windows. His mother told him, 'It is no disgrace to wash windows, James, but it is a disgrace to wash them like that.'

By the age of seventeen, James Ronald had run through all prospective employers in Glasgow, including every newspaper.

He felt the need of open space—'a lot of it'—and after various and sundry abortive departures, finally won grudging permission to seek his fortune in the New World.

For some reason, Chicago stuck in the mind of the young Ronald as a magic word. He became determined to travel to the United States of America. The main method of crossing the Atlantic Ocean in the 1920s was by steamship and ocean liner. The passengers aboard the *SS Saturnia* included seventeen-year-old James Ronald, who arrived at his destination on 6 December 1922, at the Port of Québec, an inland port located in Québec, Canada. From there he continued his journey across the Great Lakes to Chicago, Illinois, United States. He managed to survive in Chicago; the fastest-growing city in world history, with a flourishing economy approaching three million people, attracting huge numbers of new immigrants from Eastern and Central Europe. Ronald stayed in Chicago for five years, wanting to write, but unable to afford the time because he was forced to earn money to live. He was taken on and fired from a variety of jobs with monotonous regularity. Like his experiences in Glasgow, he exhausted all potential employers, dabbling in some forty jobs ranging from short-order cook and dishwasher to muslin salesman; from dance promoter and theatre manager to washing dishes again in a Greek restaurant. He edited ten trade journals at one time for a Chicago publisher; and gave new life to a women's religious magazine. A chain-smoker, he confessed slyly to have worked for the Anti-Cigarette League, his excuse being 'a man must eat don't you know'—at that time eating being the only philosophy he could afford to practise. It was in the Windy City that he learned about life.

Working in the U.S as 'a visitor' to avoid immigration may have caught up with Ronald because, in 1927, he returned to Britain on a more permanent basis, and secured a well-paid job with an English newspaper chain, and a promise of future advancement. However, during his first holiday in the job, a car accident disrupted this promising career trajectory. Whilst driving a small open two-seater Rover 8, Ronald was struck by a two-ton truck and thrown out against the radiator of another vehicle. Left with a broken hip and temporarily crippled (and without the newly acquired job), he settled down to write.

Ronald's writing developed in three stages. First, he hammered out serializations and short stories which were syndicated in newspapers, both at home and abroad; and a number were also published in obscure pulp magazines. Some stories then became lost and forgotten and this has unfortunately contributed to a lack of recognition for an impressive body of work. These early narratives were very difficult to track down, but searching has provided me with an enjoyable and rewarding task—a treasure hunt for lost tales. This was not made any easier because many of these stories were published under pseudonyms; Peter Gale, Mark Ellison, Kenneth Streeter, Alan Napier, and even women; Cynthia Priestley and Norah Banning—in addition to known pseudonyms Michael Crombie and Kirk Wales. Those I have discovered have all been gathered together for republication in this series.

A second writing stage followed; the full-length mystery stories which have made him so popular with Golden Age of Detection aficionados. They are out-of-print, elusive to find, and first editions are very expensive.

Finally, late in life, James Ronald embarked on his Dickensian-style life drama novels. He received enthusiastic praise for his ingenuity, freshness, and sharp sense of humour by many critics and writers of the time, such as August Derleth. Orville Prescott, the main book reviewer for *The New York Times* for 24 years, called James Ronald 'a born novelist', and that he 'has in full measure the two basic drives which inspire a writer of fiction—the urge to create characters and to tell stories about them. Mr. Ronald does both naturally, directly and well.' His work received praise and has been compared to William de Morgan, H. G. Wells, Rudyard Kipling, J. M. Barrie, and Somerset Maugham.

James Ronald is a writer who has not gained the long-term recognition he deserves. His work has received high praise for his ingenuity, freshness, and sharp sense of humour by many critics and writers of the time and current enthusiasts, highlighting him as one of the leading storytellers of the day, yet barely anything has been republished since his death in 1972. I hope the reader will enjoy these imaginative and entertainingly written stories as much as I have collecting them.

Chris Verner
Berkhamsted, Buckinghamshire, UK
April 2023

MURDER IN THE FAMILY

STEPHEN OSBORNE CAME out of the office building in which he had been employed for twenty-four years and walked slowly along the grey, sunless canyon which is Grave Street, the main business thoroughfare of Brancaster, that important Midland city. He walked with an unnatural stiffness, as though mind and body were concentrated on the problem of keeping himself erect. Passers-by turned to stare after him. It was a bit thick, they felt, to be as drunk as that at three o'clock in the afternoon.

He did not look like that sort. He looked like a scholar, a dreamer. Tall and thin, about fifty years of age, he had rather a fine face with a high forehead, an aquiline nose and a sensitive mouth—or perhaps it was only a weak mouth. The dark hair at his temples was sprinkled with silver. He wore a shabby blue suit which had been carefully brushed and pressed and although his shoes had seen a lot of wear they shone bravely. Hundreds of foggy rainy Brancaster days had darkened the grey felt of his hat, but it boasted a new band and showed signs of cleaning—not that anything can clean off Brancaster rain and Brancaster fog. No, he was not the usual drunkard by any means. He looked as though he had too much self-respect for that.

Of their own accord Stephen's feet led him round the first turning into Rundle Street, through which he passed nightly on his way to the station. The Labour Exchange was in Rundle Street and outside it a line of men shuffled and lounged while they waited their turns to draw the dole.

Some of them kept their eyes on the pavement, ashamed of this advertisement of their poverty; some stared at those who passed with a boldness that mocked sympathy; some seemed oblivious to everything but the door at the head of the queue. One ragged soul with frayed cuffs and patched elbows was engrossed in a racing newspaper; another was telling a funny story to his neighbour; a fourth was paring his nails with a penknife. Here a clean collar and polished shoes told of a fight against odds to keep up appearances; and there a scrubby chin, a soiled muffler, and boots caked with mud confessed the hopeless apathy of the derelict who owned them. No two faces were alike. Cheerful, callous, anxious, listless, bitter, defiant: each expressed an attitude to life, and only hope was absent. There was little hope for an out-of-work in Brancaster. The city lives on cotton and cotton is a decayed industry. Every fourth man in the city was unemployed. Stephen remembered something he had heard one shabby man saying to another in a crowded tramcar: "To lose your job these days, mate, is to be out of work for life."

Usually, Stephen looked the other way when he passed the Labour Exchange queue, but this afternoon his eyes travelled along it, resting on each face in turn. He had a new interest in this out-of-work army, a new horror at its fate—for a few minutes ago he had joined it.

"These are trying times, Osborne," his employer had said regretfully. "We're losing trade right and left...turnover a third of last year's...profit cut to the bone on the business that's left... Lord knows where it'll end...got to retrench or go under...no fault to find with your work...others in the same boat...we can manage without you immediately if you wish to be free to look for another post...cashier will give you a cheque for two month's salary...an excellent reference, of course..."

Stunned and bewildered, Stephen had put on his hat and

wandered out into the street. Mile after mile of unfriendly pavement he tramped, neither noticing nor caring where his leaden feet were taking him, and as he drifted he took stock of himself.

"We can manage without you immediately…" That stung. It stung because it was true. For twenty-four years he had served the firm of Samuel Padbury & Son to the best of his ability and yet it could manage without him at a moment's notice. His work would be parcelled out among the other clerks, who would have a little more to do than before, and that was all the difference his departure would make.

A poor recommendation to offer another employer. If others with better qualifications than his could search for work year after year in vain, what hope was there for him? He had little initiative, no confidence in meeting and talking to strangers. He did not know how to go looking for work. In all his life, he had held but one job, the one he had just lost; and it had been obtained for him through the influence of a friend.

His qualifications were few. A public-school education, three years at Cambridge, four years of idling in London, twenty-four years of clerical drudgery. Drudgery? Yes, that was what it had been; and he had hated every minute of it, although he had tried not to let Edith know. It would have hurt her to realise how bitterly he loathed the office to which he had been condemned when he married her.

Edith! How was he to tell her! And—Good God!—how were they to live? They had never been able to save. How could they, with five children to feed, clothe, educate? They had less than ten pounds in the bank; and the cheque for two months' salary, another fifty odd pounds, would not last long. When it was gone—*what?*

Stephen ground his teeth. He would find another job. He *must*. But even as he swore it, he realised that he could not hope for anything like his former salary of three hundred and fifty a year. And even that had been barely sufficient for his family's needs. A smaller salary would mean that Michael would have to go to work at once and probably Dorothy and Ann as well. Perhaps he had no right to have other plans for them, to want to see his elder son a doctor, to rebel at the thought of his daughters working in offices. Probably they should have been given an early start in the lifelong business of earning a living, like the children of most men whose financial positions were similar to his own. But the only sweetening in the bitter cup of his twenty-four years of drudgery had been the aspiration to better things for his children. And at the back of his mind there had been the thought of Octavia's money, not for himself, but for them. In the end it must come to them; there was no one else to whom she could leave it.

Thinking of his sister, Stephen frowned. '*One day you'll come crawling back to me, begging for help…*' Octavia had said that, twenty-four years ago. And now he was about to prove her right. He would have to go to her and ask her to help him. Almost he would rather die than do it. But life is not as easy as that. You don't die. You go on living. And to live you must have money, for the prime concerns of life are not love, hate, pride, and passion, but rent, rates, food and clothing.

After all, the quarrel with Octavia was a thing of twenty-four years ago. They had been on fairly friendly terms with her for twenty years and she visited them every summer. True, she had never done anything for them, but Stephen had never asked her—and she liked to be asked. Even when his finances were at their lowest ebb, Stephen had not approached her. To have done so would have seemed disloyal to Edith, who had been the innocent cause of that ancient quarrel.

This was different. This was not financial stringency but dire necessity. It would not be easy to approach her (and Octavia would not make it easier) but it would have to be done. And when he had humbled himself, Octavia would help him. It would be like eating dirt, but that was the price he had to pay for being a failure and the father of a family. She was very rich. It would mean nothing to her to allow him as much as he earned at Padbury's.

Her annual visit was due in a week. He would talk to her then. In the meantime, he would try not to let Edith know that he had lost his job. It would only worry her. He would come to town every day as usual and only break the news to Edith when he had Octavia's promise to help them.

To go home before his usual time would call for an explanation, so until six o'clock Stephen continued to walk the streets and at six, he turned his steps in the direction of the station. In the booking-hall he ran into George Bramwell, a stout, red-faced man with whom he sometimes shared a compartment. George greeted Stephen with the hearty enthusiasm with which he greeted most acquaintances; which meant, that is to say, precisely nothing.

"Hullo, old chap. You're looking seedy. Liver, I daresay. I'll put you on to a good thing I've discovered…"

They showed their season tickets, passed through the barrier, and walked along the platform. Stephen made to get into a compartment, but Bramwell drew him back.

"Not in there. Let's go further along. That was Donovan in the corner. He's on his uppers. His agency came a cropper a year ago and he hasn't earned a bean since. He'd have had some hard luck story to tell us if we'd got in with him—and I'd have been alone with him after you got out at Gay Ladies. They tell me he's touched every friend he has in the world, but he won't get a chance to touch Uncle George in a hurry. Here, this'll do.

Not many in the train tonight; we'll have the compartment to ourselves."

I wonder if you would be so pleased to have my company, thought Stephen, if you knew that this afternoon I, too, came a cropper. He dropped into a corner seat and opened his evening newspaper, without much hope that the manoeuvre would silence his companion.

"Sad affair, that suicide in Goudy Street," said Bramwell, stabbing the front page of Stephen's paper with a stubby forefinger. "Read about it in an early edition. Poor devil—lost his job—tried to get another for a solid six months—over fifty—alone in the world—living in a furnished room—down to his last bob—didn't know where to turn—stuffed door and windows with paper—put his last bob in the meter—lay down in front of the gas fire. Landlady went in to make his bed this morning; found him dead."

"Poor devil, indeed," said Stephen softly.

There, but for the grace of God— But he had Octavia to turn to. Even if she failed him, he still had Edith and the children. No matter what happened, life would be worth living while he had them.

"He wouldn't have done it if he hadn't been alone," he said. "A married man has to go on living for the sake of his family."

George Bramwell bit the end of a fat cigar and struck a match. He leaned back, exuding prosperity and self-satisfaction.

"That's all you know," he retorted cheerfully. "There was a case not so long ago, you must have read about it: fellow in Wolverhampton—forty-five years old—wife and family—two little boys and a girl of fourteen—business failed—tried to get a job—tried for two years and couldn't—no money left—no food in the house—killed his wife and the boys—cut his own throat—and left the girl to come home from school and find 'em!"

He blew a smoke ring and seemed to fill the compartment with the aura of his ghoulish triumph.

Icy fingers tightened on Stephen's heart. If Octavia should fail him— He had to muster his courage to hold fast to the fading conviction that she would not fail him. The thought that she might was too terrible to harbour. She would have to help him. He would make her.

"You'd be surprised at the things I could tell you," murmured Bramwell complacently. "Things I've seen and heard these last few years—"

"For heaven's sake," said Stephen angrily, "shut up."

Bramwell stared. What on earth had got into Osborne? His little eyes narrowed. The fellow looked worried. Money troubles, perhaps. Maybe his job wasn't as secure as it might be. Whose was, these days? He would have to keep an eye on him. He had troubles enough of his own. It was a mistake taking up with just anyone on a railway journey... With an air of offended majesty, he leaned against a window and spread his newspaper on his fat knees.

There was silence in the compartment while the train rushed through the slums of Brancaster, through the thinning suburbs, into the open country. When it shuddered to a halt at a wayside station gay with flowers, Stephen rose and opened the door.

"Good night," he said; but Bramwell did not answer.

Stephen squared his shoulders and walked along the platform. He came out into the village and his eyes softened. It was such a lovely little place. It was home.

S TEPHEN FILLED HIS lungs with the live air and stepped out briskly. Gay Ladies straggles along a country road and the back garden of almost every dwelling looks over open fields. The station, like a stranger who states his errand on the doorstep, stands at one end of the village, with a gap between it and the handful of shops which is all of the commercial enterprise that Gay Ladies boasts.

Beyond the shops the road skirts the green, flanked by lichened cottages four centuries old which look as though they were sown as seed into the soil from which they raise their weathered walls and grew up with the flowers and trees that surround them. On one side of the green the cottages huddle against the village inn, like shy children clinging to their mother, but on the other side they give more room to the stately fourteenth century church which stands in their midst. The cottages wind with the road past the green and when it leaves them the road suddenly straightens, like a drunkard who spies a genteel acquaintance, and goes straight between two rows of semi-detached red-brick villas which have an air of keeping themselves very much to themselves.

The fading sunlight shone on something that sparkled in a window of one of the villas. Stephen smiled. Miss Whipple, a middle-aged spinster, lived in that villa, and it was general knowledge that she used a telescope to keep herself in touch with the activities of her neighbours. She filled the function of village newspaper far more spicily than a newspaper would have dared. There were few sunny days when the gleam of her telescope could not be seen at the window of one of her upstairs rooms.

The road bent sharply where the villas ended, as though the

strain of going straight had been too much for it, and wavered between clipped hedges bounding the large gardens of the houses in which lived the gentlefolk of Gay Ladies, the vicar, the doctor, and a sprinkling of professional men who travelled daily to offices in Brancaster.

Round the bend Stephen came upon a sturdy boy of twelve in a grey shirt, open at the neck, and grey flannel shorts, who was kicking a ball from one side of the road to the other, and gradually—very gradually—working in the direction in which Stephen was going. The boy had fair hair which was turning from golden to brown, a cheerful sunburned face, friendly blue eyes, a short nose with a slight tilt, and a mouth which smiled readily. When he saw Stephen, the smile grew on his lips and he ran back to meet him.

"Well, Peter," said Stephen.

"Well, Daddy."

"Had a good day?"

"Splendid! I went out with Bob Dowell and his ferret and we got four rabbits. Big 'uns. He gave me two."

"You're very dirty."

"I know."

Father and son exchanged a glance which gave dirty face and hands no more than their proper importance. Peter picked up the ball and they walked on together.

"Where's Michael?" asked Stephen.

"Out on his motorbike, Daddy. I asked him to tab me, but he said he'd be tinkering with it and I'd be in the way."

They strolled along, chatting together, for a few minutes and then they spied a girl and a young man standing in the roadway a hundred yards ahead.

"Dorothy and Ted Fleming," said Peter. "They're up to something."

Stephen was inclined to agree. Something told him that this was no chance encounter. There was a guilty air about the waiting couple which suggested an ambush. He had never before noticed how really beautiful Dorothy had become. She had always been pretty, but now she was almost as rarely lovely as Edith had been at her age.

"Hello, Daddy," she said. She kissed him, a thing his children rarely did in public.

Stephen greeted the young man, who grinned awkwardly, then glanced meaningfully at Dorothy. She flushed. They all stood looking at each other in the middle of the road, then, with a cry which was not quite spontaneous, Dorothy pounced upon her small brother.

"Peter, you're filthy! You'd better hurry home and wash, or you'll be late for supper."

"I want to walk home with Daddy," Peter objected.

"You'd better run, or Mother will be cross. Give me ten yards start and I'll race you."

"All right, but I'm sure to win. You know you always get puffed half way."

They darted off up the road and Stephen and Ted Fleming were left to follow together. The young man coughed.

"Has Dorothy told you, sir: I've passed my final exam and Father is taking me into his office as a junior partner."

"I'm delighted to hear it. You're getting a splendid start in life. Your father has one of the best legal practices in Brancaster."

Young Fleming mumbled something and reddened. "I—er—I—I've something rather important I want to talk to you about, sir."

Stephen realised what was coming. If he read the signs correctly, the lad had just proposed and been accepted and they hadn't been able to resist waylaying him to get his consent without delay. It was good of them to ask his consent; he had never been the sort of parent who demanded concessions to his authority. He was glad. Ted was exactly the sort of young man he wanted for his daughter's husband. They would make a charming couple.

But would Ted's parents be equally pleased? They could not have anything against Dorothy, but they might not consider a clerk a desirable father-in-law for their only son. They were the sort of people who were certain to reduce the romance to those terms. And he was now an unemployed clerk, which made the situation a thousand times more difficult. Suddenly he felt very tired. He had too much on his mind this evening to cope with another problem.

"I'm rather tired. Won't it keep until tomorrow?"

"I—I suppose it can," said Ted Fleming dully.

At the southern end of the village, they parted at the gate of a large house, square and solid set in the middle of a fair-sized garden, like a child's building block on a pocket handkerchief. The jerry-builder who put up the red-brick villas had built it for himself. A man of ideas, he had foreseen the time when the people who worked in the cities would sleep in suburban villages. Gay Ladies was only six miles from Brancaster and a dozer trains a day stopped at its tiny station. He saw no reason why the village should not become one of the bedrooms of the city, to the profit of an enterprising builder. He bought acres of land which had grown potatoes and turnips as long as anyone could remember, planted then with bricks and mortar, and the red villas—a dozen of them—sprang up like mushrooms, almost overnight. When the first four were sold and the foundations dug for twelve more, he started his own house.

He built it solidly, of matured timber and grey stone, with large rooms, square windows, and plenty of cupboards, and the beauty of its surroundings did much to atone for the ugliness of its architecture. Beyond it lay green fields and the white road that wound between other fields to farms which drowsed in hollows among gently swelling slopes. Behind a meadow through which ran a talkative stream that a man could take in his stride, and a stretch of moorland, purple, green, and gold in the summer, melting into distant hills. Across the road in front of the house was a larch coppice which sheltered a colony of birds larger than the human population of the village.

The house was built in 1905, and a year later the jerry-builder went out at the back door and through the meadow to the chattering stream and there shot himself, having bitten off more than he could chew.

In time Brancaster proved him right by sprawling out and creating garden suburbs where before the entire countryside had been a garden, but proved him wrong by steadfastly ignoring the village of Gay Ladies, much to the satisfaction of the older inhabitants. For seven years the house stood empty and then, in 1912, Stephen and his bride came to live in Brancaster. At first, they lived in lodgings and went bicycling at weekends to get the smoke out of their lungs. On one of these excursions they discovered Gay Ladies, and fell in love with it. "If you love me, Stephen," said Edith, "bring me to live here."

The following day Stephen had consulted an estate agent and was informed that in all Gay Ladies there was but one dwelling to let—the jerry-builder's house. Prospective tenants are inclined to shy at a house which is associated with a suicide or a murder, and this one had become a white elephant. The agent, scenting a good tenant, had offered it at the tempting rental of thirty pounds a year. Stephen closed with the offer quickly and that evening Edith and he had celebrated their emancipation from lodgings in champagne and lobster at the Midland Hotel.

The Osbornes had moved into the square, ugly house, taking with them a servant girl even more young and inexperienced than themselves. In 1936 they were still living there and by that time there were seven Osbornes, the rent had been raised three times, the harsh contours of the house had been softened by a garment of Virginia creeper and hallowed by countless associations and the raw servant girl was a woman in her middle forties.

Stephen swung open the gate and went up the trim garden path. A tall, graceful woman was waiting at the open door. At forty-nine, Edith Osborne was still very beautiful and her blue eyes had a serenity born of a hundred triumphs and disasters. When Stephen met her eyes, he knew that he would have to tell her that very night about his lost job.

A T EIGHT O'CLOCK the following morning, a Saturday in early August, a boy on a bicycle rode up to the house at the end of the village. He dismounted and leaned his bicycle against the hedge, threw the garden gate back with a crash that sorely tried its hinges, swaggered up the path, and beat a rousing tattoo with the door-knocker. In a few moments the door was opened by a woman in a blue print dress and white apron who declared acidly that if it was his desire to break it in, he would have been well advised to bring an axe and do the job properly.

Her scowl changed to an anxious frown when she saw the buff envelope in his hand. In this flippant age there are those who send and receive telegrams as nonchalantly as post cards, but Hannah Gale was not one of them.

"Osborne," said the boy self-importantly, holding out the envelope and a receipt-book.

"Take your dirty boots off my clean steps, Master Ernie Piper!" snapped Hannah, but the rebuke lacked her customary fire.

She took the wire as gingerly as though it were infected, carried it to her mistress, who was laying the table for breakfast, and waited gloomily, ominously, while it was opened.

Edith Osborne uttered an exclamation of dismay when she read the message. "Aunt Octavia... Oh, dear!"

Hannah's face lit up. "Dead?" she asked hopefully.

Her mistress laughed. "Hannah, I'm ashamed of you. No, it isn't anything like that. She's had a row with friends with whom she's been staying and she's coming to visit us now instead of next week—she's arriving by the twelve o'clock train. It's going to make things rather awkward. I meant to give her the room Uncle

Simon has—he would have been gone by next Saturday—but we'll manage somehow. I do hope Simon will be civil to her. Tell the boy there's no answer."

Hannah returned to the front door where she found Ernie Piper, the tip of his tongue protruding from his mouth, drawing on one of the pillars with a chewed stump of pencil.

"Why, you little wretch—" A stinging blow from one of her large red hands sent him sprawling on the gravel path. "There's no answer," she added.

Ernie, picked himself up, felt his tingling ear, and launched on a lurid description of Hannah which terminated abruptly when she took a step forward. He took to his heels and the gate crashed behind him.

Her muscular arms akimbo, Hannah stooped to inspect the drawing. The boy had sketched a rugged, mannish profile which could only be identified as that of a woman by the bun of hair at the back of the head. A large nose with a grotesque hump in the middle of it; an ear which stood out like a jughandle; a mouth which looked ready—eager—to bite; a fierce eye, from which the artist had radiated a number of tiny daggers... Hannah realised grimly that it was not at all a bad caricature of herself. Even as a girl, she had never cherished any illusions about her own exceeding plainness.

A household may be judged by the woman in the kitchen. Hannah was a domestic servant of a type which is almost extinct. Registries do not supply them. Gold cannot buy them. Only a mistress who appreciates them can keep them.

The family that Hannah had served for twenty-four years was her whole existence. Work was her pride, cleanliness her god. A large woman in her forties, there was no superfluous flesh on her bony muscular frame; she had always been too hard a worker for that. No matter what the hour or how messy her occupation, her apron was always clean. She would rather have washed a dozen a week than have worn a soiled one.

The appetising odour which pervaded the house reminded her that she had left bacon frying on the gas-stove. She closed the front door and went into the kitchen, prodded the sizzling rashers with a fork, and turned, with her hand outstretched, to a table beneath the window. She frowned. Odd! She could have sworn she had placed some eggs, an eggbeater, and her favourite bowl on the table. The eggs were still there, and the beater, but not the bowl. Wondering if her memory was playing her a trick, she looked on the shelf on which her bowls were stacked. But it was not there.

And then she remembered that Michael had come into the kitchen by the back door at the moment when she went to answer the front door bell. And Master Michael had a habit of borrowing first and asking permission afterwards. With a belligerent look in her eyes, she went to see what he was up to with her best bowl.

Michael was in the shed at the side of the house in which he kept his motorcycle. A slim youth of seventeen with dark, curly hair, large dark eyes and a thin, eager-looking face; clad in soiled grey flannels and a much-mended pullover, he was squatting on the concrete floor, surrounded by parts from his dismantled machine. Hannah's cherished bowl was filled with a black oily liquid which smelt of paraffin and he was washing the parts in it and drying them on a grimy cloth.

Hannah uttered an outraged snort and the youth looked up, brushing a lock of hair from his eyes. "Hello, Hannah. Come to give me a hand?"

"If I do, you young ruffian, it'll be round your ears. After you broke that pudding-basin the other day, didn't I tell you to keep out of my kitchen?"

"What a mean old woman you are! Can't a chap borrow one of your blessed bowls for five minutes when he's got a job to do?"

"And how, pray, am I to beat eggs for an omelette?"

"Scramble 'em."

Hannah looked down at his curved back. The Osborne children were all as dear to her as though they were her own, but Michael was the apple of her eye. When he was born his mother had been in danger of dying and the doctor had despaired of the child as well. While doctor and nurse strove to save the mother, Hannah had tried an old-fashioned remedy on the baby. She had evoked from him his first puny cries at the moment when Edith Osborne opened her eyes again to life. And, having snatched him from Death, Hannah loved Michael as dearly as though she had borne him.

With a sigh she turned to go back to the kitchen, leaving him in possession of the bowl, but out of the corner of her eye she identified the oily cloth with which he was drying his nuts and bolts.

"One of my good dishcloths!"

She whipped it out of his hand, picked up the bowl and poured the contents down a drain, and marched off with her head in the air. A smell of burning greeted her when she entered the kitchen. She snatched the frying-pan from the gas-stove, but the damage was done. Slicing more bacon, greasing another pan, she muttered to herself things which ought to have made Michael's ears burn.

Through the window she saw Marjory wandering in the garden with a basket on her arm. Marjory was fourteen, straight and slender as a boy, with a boy's natural grace of carriage. Like Michael, she had dark, curling hair and dark eyes. She was wearing a red jersey and a short blue skirt which displayed an incredible length of leg. No matter how often her clothes were lengthened she always had too much leg.

Theoretically she was gathering raspberries for breakfast, but Hannah was prepared to bet that the basket was empty. Marjory could not be relied upon to perform the simplest task without supervision. A dreamer, she spent most of her time in a world of her own, a world peopled with characters of her own creation, in which she herself was the most important character of all.

At the moment, Marjory was a Great Lady. She was walking in the garden of a country mansion with a lovesick suitor whom she liked and respected but could never love. It was her duty to make him understand that she could never be more to him than a very dear friend (which was his cue to kiss her hand, mutter something brokenly, and stumble with bowed head from her presence to hide his sorrow in some far-flung corner of the globe) but she must break it to him gently so that he would not be driven by the agony of his despair to the point of taking his life.

It was all deliciously sad. There was a lump in her throat, a moistness in her eyes.

But there were no raspberries in the basket.

Mrs. Osborne came into the kitchen with a vase in her hand and held out the telegram to Hannah.

"Will you please take it upstairs to Mr. Osborne? I'll keep an eye on the breakfast. Oh, and Hannah, see if Miss Ann is up."

"Yes, ma'am."

Stephen Osborne was not in his room, but the sound of running water led Hannah to him. The bathroom door was ajar and she walked in without ceremony. He was standing beside the bath, shaving; and Peter, in undervest and shorts, was performing his ablutions at the wash-stand. Stephen had not worked up his usual bubbling lather and the razor was moving slowly, occasionally pausing in mid-air, a sign that his thoughts were far away. Peter was taking advantage of his father's preoccupation to wash his face sketchily and his neck not at all.

In one movement, Hannah gave the wire to Stephen Osborne and took a firm grip of his small son's neck. She plunged Peter's face into the water and picked up the soap. In spite of his squirming protests, she soaped his face, neck and ears thoroughly, rubbed them until they glowed pink, and left him to rinse and dry himself.

"Beast!" he called after her as she went out of the bathroom.

Hannah walked along the corridor and knocked at a door. There was no answer, so she turned the handle and went in. Ann, the second eldest of the family, who was nineteen, was lying in bed, propped up with pillows, reading a book supported on her drawn-up knees.

To say of a girl that she has an intelligent face is as much as to say that she has no claims to beauty. Ann had an intelligent face and she did not care who said so. In repose—and it usually was—it was plain. Her complexion was sallow and her dark eyes seemed to slumber behind thick lenses, framed in tortoiseshell, through which they viewed the world. There was often a vaguely puzzled expression in her eyes. Her Uncle Simon called it her 'questing look'. He said that she was a Joan of Arc who had not yet heard the voices and who was eternally listening for them. In her rare moments of enthusiasm her eyes came alive and seemed to light up her face, so that those who had put her down as dull and unattractive wondered how they had ever arrived at such a conclusion.

"Miss Ann!" said Hannah loudly.

Ann went on reading.

Hannah advanced to the foot of the bed. "Miss Ann!" she called, still more loudly.

"I'll be down in a sec," said Ann, without looking up.

"Your mother says—"

"Tell her you've shouted in my ear and I'm rising with all possible haste."

"If you don't, she'll be cross."

Grumbling, Ann put down the book, threw back the bed-clothes, and slid bare feet to the floor. But when Hannah left the room with a satisfied grunt, Ann went back to bed and her book.

She was lost in it again when the door opened once more and Dorothy came in. Dorothy, the eldest of the family, was twenty-three. She was also the handsomest, and was well aware of the fact. The others, except Peter, were dark like Stephen, but Dorothy had inherited her mother's glorious golden hair and lovely complexion. This morning she was wearing a white tennis frock and carrying a silk scarf of many colours.

"Not up yet! You *are* a lazy pig!"

"Go away," mumbled Ann.

Dorothy crossed the room to the dressing-table, tied the scarf about her neck with a studied effect of carelessness, and admired herself in the mirror.

"Ann!"

She repeated her sister's name twice before Ann heard her.

"What is it?" Ann asked testily.

"My new scarf. Do you think it goes with this dress?"

Ann looked up. "Where'd you get it?"

"A present from Ted."

"What taste the lad has! You certainly can't wear it with that frock. Much too gaudy. Looks as though he cut himself shaving and bled on it."

"Don't be vulgar," said Dorothy, without heat. She was too accustomed to the frankness of her brothers and sisters to take offence at it.

"Why on earth you want to put that red muck on your nails, I don't know."

Dorothy looked at her hands. Nice hands, she reflected complacently. Small, white, shapely. "Everyone does. It's the fashion."

"I don't."

"Oh, *you*! You never care how you look."

Ann could think of no reply to that perfectly true remark, so she lowered her eyes to her book.

Dorothy stood looking at herself in the mirror. Yes, perhaps the scarf was a little too—not gaudy, bright was the word—to be worn with a simple tennis frock. And yet Ted would expect her to wear it today. Ted... It was no longer her own face she was seeing in the mirror, but his.

Funny... Until a little while ago she would have laughed at the thought of being in love with Ted. It would have seemed like being in love with one of her own brothers. An only child, he had first come to play with her when he was six and she was four. Always since then he had been free to come over when he chose and join in whatever was going on, whether it was a game or a fight. Dorothy could remember pulling his hair when he tried to put on airs with her when he came home for the holidays after his first term at Eton. And now they were in love. Funny...

It had happened so suddenly. She had called him a silly ass, she forgot why. She had called him that before, more times than she could count; but this time he had flared up in a rage. Before she quite knew what it was all about, she had lost her temper too; and they were both saying things, biting things, trying to hurt each other. And nothing was the same as it had been; for suddenly they realised that the things they were saying really *were* hurting, as no words between brother and sister could hurt. That was how they found out that they were in love. It seemed a silly way to find out. Afterwards they wondered how they could have helped knowing it long ago.

*

Edith Osborne filled her vase with flowers, carried it to the dining-room, and placed it in the centre of the table. The room was large and sunny, papered in apple-green, with cream woodwork. The table was pleasingly laid, with a fresh white cloth and shining cutlery, for Edith held that how one ate was almost as important as what one ate. She opened the French windows and walked out on to the lawn. From a cloudless sky the sun smiled on a smiling world. The air was sweet with the scent of the gently nodding flowers. A bee droned by on his way to an assignation with a rose.

"It's going to be a lovely day," said Edith softly.

Chapter 4

Before breakfast was served in the dining-room Hannah took a tray up to Mr. Simon Osborne, an elderly cousin of Stephen's who had been staying with them for two weeks. 'Uncle' Simon was a visitor of whom Hannah entirely disapproved. He had all the vices she could not tolerate: he was lazy, dirty, unpunctual, careless, untidy; worst of all, he drank enough whisky at a sitting to incapacitate any normal man and was not affected beyond a slight thickening of his speech, which proved him to be a hardened and unregenerate reprobate.

There were never any buttons on his underwear and pyjamas and always large holes in his socks. On the visit he had brought only one shirt, which he would cheerfully have worn throughout his stay, had not Hannah stolen it away to be washed while he slept and replace it with an old one belonging to her master.

After a loud, unanswered knock, she marched into his room and placed the tray noisily on the table beside the bed. All that could be seen of Uncle Simon was his bulging outline under the bedclothes and a stray lock of wispy grey hair protruding above them. He was snoring un-melodiously into the pillows. Hannah stalked across the room and pulled up the blinds, admitting a flood of sunshine which evoked muffled protesting grunts from the bed.

"Your breakfast, sir," she said loudly.

"G'way," mumbled Uncle Simon sleepily.

Grimly Hannah eyed the accumulation of cigarette ash and spent matches on the carpet beside the bed; loudly she sniffed the air, redolent of stale tobacco and whisky; with an emphatic "humph!" she went out of the room banging the door behind her.

Uncle Simon rolled over, away from the searching fingers of the sun, and again his snores punctuated the silence.

*

The clamouring young appetites of Peter and Marjory brought them to the table before breakfast was served, and Dorothy was hardly less punctual, but Michael had to be called in from the shed where he was tinkering with his motor-cycle, and Ann appeared in belated haste five minutes after the others were seated, wearing a jersey and skirt which had the appearance of having been thrown on, and carrying a book under her arm.

"Ann!" said her mother quietly, when she placed the book, open, on the table beside her plate.

With a heavy sigh, Ann closed it and put it aside.

"I'll bet you haven't washed," said Dorothy, eyeing her suspiciously.

"No lady," retorted Ann coldly, "would offer to bet on a certainty."

"No lady," snapped Dorothy, "would neglect to wash."

"Someday," said Ann, through a mouthful of toast, "I'll have a flat of my own and it'll be nobody's business but mine if I read at every meal or neglect to wash before 'em."

Toward the end of the meal, Edith folded her napkin and looked round the table until she had arrested the attention of all her children.

"We've had a wire from Aunt Octavia," she announced. "She is arriving at twelve today instead of next Saturday."

"Oh, Lord!" muttered Ann. Marjory and Peter groaned in unison. Dorothy said quickly: "I shan't be able to meet the train. I'm playing tennis with Ted."

And Michael added hastily: "I needn't either, need I, Mum? I want to finish tuning up the old bike."

Edith's lips set firmly; a danger signal they knew of old. "I want you all to be nice to her while she's here. It will only be for a week. You simply must be on your best behaviour. No grumbling. No quarrelling. No fighting."

"Why on earth does she come, anyway?" asked Dorothy. "She hates the sight of us and she can't possibly enjoy her visits here anymore than we do. She's only happy when she's finding fault with us."

"And that's all the time," said Michael gloomily. "What I'd like to know is why we put up with her."

"That's easy," replied Ann. "She's filthy with money and hasn't anyone else to leave it to."

"Ann!"

"Well, Mother, I ask you, *would* we put up with her beastly temper if she were a poor relation?"

"If she were a poor relation," remarked Dorothy wisely, "she wouldn't have it. A temper is a luxury only the well-to-do can afford."

"Was she always the same, Daddy?" asked Michael. "Or is it old age that's made her such a bear?"

"Old age, I think," replied Stephen soberly. "I can remember a time when she was the best sort in the world when I loved her as much as I love all of you. But she's been alone a lot since then, and loneliness often sours people. I'd like you to be nice to her, if you can, for my sake."

"We'll be like kittens round a saucer of cream," Dorothy assured him. "But as long as *I* can remember she's always been the same. Do you remember the letter Peter wrote her, when he first learned to print capitals? And how she sent it back to him with all the errors, spelling and grammar marked? It was a beastly thing do. He was so proud of his first letter, poor kid!"

"I suppose there's some good in her," said Ann. "Her companion—that poor Miss Mimms—adores her."

"Miss Mimms!" said Dorothy. "She's like a frightened stray; she'd worship anyone who gave her shelter."

"I hope you all quite understand," said Edith, cutting short the discussion. "I want you to show her how really nice you can be when you try."

Michael rose to return to his beloved motorcycle and his mother picked up his crumpled napkin. She spread it out with a gasp of annoyance.

"Michael!"

"Yes, Mother?"

"It's really too bad of you. Look at that napkin!"

In abject silence the youth regarded the oily streaks on the white linen.

"Show me your hands."

Shamefacedly, he spread them for inspection. They were grimy—but not as grimy as they would have been had he not wiped them on the napkin. A sarcastic remark trembled on Edith's lips—*"I'll ask Hannah to wash them for you in future before you come to the table"*—but she suppressed it. She had learned how to discipline her children without hurting their pride.

"I'm sorry, Mother."

"You are getting into the habit, Michael, of wiping your hands on the first thing you come across, after you've been working with your engine. It isn't a nice habit."

"I—I'll try to get out of it, Mother."

Edith sighed. "I wish you would."

Chapter 5

A T HALF PAST TEN when Ann entered Uncle Simon's room, he was still fast asleep. Snoring. The breakfast tray lay untouched on the table. The sheet had worked up from the foot of the bed and he had pulled it over his head to keep the light from his eyes. The blankets had slipped down from his shoulders and his unbuttoned pyjama-jacket revealed a greyish-white chest thatched with dark hair and an immense round stomach. Stomach and chest rose and fell rhythmically, every rise accompanied by a snore, every fall punctuated by a whistle.

Ann pulled the sheet away from his face and looked down at him. The round head, the round body, were like a small butterball stuck to a larger one, but they lacked the attractiveness a rich yellow colour gives to a butterball. Uncle Simon's flesh was tinged with yellow, but it was the pale yellow of a disordered liver. 'A disordered liver'—the words admirably described him. His had been a disordered life, if ever there was one. Ann had no illusions about her uncle. At the age of ten she had seen him as a glamorous and amusing figure but although he was still amusing, the glamour was gone. With the pitiless eyes of youth growing to maturity, she saw him for what he was: a fat, rather soiled old man who led a messy life and garbed his failure in a tattered cloak of rakish impudence.

The reason for his visit to Gay Ladies, she knew, was that he had been forced to leave London to escape his creditors; and Stephen Osborne's home was the only place where he could count on free board and lodging for an indefinite period. Years ago, Ann had regarded him with awe because he was an author and that was the one thing in all the world that she wanted to be. Now she realised that although he had genuine talent, he had never done anything with it; never would do anything with it. He was too lazy.

When he had no money in his pocket and could persuade no one to lend him any; when the tradesmen stood out for ready money and the publican refused to add more items to the slate; then Uncle Simon would force himself to sit all day and half the night at his desk, scribbling furiously, churning out in a few days a thriller for the publishers of twopenny bloods who were his only sources of legitimate revenue. At other times he was content to idle his life away in a frowsty, alcoholic semi-coma. No, Ann had no illusions about her uncle. And yet, the one person she loved, apart from her immediate family, was that graceless reprobate, Simon Osborne.

She shook his shoulder vigorously and he rolled over, pawing the air. He opened one bleary eye.

"Go 'way," he growled.

"Wake up. It's morning."

Uncle Simon sat up and scratched his head. He yawned. Not a pretty picture, Uncle Simon, with his unshaven chin, bloodshot eyes, wispy grey hair, and slack grey lips. He rubbed his head, making his hair stand up in wilder disorder than before, and gave his niece a malevolent look.

"Why the devil don't you leave me alone? I'm tired."

"The morning after the night before," said Ann.

"No," he answered dryly; "the morning after a lifetime of nights before."

"You were pretty tight last night. I heard you falling upstairs when you came in."

"'Tight'," said Uncle Simon, doing his best to assume the righteous severity with which the respectable old admonish the impertinent young. "'Tight' is not a suitable word for a young girl to use."

"It isn't a suitable condition for an old man to be in, and it isn't fair. Father goes to the trouble and expense of getting in beer for you; and yet you insist on spending your evenings boozing in the local pub."

"I hate bottled beer," said Uncle Simon peevishly. "It's poisonous muck."

"Perhaps. But no one except labourers and workmen ever go into the village pub. What do you suppose people think when they see you staggering out of it?"

"Not staggering. I can carry it as well as any man. And"— Uncle Simon curled his lip—"I hope I'm sufficiently intelligent not to care a tinker's damn what people think."

"That's all very well for you. But we have to keep up appearances. I don't care two-pence for other people myself. But Father and Mother do. Dorothy does. And you're letting them down."

"If the lecture's over, perhaps you'll be good enough to let me sleep."

"You might at least button your pyjama jacket," said Ann striking off at a tangent; "after Hannah's gone to the trouble of sewing all the buttons on."

"I wish she'd minded her own business. I don't like buttons on my pyjamas. I'm not used to them. They scratch."

"They wouldn't scratch if you buttoned them."

Uncle Simon gritted his teeth and rolled his eyes. "I've had this pyjama jacket for twelve years. I've grown round the middle. It won't button. *It—will— not—button!* Now are you satisfied? A man of my age lying here taking lip from a chit of nineteen! Ye Gods!"

Ann giggled. "It's amusing to find that all I've read about the helplessness of grown men is absolutely true. You're like a baby. You need a woman to take care of you—a woman of tact, who can do things for you without getting your back up."

On a flying visit to London, Ann had once called for her uncle at his house in Battersea. She would never forget it. The front steps, from which the tracks of countless muddy feet had not been washed for years. An area littered with rubbish. The paint of the front door, blistered and scarred. The doorbell green with tarnish. The bare floorboards of the hall, on which one left footprints in the dust as one walked across them. The smell. The dirt. Age-old dirt, everywhere. Over the house presided Mrs. Glott, an elderly slattern, with a red nose, who charred Uncle Simon's food, drank his whisky, robbed him; and considered her work done for the day when she made his bed.

"You need someone to look after you," she repeated. "Why not me?"

"In the first place," said Uncle Simon, instantly wary, "you're not a woman of tact. There's no such thing as a woman of tact."

"I've always wanted to live in London. Maybe I'd find a job on a London newspaper—that's my ambition. Oh, it's a grand idea. I'll come and keep house for you. I'll be shot if I can't make a better stab at it than that awful Glott woman. I won't drink your whisky. And I can cook. I'll see you get decent food at regular hours and mend your clothes."

"No!" shouted Uncle Simon. *"No! No! No! No!* I like dirt. It's liveable. I don't want to be scrubbed and polished out of house and home. I like to drop things on the floor and find 'em there next time I look for them. Mrs. Glott suits me. She leaves me alone. No, thanks! I'm quite happy the way I am."

"If that's the way you feel—"

"That's exactly the way I feel. And now, I want to sleep."

Uncle Simon turned on his face and pulled the crumpled sheet over his head to indicate that the interview was over. Ann sat on the edge of the bed. "Aunt Octavia's coming today!" she breathed into his ear. Uncle Simon bobbed up like a jack-in-the-box.

"No!" he cried. Then, more calmly, he said: "You infernal little liar, giving me a shock like that. You know perfectly well she's not coming until next Saturday."

"She sent a wire to say that she's changed her mind. She's coming today, and you'd better get up. You can't expect to hog the best bedroom when our rich auntie is here. We're putting you in the boy's room and Michael and Peter in the attic."

"Not me. If Octavia's coming, I'm going. I wouldn't spend a night under the same roof as that—that—acid-tongued, sniffy-nosed old megalomaniac for all the gold in China!"

"You don't like Aunt Octavia," remarked Ann dispassionately.

"Your perspicacity is amazing. I do *not* like your Aunt Octavia. I hate her. I loathe her. The very thought of the woman gives me a dark brown taste in my mouth and spots before my eyes. She makes me sick. I'm a lifelong bachelor because I don't like women. It's the Octavia in 'em that I can't stand. Every woman's got a touch of Octavia. Every woman wants to manage people, to poke, to pry, to stop 'em doing whatever makes 'em happy and set them at what's supposed to make 'em good. No woman is content to leave things as they are: she wants to take them apart and put them together again in a new way of her own. Women are born interferers. You're one, and you know it. No sensible man likes women. Most men get entangled with 'em—poor devils!"

"Why this lecture on my sex? I thought we were talking about Aunt Octavia."

"We were. We're not. We're not talking about anything. I'm sick and tired of talk. I want to sleep. Call me about two. Don't bang the door as you go out."

"Don't be silly. You've got to get up this minute. She's coming at noon."

Uncle Simon groaned. "She would! Trust Octavia to make

things awkward for everyone. That means I've got to catch the quarter to twelve train for Brancaster. And—Good Lord! —this *is* going to be awkward! I suppose your father is at the office?"

"No. He's in the garden."

"Good!" said Uncle Simon, brightening. "Run along, child. I'll be down to have a word with him in a minute."

"No, you don't!" said Ann sternly. "I know what you want to see him about. You're going to touch him for some money. It's no good giving me that nasty look. You can't touch Daddy. He's lost his job."

"Lost his job!" Uncle Simon repeated it in the incredulous tone he would have used had she said: "The skies have fallen."

"Yes. I'm not supposed to know, but I heard Father and Mother talking. They're pretty sick about it. I suppose it *is* rather awful, although he always hated his work."

"Awful? It's catastrophic! At his age with a wife and five children—What on earth is he going to do?"

"I gather they plan to touch Aunt Octavia."

Uncle Simon laughed; a hollow, mirthless laugh. "That's good. That's great. They're going to touch Aunt Octavia—just like that! The poor innocents, have they any conception of the magnitude of the task? Touch Octavia? Ye Gods!"

"You've been there, I gather?"

"Many a time and oft. And I'm an old and hardened toucher. I know all the approaches, all the opening gambits. If blood could be coaxed from a turnip, I could coax it. But I've never succeeded in separating your Aunt Octavia from a red cent."

"Yes, but this is different. Daddy's her only brother. He's a respectable married man, and he'll use the money wisely. After all, Aunt Octavia is bound to know what you'd do with any money she was misguided enough to let you have."

"We'll let that pass. It stings—coming from my favourite

niece—but we'll let it pass. You listen to me, miss: I'll give you a hundred to one in anything you like from old boots to fivers that Octavia turns your father down flat."

"It's a bet. She couldn't do it. I know she's as hard as nails, but after all, Daddy's her brother. She can't let him starve. Blood's thicker than water."

"Not Octavia's blood. Her veins flow with vinegar."

Ann drew her knees up and rested her chin on them. She gazed thoughtfully at her uncle. "Why is she so rich and Daddy so poor? Didn't she get her money from Grandfather?"

"She did. Seventy thousand jimmy-o'-goblins. And she's bound to have twice that by now. I don't suppose she's spent a third of her income during the past twenty years."

"Why didn't Grandfather leave Daddy any?"

"It's a long story," said Uncle Simon, closing his eyes.

"I like long stories."

"Very well," he sighed. "As a boy, your father was a trifle wild. Don't look so interested. You aren't going to hear any scandal. When I say wild, I mean—oh, I don't know—fond of fun, perhaps; irresponsible, I suppose—"

"I don't believe a word of it. It doesn't sound in the least like Daddy. But go on."

"When your grandfather was alive, they were always rowing. He was an earnest-minded old boy, who took life a damned sight too seriously. He'd been married twice, so perhaps you can't wonder at that. Octavia was the only child of the first marriage, your father the only child of the second. At the time I'm talking about, the old boy was a widower for the second time, and an enlarged heart was slowly but surely taking him to join his spouses. Your father was a lad of twenty, or thereabouts; Octavia was forty-odd. You won't believe it, but she loved your father very much. She was like a mother to him. And when your grandfather died, he left all his money to Octavia, knowing that she'd take care of it. There was some sort of direction that she was to consider half the money her brother's and administer it on his behalf, but it was left entirely to her in what amounts he was to receive it and she was allowed to withhold both capital and income if at any time she saw fit. I never read the will, but that's roughly the gist of it."

"So that, morally, half the money is Daddy's?"

"Yes, but legally it's Octavia's. And if you depend on your moral rights in this world, you'll have a thin time. At first Octavia played fair. She gave your father a generous allowance and promised to make over half the money to him—someday. But before that day came, he met your mother and fell in love with her. Octavia was furious. There wasn't anything she could say against your mother. She'd have felt the same way about any woman her brother wanted to marry. She wanted to be the whole world to him, which is roughly what *he* was to *her* at that time. She behaved more like a jealous mistress than a loving sister. Her trump card was the money. If Stephen married without her consent, she declared, she'd cut him off without a penny. He did marry. She cut him off. It happened twenty-four years ago, and he's still cut off. That's why he's been slaving his heart out on an office stool all these years."

"But they've made up their differences. She comes every year to visit us."

"There's no making up with your Aunt Octavia. With her quarrels may slumber, but they never die."

For a long time, Ann was silent. Her father, her mother, had loved like that, all those years ago. As long as they could have each other, money hadn't mattered. An office stool had been bearable. Poverty had meant nothing. It was rather splendid. Ann wondered if she would ever know love like that; and thought she never would. For money was so terribly important; and love—to Ann—so very remote.

"If I were your father, I'd cut Octavia's throat," said Uncle Simon. "I've a good mind to do it anyway It would solve a lot of problems. Your father would inherit her money—and I'd be able to touch him regularly for the rest of my life."

"Do you really think she'd leave it to Father?" asked Ann thoughtfully.

"To whom else could she leave it? Not me, that's a certainty; and she hasn't any other relatives. She can't stand dogs. She hates cats. She's never taken any interest in charity. Oh, I expect your father will get it in the end. But although she's over seventy, she'll probably hang on for another ten years—unless someone arranges otherwise. I've a jolly good mind to do it myself."

"And be hanged for murder," said Ann shrewdly.

"That," replied Uncle Simon, "is the snag."

Ann stood up. "You didn't touch your breakfast. Shall I make you some tea?"

"Tea? God forbid." He looked up at her with a wheedling smile. "Now, if there's a drop of whisky in the house—"

"There is," said Ann coldly. "For emergencies."

"This is an emergency, my dear child."

"I mean if people are ill."

"I'm ill. I'm a sick man."

"Let me see your tongue."

Uncle Simon opened his mouth and put out some inches of thick furriness. Ann took one look at it and ran to fetch the whisky.

MARJORY SAT ON the wall which divided the garden from the fields, her long legs dangling down its mossy sides. Her brooding eyes gazed at the distant hills, but she did not see them. She saw sparkling blue water, laced with white ruffles; and the spreading sails of yachts, swelling in the breeze. She saw a terrace dotted with tables at which gay, sophisticated men and women were sipping aperitifs under striped umbrellas; and an immense white casino, shining in the sun, against a background of tropical foliage. Tall, slender, and very beautiful; gowned with a perfection only Paris can offer, Marjory sauntered gracefully along the terrace, and all the males turned their heads to look after her.

Marjory was at Monte Carlo—or as nearly at Monte Carlo as an imaginative young girl can be who is sitting on a wall in a Midland village.

A sudden clamour broke in upon her day-dream. Marjory tried to ignore it, but it compelled her attention. Sliding off the wall, she went to see what was going on. Rounding a bend, she almost fell over a jumble of arms and legs that was threshing about in the road in a flurry of dust. It had two tousled heads, two fiercely struggling bodies. One of the bodies came uppermost and squatted on the chest of the other, pounding at it lustily with clenched fists. Marjory recognized the grimy, exultant face of Ernie Piper, the post office messenger; and in a swift glance saw that the form he was belabouring was that of her younger brother, Peter.

She ran forward and clutched Ernie Piper's hair, in both hands, tugging as though she were trying to part it piecemeal from his skull. The youth gave a yell. Still kneeling on Peter, he jabbed at Marjory with his elbows. Dodging his clumsy backwards lunges, Marjory hung on to his hair. Master Ernie swore most horribly and, in a pain-thickened voice described a few of the things he intended to do to her as soon as he was free. Marjory took a firmer grip and yanked, dragging him off her brother and on to his back on the road. She released him and wiped her hands—sticky with cheap hair-oil—on a clump of grass.

"There!" she panted. "Let that be a lesson to you!"

Ernie Piper scrambled to his feet and made a wild rush at her. Marjory swung her open right hand and hit him a resounding smack on the left cheek. She followed it up with a similar blow on the right cheek, dealt by her left hand. His cheeks aflame, the boy stumbled back, a new respect for her in his startled eyes.

"If you want any more," said Marjory calmly, "come and get it!"

Master Ernie did not want any more. From a safe distance he started to throw stones and was enjoying the fun until Marjory began to throw them back and shattered his fond delusion that girls could not throw for toffee by scoring three painful hits out of four throws. Ernie hated games that two could play, so he picked up his bicycle and started for the village. Over his shoulder he called back:

"You wait, young Osborne! You wait! One of these days I'll run into you when you haven't your big sister to hide behind; and won't you *just* catch it when I do!"

Peter picked himself up, with a bruise on one leg and a swelling under his left eye, and turned furiously on Marjory. "See what you've done? Why couldn't you mind your own business? Now he'll tell everyone that I'm a coward and need my sister to fight my battles for me."

"Well, don't you?"

"No, I don't! I can lick him with one hand tied behind my back!"

"Oh, can you? Then why did you let him put you on your back? You were resting, I suppose?"

"Well, anyway, I'd a thousand times rather be beat than rescued by a girl. And pulling hair's a caddish trick."

"What an ungrateful little beast you are! Next time I'll let him do what he likes with you. What was it about, anyhow?"

"He said Hannah's face would sour vinegar."

Marjory considered the point. "Well, so it would," she said judicially.

"I know, but I couldn't have *him* saying so."

That was unanswerable. Hannah was one of the family and you can't let outsiders criticise your family, no matter how well-founded the criticism may be.

"Well, at your age, Peter," said Marjory loftily, "you ought to be able to settle your differences with other boys without behaving like a savage."

"*Well*, I like that!" exploded Peter; but before he could express himself further, Hannah came round a bend in the road and hailed them.

"You're wanted, Peter and Marjory."

"Blow!" muttered Peter. "I know what that means."

"So do I," groaned Marjory. "I'll bet we're booked to meet Aunt Octavia."

They were right. In spite of their protests, they were made to wash and change their clothes and despatched to the station with shining faces and shining shoes and strict orders not to soil either on the way. For days Hannah had been too busy to bake, so Marjory was given a two-shilling piece and instructed to buy a cake in the village for tea.

At first, they walked along almost primly, but Nature won't have boys and girls behaving like ladies and gentlemen on a winding country road. Peter produced a ball and they kicked it back and forward as they sauntered along. In the heat of the game, they scuffled and collided and arrived in the village looking pretty much as they had done before they were called in to wash and change.

There was a quarter of an hour to wait for the train, of which they spent five minutes gazing in the window of the village baker's shop, wondering which of the limited assortment of cakes to buy. Peter favoured one coated thickly with chocolate icing and surmounted by a large frog in green marzipan; but Marjory pointed out that it wasn't in the least an Aunt Octavia kind of cake. Regretfully, she declared that a solid-looking seed cake of indubitable—but undecorated—worth would be much more in Aunt Octavia's line.

"Well, there're seven of us and only one of her," said Peter, in a tone of utter reasonableness. "Seems to me we ought to please the majority. And I don't see how anyone could help liking the choc'late one."

"Aunt Octavia wouldn't touch it."

"All the more for us, then."

"Mother will be cross if we get something aunt won't like."

"Well, she didn't tell us what to get. She said to choose something nice—and you can't call that seed thing nice!"

Marjory wavered.

"Let's toss for it," coaxed Peter. "Heads, the choc'late cake; tails, the seed cake."

The gamble was irresistible. Marjory capitulated. She spun the coin and both heads bent quickly to look at it as it fell. Tails!

"Best of three," said Peter quickly.

They tossed again. Heads this time. Anxiously, Peter watched Marjory spinning the coin for the third time. "Heads, heads, heads, heads," he muttered under his breath.

The coin dropped on its edge and rolled across the pavement. With a mocking tinkle it fell down a drain and was submerged in thick black mud.

"Now we've done it!" cried Marjory, in a stricken tone.

Peter went down on his knees and made frantic attempt to salvage the coin. With a long face, he rose at last.

"No go," he mumbled. "Sorry, Marje. It was all my fault."

"It was as much my fault as yours; more, because I'm the elder. Oh, *Peter!* —just look at your hands and knees!"

Peter looked. They were filthy. He wiped off some of the dirt with his clean pocket handkerchief. Crestfallen, they hurried to the station in time to see Aunt Octavia descending from a third-class compartment.

It was a smoking compartment, but the young man who was handing out Aunt Octavia's suitcases with sardonic politeness was not smoking. He had not smoked throughout the journey. Aunt Octavia could not bear smoke. The young man had brought out his cigarette-case when the train started, but by sheer force of character Miss Osborne had made him put it away without extracting a cigarette.

"But, madam," he had protested, pointing to the window, "that sign says: 'Smoking.' You can see that for yourself."

"Sir," replied Miss Osborne stiffly, "no matter what sign may authorise him to do so, no gentleman will smoke in the presence of a lady who objects."

Her fierce stare dared him to carry the matter further, I'm ready for you, it seemed to say, if you do. Like most people who found themselves in opposition to Miss Osborne, he had subsided into sullen obedience to her wishes. She gave one the feeling that no matter how rude one was she could always be a little ruder, in the most ladylike way in the world.

Miss Osborne was a tall, erect old lady, with a dominant nose, a thin, tight mouth, and a pair of icy blue eyes whose scornful gaze (one could readily believe) would make a raging lion slink dejectedly back to his jungle. She wore a tailored coat and skirt of a serviceable dark grey material, grey woollen stockings and grey leather gloves; and a grey pork-pie hat perched on top of her bunched-up white hair. Of lighter grey was her severely-cut silk blouse, which terminated at the neck in a tight collar of lace and whalebone, encasing to the chin her wrinkled throat. In one hand she held a grey silk umbrella, and in the other a handbag quite large enough to hold the average person's weekend requirements.

Behind her stood a tired-looking little creature, a human mouse, who had received the three suitcases as the sardonic young man handed them out, and who now waited patiently for orders. Clad in a drab suit which had been cast off by her mistress and "made over" by an incompetent dressmaker—and looked it—Miss Mimms resembled nothing so much as the humble shadow of Octavia Osborne.

While the guard waved his flag and blew his whistle, Marjory and Peter timidly approached their aunt. She eyed them coldly from head to foot, and they were agonisingly aware that she was itemising the defects in their appearance. She pecked at each smooth young cheek with pursed lips; it was like the kiss of an ancient crocodile.

"Well, I must say you don't seem very pleased to see me. Where are your tongues? You're not always so quiet, I'm certain."

Marjory blushed and Peter scraped one shoe over the other.

"You might at least have washed before you came for meet me. And surely your mother did not send you out with shoes like that?"

"We—we played along the road," gulped Marjory.

"That," said Miss Osborne grimly, "is obvious. You made

mud-pies, too, by the look of you. Surely you are both a little old to enjoy wallowing in dirt?"

"I—I'm sorry, Aunt. We—we didn't think."

"You didn't think! I can quite believe it. I should be greatly surprised, indeed, to find either of you showing signs of thoughtfulness."

"Shall I—shall I tell the porter to have your luggage sent up?" Peter blurted out. "Or shall I run for the village taxi? It—it's rather a long way, you know."

"It's no distance at all. We shall walk. Mimms will take one suitcase and you children must manage the others. Well, what are we waiting for?"

Hefting the luggage, the children and Miss Mimms trailed out of the station at the heels of Miss Osborne who marched like an officer of the Guards. While they walked, she chided them for not being more lively company, but when Marjory ventured a shy remark, she snatched at the words almost before they were out of the girl's mouth and worried them like a dog with bone.

When they were passing the village green a motor-cycle roared by and disappeared round a comer in a cloud dust and smoke.

"Was not that your brother Michael?" Miss Osborne demanded sharply.

Silence. She repeated the question.

"I—I don't know," mumbled Peter. "I—I wasn't looking."

"Does your brother possess a motor-cycle?" she insisted, pursing her lips.

"W—e—ell, yes."

"Indeed. Then I have no doubt that it *was* him. And I shall have something to say to the young man when we meet!"

EDITH OSBORNE WAS waiting in the hall to receive her sister-in-law. She looked cool and very lovely in a pale-yellow frock.

"I'm so glad to see you, Octavia. You're looking very well."

"What pretty speeches you always make, my dear Edith," said Miss Osborne, presenting a withered cheek to be kissed. "A new dress, I see. What a lot of clothes you manage to afford!"

"It's only a simple little frock I ran up on my sewing-machine. I hope you like it."

"I must admit it looks quite smart, although not very serviceable; and hardly suited to a person of your years. Stephen, I presume, is not home from his office?"

"Stephen... No, he—he didn't go to the office this morning."

"He is not ill, I trust?"

"Oh, no. He's quite well."

"Indeed. In that case it would have been a reasonable politeness on his part to have met me at the station. But I daresay he would consider that too much trouble. He might at least be here to receive me."

"He's in the garden. He won't know you're here yet; he loses all account of time when he's working in the garden. I'll call him."

"Pray don't trouble. It would be too bad to drag him away from his beloved garden for no better reason than to greet his elder sister."

The door leading to the kitchen opened and a head appeared and bobbed back again almost in one movement—but not quick enough to escape the gimlet eyes of Miss Octavia Osborne.

"Ah, Michael!"

Spotted, Michael came forward, pink to the tips of his ears. "Oh, hello, Aunt."

"I cannot commend you on your manners, young man. Do you know no better than to pass your relatives on the street without recognition? And was it necessary for you to career past at such a speed as to throw up a positive fog of smoke and dust?"

"I'm—I'm so sorry, Aunt," he stammered. "I didn't notice you until I'd passed."

"Then it was you," she said dryly. "I thought so, but I couldn't be sure."

Michael was cold with fury. How dare she lay traps for him before she had been in the house two minutes? Miss Osborne eyed him from head to foot with a disapproving air that made him feel like a naughty child of six.

"Are your hands always as grubby as that?" she enquired dispassionately.

The boy looked down at them. "Sorry," he muttered. "I'll go and wash."

Relieved at the opportunity of escaping, he took the stairs two at a time. Miss Osborne sighed and closed her eyes. "I can't bear noise. It gives me a headache."

She's started already, Edith thought desperately, and she'll go on like this for seven days. Seven whole days! Every day she'll become a little sharper, a little more acid. A dozen times a day she'll make my gorge rise; and I'll have to smile and be nice and turn the other cheek. Whatever she says, I'll have to be patient. She'll pick all the children to pieces and I mustn't complain. For during those seven days, I've got to ask her to help Stephen; and beggars must be hypocrites. Beggars must swallow every insult with a smile.

"You must be tired, Octavia. I'll take you to your room."

"Thank you, I prefer to remain down here for the present. At my age, one can't race upstairs like a colt at the end of a long train journey."

"How thoughtless of me! Do come into the drawing room and sit down. Hannah will attend to the luggage and look after Miss Mimms. By the way, how are you, Miss Mimms?"

"I'm quite well, thank you."

Edith touched a bell and led her visitor into the drawing-room.

Hannah came out of the kitchen. "Back again?" she said, beaming good-naturedly at the drab little figure standing among the suitcases by the front door. "Here, let me take that. I expect you've had about enough of lugging bags about." Hannah gripped the handles of two suitcases in one large hand and picked up the third with the other. "When you've as much brawn as I have, you can run upstairs with this little lot."

She led the way to the room Simon Osborne had vacated less than an hour before and dumped the luggage on the floor at the foot of the bed. As soon as Uncle Simon was out of it she had gone through the room with brush, mop and polish like a whirlwind and it was now shiningly clean and tidy. The window was wide open, but Miss Mimms sniffed the air nervously.

"Oh dear, there's a distinct odour of tobacco, and Miss Osborne can't bear it!"

"Then I've a good mind to shut the window and let her have the full benefit of it," said Hannah grimly. "Don't you fret, my dear. There's a fresh breeze blowing and the smell will be gone before your precious mistress has a chance to notice it. You look all in. Come downstairs and I'll make you a nice cup of tea."

Meanwhile in the drawing-room, Miss Osborne was taking inventory. She did not appear to look directly at anything, but not even the minutest trifle escaped her, within two minutes of entering the room she could have recited from memory its entire contents. The ink spot on the carpet which Edith thought was camouflaged by a chair; the neatly repaired tear in one of the curtains, almost hidden by a fold; the cracked vase, so cunningly glued, which stood on the mantelpiece with the crack turned to the wall; Miss Osborne spotted them all in one sweeping glance. She was looking for some evidence of extravagance on which she could comment, but it was denied her. Sofa and chairs had seen over twenty years of hard service and Miss Osborne recognised from her previous visit the gay chintzes—bright and freshly laundered—with which they were covered.

"What masses of flowers!" she exclaimed. "How can you afford them? I'm sure I couldn't."

"They come from the garden. Stephen works so hard in it, you know."

Miss Osborne walked to the window and looked out. Half-way down the garden she saw her brother standing with a trowel in his hand, looking into the distance.

"He isn't working very hard at the moment," she commented dryly. "Dear me, how worried he looks! Really, he looks older and less robust every time I see him. How thin he is! And what a dreadful stoop he is getting! His hair is going grey very rapidly."

Miss Osborne turned suddenly. "You didn't say why he isn't at his office. I thought he always went in on Saturday mornings?"

Edith hesitated. If she evaded the issue now, Octavia would be furious at the deception; while, if she told the bald truth, it would precipitate the moment she was dreading, the moment when she must beg Octavia to help them.

"What are you frowning about?" asked Miss Osborne sharply. "And why don't you answer me? Something is wrong, I suppose. What is it?"

"Stephen has lost his job."

"Has he, indeed? *Well!*" Although she tried to make her voice sound calm and impersonal, Miss Osborne could not keep out of it a note of extreme satisfaction. This was the moment for which she had been waiting for twenty-four years.

"You mustn't blame Stephen. It isn't his fault. Times are hard. A good many firms are being forced to economise to keep going with a reduced turnover, and that means the dismissal of employees. Stephen is one of the unfortunate ones."

"Stuff and nonsense, my dear Edith! When firms reorganise, they do not discharge valued employees. I know enough about business to realise that! If Stephen has been dismissed after twenty-four years with his firm, his services cannot have been of any great value to it."

"I admit that he has never been suited to his work. After all, he was not trained for business. He was pitch-forked into it when he married me. He has worked hard, uncomplainingly, all these years. That surely counts for something."

"He is a failure. Say what you will, that's what it comes to. Do you think I don't know my own brother? His nature is inherently weak."

"He isn't hard, I agree."

"In the eyes of the world he's a failure," Octavia returned.

"The world! What the world thinks of a man doesn't matter. It's the verdict of his family that counts."

"What does he propose to do? He won't find another post in a hurry!"

"No," said Edith wearily; "I'm afraid he won't. At fifty, it isn't easy to make a fresh start. Few employers will even consider a middle-aged man."

"I presume you have saved?"

"How could we?"

"Anyone can save who wants to. It is simply a matter of cutting your coat according to your cloth. If you had been prepared to do without—"

"Have you any idea of the things we have been forced to do without? I can count on my fingers the number of theatres

Stephen and I have been to since our marriage. I make my own clothes and most of the girls' frocks. Stephen has to make a suit last three years and an overcoat five. He rations his tobacco and walks quite long distances to save fares."

"You have a wireless!" snapped Miss Osborne, almost as accusingly as though it were a pearl necklace.

"Michael made it. He earned the money for the parts by repairing other people's sets."

"Michael has a motorcycle—surely an unwarrantable extravagance for a boy his age."

"The boy earned it by helping Doctor Fleming with his car. He has a strong mechanical bent and does all his own repairs."

"Well, I must say you live extremely well for people who cannot save."

"We've done our best to bring our children up decently, if that's what you mean."

"Your three elder children ought to be contributing to their support."

"We want Michael to be a doctor; and neither Ann nor Dorothy would be happy in offices."

"Happy! I do not consider it important for young people to be happy. You are giving them ideas far beyond any station in life their father can offer them. You keep a far more elaborate ménage than many of my friends whose incomes are considerably larger than Stephen's."

"You are simply accusing me, Octavia, of being a good manager."

"Good manager or not, a pretty mess you and Stephen have made of your lives. Jobless at fifty, without a penny saved! How do you propose to live?"

"Well…" Edith took the bit between her teeth. "We hoped that you—"

"You hoped that I—! Go on, pray. What did you expect of me?"

"You have so much, Octavia. It would mean nothing to you to allow Stephen a few hundred a year."

"*So!*"—all the bottled-up bitterness of twenty-four years was in that one word. "You defy me and scorn my judgment when it suits you, but you come running to me for help when the shoe pinches. I knew you two would never make a success of life—I knew it!—but neither of you would listen to me. Oh, no. You knew better! You could manage without me and my money—or so you thought. But you can't manage without me and my money now. Do you suppose I haven't known this would come?"

"I assure you neither Stephen nor I would ask you for a penny if we had only ourselves to consider. If we are pocketing our pride, it is for the sake of our children."

"Your children! What right have you to have children you can't support?"

"I had not intended to mention it, but after all, Stephen has a strong moral claim on you."

"Indeed! I don't recognise it."

"You are hard, Octavia, bitter, unforgiving. Well, I suppose there is no more to be said."

"On the contrary, my dear Edith, there remains a great deal to be said. But I prefer to say it later, after I have given the matter the fullest possible consideration."

MEALTIMES IN THE Osborne household were usually festive occasions with a great deal of airy chatter but luncheon on the day of Miss Osborne's arrival was as gloomy as a funeral. It was as though the family skeleton had been brought from its cupboard and seated at the table. Stephen tried to keep the talk alive, but it languished and died in spite of him. To know that whatever one said would be seized upon, shaken to bits, and held up to ridicule was enough to silence the most wagging tongue.

Hannah had exerted herself over the meal, but no one had much of an appetite. Waiting on table, Hannah removed each half-eaten course as though it were a personal insult. She trod more heavily on the floor every time she entered the room and it was really a wonder that the scorching gaze she directed at Miss Osborne did not burn through the autocrat's garments and blister her stiff back.

Towards the end of the meal Miss Osborne took some folded pieces of paper from her handbag and, adjusting her pince-nez, shot an arresting glance round the table.

"I have something to say to which I want you all to listen carefully. It is concerned with the—I suppose one would say misfortune—which has befallen you father."

Edith looked at her sister-in-law sharply. "I must ask you, Octavia, to permit my husband to explain to his children as much of his affairs as he sees fit in his own good time."

"In the name of your children, you have appealed for my financial assistance," replied Miss Osborne acidly, "and I intend to explain to them why I cannot grant it. The reason is simple; I do not consider my brother deserving of assistance. He has always been weak and lacking in the qualities which are essential in a man if he is to conduct himself with dignity and be regarded with respect.

"It is with no pleasure that I am forced to consider him a failure. He has proved himself incapable of holding a post which entailed little initiative and less mental effort, and although for over twenty-four years he has enjoyed what most people would regard as an adequate income, he has failed to take the elementary precaution of providing for his family's future. With sublime inconsequence he throws the problem of his children's support on my shoulders as though the responsibility for their existence were mine. Lacking the manhood to approach me in person, he even delegated to your mother the doubtless unpleasant task of seeking my aid. Such shiftlessness merits no consideration."

Edith stood up. "Octavia, have you gone mad? I must ask you not to say another word!"

"Let her go on," muttered Stephen brokenly. "She's right. I am a failure. I've failed you all."

"Little remains for me to say," continued Miss Osborne blandly. "I have no intention of encouraging my brother's children to become as lazy and inefficient as their father. The possession of money is a sacred trust, not to be considered lightly. I should be false to my trust if I advanced my brother funds to fritter away in indolent and extravagant living." She unfolded the papers she had taken from her bag. "Not only do I consider it my duty to withhold the assistance he demands, but since my talk with your mother I have taken the step of drafting a new will which I shall instruct my solicitor to put into legal shape as soon as I return to London.

"My existing will leaves the income from the bulk of my estate to your father for life, the capital to be divided equally among his children at his death. In my new will, with the exception of a legacy of one thousand pounds a year for life to my servant, Catherine Emily Mimms, I intend to leave my entire fortune to various charities which I shall not trouble to enumerate at this time."

Hannah had come into the room while Miss Osborne was talking and stood behind her, holding a tray, and breathing heavily on her neck. "You mean, wretched old woman!"

"*Hannah!*" cried Edith.

For a moment it seemed that Hannah would not be silenced. She glared at the poker-back of Miss Osborne and Peter held his breath in the delirious hope that she was going to bring her laden tray down with a resounding thwack or his aunt's erect head. But without another word she turned on her heel and left the room, slamming the door behind her. She swept into the kitchen and set down the tray with a bang.

"The miserable old buzzard!" she exclaimed. "What do you think? She's going to make a new will! She's cutting out her own flesh-and-blood and leaving her money to charity! Charity! Her that hasn't an ounce of charity in her whole shrivelled carcase."

"Oh dear!" breathed Miss Mimms. "And the Osbornes seem such nice people, too!"

"If you knew them as I do! My blood boils when I think of that dyspeptic old crow sitting at their table, eating their food, and telling them what she's going to do with money that's as much theirs as hers, if there was any justice in this world! But you'll be all right when she dies—if you can hold on long enough. I'd never have believed it of her, but she's actually spared you a thought. Take a deep breath, my dear, you're in for a surprise. When she makes this new will, she's going to leave you *a thousand pounds a year for life.*"

Miss Mimms turned very white. The fork with which he had been picking at an omelette dropped with a clatter.

"A—*a thousand—pounds*—a—year—"

"For every year of your life! You'll be rich, my dear!"

"For life," repeated Miss Mimms, as though she hardly comprehended. "For life…" She swayed and would have fallen had not Hannah caught her.

"Poor dear, you're exhausted. Hannah's going to take you upstairs and tuck you into bed with a hot-water bottle."

"M—Miss Osborne may want me."

"If she does," said Hannah grimly, "it's Hannah Gale who'll give her her answer!"

*

"There's no need to apologise," said Miss Osborne stiffly. "If my own brother's family cannot treat me with respect, is it likely that his servant will?"

"Respect!" cried Ann scornfully. "You insult and humiliate my father at his own table, and sit there blithering about respect!"

"I won't have that, Ann," said Stephen sternly. "You will apologise to your aunt immediately."

"Please don't interfere, Stephen," retorted his sister. "Go on, miss. Let us understand each other. It will be interesting to learn once and for all, exactly what my niece thinks of me."

Stephen rose unsteadily and stumbled from the room. His sister hardly noticed his going; she was facing her niece with a mirthless smile.

"I'll tell you gladly," said Ann, trembling with anger. "You're a purse-proud, egotistical megalomaniac. You talk about your wretched money as though you had it by some divine right. You imagine God gave it to you because you are infinitely superior to the ordinary run of people; and that those who have no money have none because they don't deserve it. God didn't give it to you. Grandfather left it in your charge because he was misguided enough to think that your brother's future would be safe in your hands."

"So! *So!* Your father told you that, did he?"

"Daddy didn't tell me. I heard the whole story from Uncle Simon. And I know as well as you do that you have absolutely no moral right to give away money that is as much Daddy's as yours."

"Simon! That drunken scapegrace! I might have known it."

"Yes, he's a drunkard. He doesn't pay his bills. He doesn't even wash regularly. But I'd rather model myself on him than on you. At least, Uncle Simon has a heart and a sense of humour. He has no inflated ideas of himself. But you!—you are a monument of conceit. And why? What are you? What have you done with your life? You call Daddy a failure, but he's brought five healthy children into the world and made us happy. He's never spent a penny selfishly or uttered an unkind word as long as I've known him. A failure! If Daddy's a failure, what on earth is success? What have you done with your life that can begin to compare with the achievements of his?

"There isn't a charwoman scrubbing floors on her knees who isn't of more use in the world than you. There isn't a mother in a slum who hasn't justified her existence a thousand times more than you ever will. You've done none of the work of the world, you've brought no life into it; you've contributed nothing to its happiness. You eat, sleep, dress and undress, quarrel with your acquaintances, nag your maid: that's your whole life. And when it's all added up, it amounts to zero. Seventy years of life! —seventy years of empty futility. And yet, you think you're wonderful. And why? Why? Why? Simply because you've got money. And what gave you the money? Your intrinsic worth? Bah! That's what you think, but it isn't so. An accident of birth, that's what gave it to you. If I'd been born fifty years earlier and you fifty years later, I'd be the aunt and you'd be the niece—and *I'd* have the money."

"You ought to stand for Parliament in the Labour interest," said Miss Osborne dryly. "You have all the tricks of rhetoric, and it would be a pity to waste so much energetic venom. But I'm not a fool, you know. I've known all along that I was merely tolerated in this house for the sake of my money."

"Do you think anyone in the world would put up with you if it weren't for your money?" demanded Dorothy suddenly. "You make no effort to be pleasant. You delight in picking holes in everyone. Why, you wouldn't dare behave the way you do if you weren't stinkingly rich. There isn't a hotel or boarding-house in the country where you'd be welcome for a single night if you couldn't pay well enough to make it worthwhile to put up with your tantrums. Uncle Simon has no money, but we all love him. There's nothing mercenary about our love. When he comes to visit us he comes empty handed, but we're all glad to see him. We'd be glad to see you, too, if you'd only be half-decent, but you won't be, because money has swollen your head so much that you think you can look down on everyone."

"You express yourself less vehemently than your sister," purred Miss Osborne; "but I see you hold the same views. And, you, Michael, have you no desire to give your aged and despised aunt what—I believe—domestic servants and people of that class call 'a piece of your mind'?"

"Oh, what's the use of chewing the fat?" muttered Michael. "Ann's said it all—well, all but this: if you'd earned the money, you'd have a perfect right to do what you like with it, and we couldn't grumble. But you didn't earn it. You inherited it from a member of the family and you've no right to do anything with it when you die except pass it on to another member of the family.

If Grandfather had wanted it left to charity, he'd have left it to charity himself. Don't think *I* care what you do with it, I don't want it. We'll probably be happier without it. I can't see that it's made you happy. If you'd spent it all and had a good time, I'd say good luck to you. If you gave it away during your lifetime and made some poor devils' lives more bearable, I'd applaud your goodness of heart. But to hoard it like a miser all your life and then toss it to charities for which you don't care a button simply to spite Daddy—well, that's not my idea of fair play."

Hannah stamped into the room, whispered in her mistress's ear, glared at Miss Osborne, and stamped out. Peter was squirming in his chair as though he had something on his mind. Miss Osborne turned on him a caustic glance.

"You, too! Well, what is it? I may as well hear what the twelve-year-old thinks of me."

Peter looked at his mother. "Please," he said, "may I go out to play?"

Edith's gaze, stricken and sorrowful, travelled round the table, resting in turn on the faces of each of her children.

"You are all excused," she said at last.

I<small>T IS QUITE</small> out of the question for me to remain under your roof after what has transpired," said Miss Osborne, with tremendous dignity. "If you will be so good as to instruct Mimms to repack my luggage and procure a vehicle to convey it to the station. I shall leave at once."

"I don't think Miss Mimms has unpacked," replied Edith, with all the calmness she could muster. "She felt faint at luncheon and Hannah gave her some aspirin and made her lie down. I understand she's asleep. There is no train until four o'clock, so perhaps until then—"

"I can wait at the station."

"On the platform? There's no waiting-room. Gay Ladies is no more than a wayside halt, you know. And I hardly think you would find the atmosphere of the village inn congenial. Let us be reasonable, Octavia. The scene at luncheon was ghastly. I shall never forgive myself for failing to step in at the outset and end it there and then. I am not apologising for my children; you practically forced them to express themselves as they did; but I do blame myself. As your hostess I ought to have been able to protect you from insult; as a mother I should have safeguarded my children from a scene which is bound to have its effect on their minds. But the scene is over. We are neither of us children, and we claim to be civilised. Your train does not go for two hours. Surely, we can submerge our differences for that short period?"

"Very well. I shall wait in the drawing-room."

Like a stark and awful spectre, Octavia Osborne stalked from the room. In silence Edith watched her go, and then she reeled and clutched at a chair for support. The room seemed to revolve dizzily about her. I mustn't faint, she thought, clinging desperately to the chair, I mustn't faint.

"Mother!" It was Ann's voice, tense and anxious. Edith managed to raise her head and force a smile. "I'm all right, child. For a moment I felt giddy, but I'm better now. Don't look so worried, dear, it was nothing."

"You'd better come and lie down. I'm sorry about that awful scene, Mother, but I couldn't help it. She was so beastly to Daddy. Oh, I'd like to kill her!"

"So should I!"—the words shuddered out of Edith's lips—"God help me, so should I! To sit there and watch poor Stephen's face while she ranted on—what am I saying? Ann! We mustn't talk like this."

"You're upset, Mother. Do come and lie down."

"No, my dear, I'm perfectly all right. Besides, I must find your father."

On her way out to the garden through the French windows, Edith paused and looked back anxiously at her dark, scowling daughter. "Ann...your aunt's in the drawing-room. We can't let her sit there alone. After all, she's going at four, and we shall probably never see her again."

"She can sit there alone till she rots for all I care!"

"Ann, dear, we've got to be polite."

"Polite? Hah!"

"For me, Ann."

"Oh, all right."

Ann went into the drawing-room and dropped into a chair facing her aunt. Miss Osborne was sitting very straight, her back arched, her head held high, her withered neck stiffer than its rampart of net and whalebone, her hands folded on her lap. Her face was sharp and hard, her blue eyes as icy and pointed as ever. The heightened colour of her thin cheeks was the only sign of emotion she displayed.

"I presume your mother sent you to keep me company. How very thoughtful of her!"

You are my own flesh-and-blood, thought Ann; and how I hate you! I hate you so much that my eyes are burning in my head. I often wondered what it was like to 'see red' and now I know. Every bit of me is tense with hatred of you.

In a silence so heavy that it seemed to close in on them like an encircling wall, they glared at each other. Acid blue eyes. Smouldering dark eyes. Bitter age. Contemptuous youth. The room was like a sky black with clouds, thunderous, stifling, that at any moment might be ripped jaggedly by flashes of lightning.

"You are hardly very lively company, niece," said Miss Osborne dryly.

Ann stifled the desire to laugh. If she once started, she would go on laughing wildly, hysterically, until the end of time.

"I have no doubt you would rather be reading a book."

"Much rather," retorted Ann.

"I am not surprised. Pray read, if you are so inclined."

"Very well, I shall."

"Do."

Ann took a book from the shelf at her elbow without glancing at the title and opened it at random. The printed lines were a meaningless blur before her eyes, but she stared at them and tried to concentrate.

"You would probably manage better," murmured her aunt, "if you turned it up the right way. Or is it your custom to read a book upside down?"

Without raising her eyes, Ann swung the book the other way up. But it might have been written in Chinese for all she understood of the lines her eyes raced along. Hatred, like a dark blanket, pressed smothering her mind.

"Sword is an oath, and oaths must have their course…"

Ann read the line four times before she made head or tail of it. Her eyes were at last breaking up the lines into words—and Ann loved words—but her brain was not yet taking the words and making sense of them. *"Sword is an oath..." "...Oaths must have their course..."* What on earth had she got hold of? *King Henry the Fifth.* That was Shakespeare. Well, any port in a storm. Let's see if Shakespeare can make me forget that awful Gorgon who's sitting there goggling at me.

She read on. Reading was second nature to her, and books more important than food. Under the spell of Shakespeare's glowing verse, she fell into a trance in which Bardolph, Nym, and Pistol; King Henry, Lord Scroop, and Isabel, Queen of France, were real and very much alive; and the world about her was as far forgotten as though it had no existence. "When Ann has a book," her father sometimes said, "you could fire a cannon at her ear and she'd never hear it." That was almost true.

Time ticked away unheeded. Her eyes devouring the pages ravenously, she saw nothing, heard nothing; knew nothing except the pageantry of Shakespeare's characters and the drawing on of their destinies. She was not even conscious of the irritable tap-tap-tap of her aunt's foot; nor was she aware when the tapping ceased.

A sudden piercing scream brought Ann back to earth with a jerk. It tore the air, like a cloth ripped up the middle.

Ann dropped the book and started up. In the doorway stood Miss Mimms, her meagre, black-clad frame wavering as though she were drunk. Her eyes were starting out of her wrinkled yellow face; her mouth hung foolishly open, making a round O. One bony finger, palsied, trembling, was pointing—pointing—

Pointing at the chair opposite that from which Ann had risen. Aunt Octavia still sat in it. Her back was as straight as ever, her expression as chillingly unpleasant. But *her* eyes, too, were starting out of her head; and her cheeks were livid. *About her neck was tightly knotted a gaudy silk scarf.*

"She's dead!" screamed Miss Mimms. "*Dead!*"

"Yes, she's dead," said Ann, mechanically. "For God's sake shut up!"

Chapter 10

A T SIX O'CLOCK that evening, at the close of a strenu-
ous day's shooting, Major Blackett drove home in the
mood for a whisky-and-soda, a warm bath, a good dinner,
and an early adjournment to bed. The Major was a tall, spare,
broad-shouldered, soldierly man a year or two over fifty. He had
a lean, intelligent face, deeply lined; tanned from a lifetime spent
in the open; with blunt features, a firm mouth, and a squarish
jaw. A closely-clipped moustache bristled above his upper lip.

Entering his house, Major Blackett found a police constable
sitting in the hall, who had been waiting there for considerably
more than an hour. The Major sighed. The greatest drawback to
being Chief Constable of the county was that he was never able
to take a day off with any certainty that he would be allowed
to enjoy it in peace.

"What is it, Jenks? Nothing urgent, I hope?"

"Murder, sir," replied the policeman stolidly.

"No rest for the wicked! When was it committed, and where?"

"The village constable at Gay Ladies 'phoned through to
county headquarters two hours ago, sir. An old lady was strangled
this afternoon at a house in the village."

"Has he made an arrest?"

"No sir."

"Come into the dining-room." Major Blackett strode in ahead
of his subordinate and poured himself the keenly anticipated
whisky-and-soda. That at least he would have, murder or no
murder.

"Who is on the job?" he asked, glancing over the rim of
his glass.

"Divisional Detective Inspector Burrows, sir, and Sergeant

Feathers. They left headquarters directly word came. Inspector Burrows tried to get you on the 'phone, sir, and when he failed instructed me to get in touch with you at the earliest possible moment."

"I see. You drive, don't you, Jenks?"

"Yes, sir."

"Know the way to Gay Ladies?"

"Yes, sir."

"Then you'd better run me over. My car's outside. Half a minute while I change."

In a surprisingly short time Major Blackett returned clad in a suit of Saville Row tweeds and a green felt hat and they went out to the car. The Major fell asleep as soon as he entered the vehicle. He awoke refreshed when it drew up at the gate of Stephen Osborne's square solid house. Three other cars and a motorcycle were parked at the edge of the road and at the gate stood a uniformed constable who was turning a deaf ear to the blandishments of a group of newspapermen, some of them with press cameras slung over their shoulders, who were clamouring for admittance. He saluted and stood aside to let the Chief Constable go in. Major Blackett heard several cameras clicking as he strode up the gravel path to the front door, where another policeman was on duty. He cocked an inquiring eye at the man.

"In the drawing-room, sir. The door to the left at the rear of the hall."

As Major Blackett entered the room a flashgun went off, lighting up the place for an instant with a blinding white flare. A plain clothes officer near the window took a plate out of a large camera which was focused on the chair in which sat the corpse.

"That's five exposures from different angles, Inspector," he said. "Want any more?"

"No, five'll do. Now go outside and get me one of the room as a whole through the French windows. Oh, good evening, sir."

"Evening, Burrows."

Major Blackett came forward and looked down at the body of Octavia Osborne. "Poor devil! Any idea who did it?"

Inspector Burrows fingered his chin. A stocky, thickset, middle-aged man with a broad, homely face, he was dressed in sober grey. "One of eight people, Major," he replied, "but which one is the point."

"Eight, Inspector? How do you arrive at that figure?"

"There're eight in the family, sir."

Major Blackett eyed him keenly. "Like that, is it?"

Inspector Burrows nodded grimly. "Just like that, Major. Oh, by the way, this is Doctor Denham. He's been hanging on to see you."

"Doctor Denham and I are old friends. Good evening, Denham. Nasty business, eh?"

The doctor coughed and fingered his dangling pince-nez. "Particularly unpleasant, Major," he replied, "since the people concerned are neighbours of mine."

"The death was caused by strangulation, I believe?"

"Not precisely. Heart failure was the actual cause. The shock of having the scarf passed round her neck and drawn tight killed the old lady almost before her breath was cut off."

"Oh...Then no particular strength was exerted in the commission of the crime?"

"None. The scarf was tightly knotted, but as the victim did not struggle that would be a simple matter."

"Even for a child?" asked Inspector Burrows sharply. Doctor Denham hesitated and a heightened colour flushed his pale cheeks. "Well—I suppose—yes, even for a child," he said huskily. "But—good heaven's man! You're not suggesting—"

"I presume the victim's heart was weak?" put in Major Blackett. "Or she'd hardly have conked out so easily?"

"It wasn't," replied the doctor. "I can be quite definite on that point, because she came to see me about some slight indisposition this time last year and I was amazed to find a woman of her years so organically sound. I can only surmise that she was in an agitated state at the time and when the scarf was thrown about her throat, she realised instantly that murder was intended. So terrible a realisation would probably be sufficient to stop the hearts of most elderly people."

"I see."

Doctor Denham looked distressed. He put on his pince-nez and took it off again. He fumbled with the catch of his bag. He coughed.

"Something on your mind, Doctor?" asked Major Blackett casually.

"Well—I hardly like to— Look here, Blackett, this sort of thing isn't in my line at all, but— Oh, I suppose it's my duty to tell you. When I arrived at the house this afternoon, summoned by Mrs. Osborne, the maid led me straight in here. There were two people in the room: Mrs. Osborne and her daughter Ann. Ann was in a hysterical condition. She was fumbling with the scarf that was tied round the dead woman's neck and when her mother tried to pull her away, I heard her cry out: '*But Mummy, it's Dorothy's scarf! It's Dorothy's. We've got to get it off*'!"

"Oho!" said Major Blackett. "And where was the village bobby?"

"He hadn't been called in then. I summoned him as soon as I realised that it was murder."

"And Dorothy? Who is she?"

"Dorothy is Mrs. Osborne's eldest daughter."

"Thanks, Doctor. Yes, it was your duty to tell me."

"A very painful duty I assure you, Major. I think I'll go now, if you'll excuse me. I'll let you have my report first thing in the morning."

"Very good, Doctor. Good night."

"Good night, Major. 'Night, Inspector."

When the doctor had gone, the Chief Constable turned to Inspector Burrows. "Let's hear about your eight suspects."

"Well, sir, there's Stephen Osborne, the father, Edith Osborne, the mother, five children—"

"Ages?"

"The parents, about fifty, I suppose. The children, I'm informed by the village constable, range from twelve years to twenty-three."

"We can wash out the younger ones."

"I'm not so sure, sir. You heard what the doctor said. A child could have done it. And children of twelve have committed murders before this."

"Well, go on. Who's your eighth suspect?"

"Hannah Gale, sir, the cook-general. She's fortyish."

"A servant? Do you think a servant is likely to have—"

"I'm told she's devoted to the family, Major. And according to the village policeman she's a regular terror. You'll hardly believe it, but when he was summoned, she actually tried to make him come in the back way—with a murdered corpse in the house! Told him to 'take his dirty boots off her clean doorstep'!"

"A card, evidently. Have you questioned these people?"

"Not very thoroughly, sir. I thought you'd like to be present when I did. I had a few words with the mother, the daughter Ann, a Miss Mimms who was a sort of companion to the dead woman, and the village policeman; but that's all."

"This Miss Mimms doesn't figure in your list of suspects?"

"If you'll come over here, sir, I'll show you why." Inspector

Burrows led his chief to a table on which were spread some sheets of paper covered with writing in a thin, precise hand. They were charred at the edges, but still legible. Major Blackett bent over them.

"'...*to the S.P.C.A., twenty-five thousand pounds...*' Looks like a draft of a will."

"That's what it is, Major. And when the village policeman was called in, he found it blazing merrily in the grate. If he hadn't had the presence of mind to drag the papers out and stamp on 'em, they'd have been burned to ashes. Look at this page, sir: '*...to my faithful servant, Catherine Emily Mimms, one thousand pounds a year in trust for life...*' Now, sir, if the will had been legally drawn up and signed *before* the murder, I should be very suspicious of this Catherine Emily Mimms, for apart from a number of charities, she is the only person to benefit from it—but would she be likely to murder her employer before the will was in proper shape, thus doing herself out of a thousand a year? Would she, sir? I ask you!"

"And the answer is: not bloody likely!" replied Major Blackett. "But this drafted will looks fishy. I'll bet my boots it has a good deal to do with the case."

"That's what I've been thinking, sir. *Someone did not want it to be drawn up and signed!*"

All this time, a burly figure in navy blue had been moving about the room, examining furniture with a magnifying glass and dusting powder on selected spots. "What's Feathers up to?" asked Major Blackett.

"Looking for fingerprints, sir," replied Sergeant Feathers.

"You'll find plenty, I expect," said the Chief Constable dryly. "Looks as though this room were used a good deal."

"Yes, sir," said Inspector Burrows. "But my idea is this: we'll take a photograph of every fingerprint in the room, then we'll ask every member of the family to let us take their prints. We'll compare 'em. If we find one that doesn't match, then an outsider has been in the room today. If not, well—it leaves it up to the family, doesn't it?"

"It does," said Major Blackett thoughtfully. "Unless the murderer wore gloves. That would be a dirty trick, but you can hardly expect a murderer to play fair with us."

"Look at this, sir," said Burrows, ignoring the mild pleasantry.

He picked up the silk scarf with which the murder had been committed and spread it out. There were many black smudges on the shiny fabric.

"Oil," commented Major Blackett.

"Exactly, sir. And where would you expect to find thick black oil in a house like this?"

"In the garage, I suppose."

"There isn't a garage, Major—but there *is* a motorcycle, belonging to the eldest son, Michael, aged seventeen, in a shed at the side of the house. *And* the floor of the shed is slimy with oil. *And Michael has been tinkering with the motorcycle all day!*"

"Looks black for Master Michael! I see you've been busy, Burrows. If you carry on like this, you'll have the whole business in your pocket in no time."

"I'm not so sure of that, sir. In most murder cases there are a few witnesses who can be relied upon to tell the truth. In this case all the witnesses are members of the family. When they've had time to think the matter over—if they haven't done so already—they'll come to the conclusion I've already reached: that one of them must have done it. And do you think they'll help us find out which?"

"Not bloody likely!" said Major Blackett again. "Well, let's have 'em in, one at a time. Whom do you suggest first?"

"Catherine Emily Mimms, sir. She discovered the body."

"Very good. Oh—wait a minute. Throw something over the body, will you?"

"You don't think it would be better to leave it as it is, sir, for the psychological effect?"

"No, I don't. Confound it, this isn't the United States or France. We don't want any of these third-degree tricks. And I'm sick of looking at it myself."

Chapter 11

MISS MIMMS CAME in more than ever like a frightened mouse. Her scared eyes darted to the draped form of her dead mistress and she drew in her breath with a hiss. The bony structure of her face showed sharply through the tight yellow skin, making it look like a fleshless skull. She looked ill and very pitiful standing just inside the door, blinking timidly at the police officials.

Major Blackett put on his most disarming smile. "Come in, Miss Mimms. Please don't be frightened. No one is going to worry you. I only want to ask you one or two questions. Please come over here."

He led her to a chair facing the window, on the edge of which she perched with her back to the shrouded corpse.

"In the first place, do you mind if we take your fingerprints? We shan't if you object, you know. It's only a formality. You don't mind, do you?"

She shook her head wordlessly.

"Feathers," said Major Blackett quietly.

Sergeant Feathers came forward with a white card and a black inked pad. He took her fingers one by one, moistened them on the pad, pressed them on the card, then cleaned them with a petrol-soaked rag. He placed card and pad on a table and sat down behind Miss Mimms with an open notebook before him and an indelible pencil poised above it.

"You were the dead woman's companion?" began Major Blackett pleasantly.

"Well, sir, more her personal maid."

"How long have you been in her employment?"

"Eighteen years in October, sir."

Sergeant Feather was writing busily in his notebook "Was she a kind mistress?"

"Yes, sir. She had her little ways and she did not get on with everybody, but she was quite kind to me. Now that she is gone, I don't know what I shall do."

"With a record of eighteen years' service in one post, you ought to find another quite easily."

"I hope so, sir. But—you see—I have never worked for anyone but Miss Osborne. Until my father died it was not necessary for me to earn my own living. I'm afraid I'm quite stupid in many ways. It isn't everyone who would be patient with me."

"I suppose it surprised you to learn that your mistress intended to leave you a thousand pounds a year for life?"

"I was overwhelmed, sir."

"Oh, then you knew about it?"

"Mrs. Osborne's maid heard the matter discussed the dining-room at lunch today, sir, and she told me. She was upset, there had been rather a—" Miss Mimms stopped talking and looked more frightened than ever.

"Go on. Rather a—what? Rather a row, eh?"

"Yes, sir," she mumbled, almost inaudibly.

"What was the row about? Didn't Miss Osborn relatives like the terms of the new will?"

"No—no, sir, they didn't. And it *did* seem very unkind of her. They are her only relatives, and not very well off. It wasn't very fair to propose leaving all her money to charity, with the exception of—"

"With the exception of your legacy? Your mistress was very rich, I presume?"

"Yes, sir, very rich indeed."

"In that case, there is sure to be a will in existence?"

"Yes, sir, there is."

"Have you any idea of its terms?"

"Well, sir, she never confided very much in me, but I gathered that her existing will leaves most of her property to her brother."

"Do you benefit under it?"

"No, sir. Miss Osborne told me many times that she had not left me a penny."

"H'm. And the old Will stands. Hard on you, isn't it? Especially since you would have inherited a thousand a year had your mistress lived to put the new will into effect."

"Y—yes, sir. It is rather a disappointment."

"A thousand a year would mean a great deal to you?"

"A very great deal, sir."

"Tell me, was Miss Osborne on good terms with her brother's family?"

"I—I am afraid not, sir. But then—you see—well, she was seldom on good terms with anyone."

"I see. Now, where were you between luncheon and the time you discovered the murder?"

"In bed, sir. When Hannah Gale told me at lunch about my good fortune I was quite overcome and she made me go upstairs and lie down. She gave me some aspirins and a hot-water bottle and I fell asleep. Hannah woke me at half-past three and I came down to find my mistress. I found her in here"—her voice broke—"*dead!*"

"Was there anyone else in the room?"

"Yes, sir. Miss Ann Osborne."

"What was she doing? Why didn't *she* give the alarm?"

"Well, sir, she was reading a book."

"*Reading a book!*"

"Yes, sir. She is very fond of reading."

"She must be," said Major Blackett ironically. Inspector Burrows snorted.

"That is all for the present, Miss Mimms."

The little woman scurried out of the room, casting a terrified glance over her shoulder at the covered chair. Major Blackett turned to the Inspector.

"Summon Miss Ann Osborne. No—on second thoughts, I'll see her father first."

"Reading a book!" repeated Burrows scornfully. "That's a likely yarn, that is!"

"I said I'd see Mr. Osborne, Inspector," replied the Chief Constable.

"Yes, sir. I'll fetch him."

Stephen Osborne, too, looked shaken as he passed the draped corpse. His thin, intellectual face was very white, and he moistened his dry lips nervously with the tip of his tongue.

"This is a dreadful business, Mr. Osborne," said the Chief Constable, when Stephen had seated himself.

"Dreadful? It's ghastly! I can hardly believe it."

"It must have been particularly painful for you that it should have happened in your house."

Stephen groaned and covered his face with his hands. "We should like to take the fingerprints of the various members of your family," Major Blackett continued blandly. "You have no objection, I hope?"

"I won't have it!" declared Stephen, looking up. "Do you hear? I won't have it. You're not going to treat my children like criminals!"

"You mustn't look at it like that, Mr. Osborne. We merely want the fingerprints to check them with those we find in the room. Naturally, we shall find prints of each of you on the various articles of furniture, for this room is obviously in constant use. We want to be able to eliminate all the prints that have been made by your family, so that we can tell if an outsider has lately entered the room. It is only a formality, but it will assist us greatly. Surely you cannot possibly object? You want to help us find out who killed your sister, don't you?"

"Yes…yes…Of course, I do. What are you suggesting?"

"Then I presume you do not object? Thank you. Feathers!"

Sergeant Feathers came forward and took Stephen Osborne's fingerprints. Stephen did not resist. He seemed stunned, numbed.

"Now, tell me, Mr. Osborne," said Major Blackett suavely; "your sister did not reside with you permanently?"

"No, she lived in London. She spent a week with us every summer."

"And she arrived on her annual visit at noon today? How unpleasant that a quarrel should have arisen so shortly after she entered the house!"

"A quarrel!" Stephen stared at him. "How did you know there was a quarrel?"

"We shan't go into that. The point is that there *was* a quarrel; a violent one. Over her new will, wasn't it?"

"Then you know that, too."

"We know a great deal already, Mr. Osborne, and we shall know much more before we are finished. It will be in your best interests to tell us all you can."

"What can I tell you? I know nothing about this—this terrible affair."

"Where were you after luncheon until the time the murder was discovered?"

"Where was I? In the garden, I think. Yes, in the garden."

"You aren't very definite."

"I was in the garden, I tell you, until I heard Miss Mimms screaming."

"All afternoon?"

"Yes. No. I was upset. I may have wandered into the field behind. I think I did."

"Did you see any stranger approaching the house?"

"No."

"Or anyone you knew?"

"No. I was thinking. I was too abstracted to have noticed anyone."

"What is your occupation, Mr. Osborne?"

"I am a clerk."

"Where are you employed?"

"In the office of Messrs. Samuel Padbury and Son—" Stephen stopped short.

Major Blackett looked at him with raised eyebrows.

"Yes? You were saying—"

"That is, I *was* employed by Messrs. Padbury. For reasons of economy they are cutting down their staff. They dismissed me yesterday."

"Oh." Major Blackett fondled his moustache. "What was your salary with Padbury's?"

"Three hundred and fifty pounds a year."

"It must have taken every penny to keep up this house,"

"It did," agreed Stephen.

"Have you any private means?"

"None."

"Then you must have felt pretty blue when you lost your post."

"I did!" groaned Stephen.

"How did you propose to live until you found another?"

"I—I don't know."

"You must have had some plan. Your sister was very rich. It would be natural for you to ask her to help you."

"Yes, but…"

"Go on, Mr. Osborne."

Stephen was silent.

"You did ask her, but she refused. Isn't that so? That was what the quarrel was about, wasn't it? Not only did she refuse, but she proposed to make a new will, and you stood to be cut off without a penny. That would have been serious for you, a man without a job. Pretty convenient for you, eh, that she died when she did?"

"Damn you!" cried Stephen, starting up. "What the devil are you trying to insinuate?"

"Under the terms of her existing will, her death makes you rich. If she'd lived a few days longer—"

"I see. You—you—" Stephen panted, his eyes wide with horror; "you think I did it. I can see you think that. I killed my only sister for her money; that's what's in your mind. Well, you're wrong. I didn't do it."

"I think that will be all for the present, Mr. Osborne."

Stephen stood stock-still for a moment, staring from the lean, thoughtful face of the Chief Constable to the frankly suspicious face of Inspector Burrows, then with a gasp he hurried from the room. Major Blackett and the inspector watched him go, then their eyes met—

"What do you think, Burrows?" asked the Major softly.

"I'd say, sir, that we haven't much farther to look for our man."

"H'm. Perhaps you're right." The Chief Constable tapped his strong white teeth with a long forefinger. "And now, Inspector, let's interview the young lady who was reading the book!"

Chapter 12

THERE WAS NOTHING hysterical about Ann when she preceded Burrows into the room. Major Blackett thought he had seldom seen a young lady calmer and more self-possessed. To Inspector Burrows' intense disappointment, she did not even glance at the corpse. Burrows had been reading applied psychology and he had hoped for a display of emotion on Ann's part which would give him clue to her inner feelings. But what can you gather from a girl who strolls past a draped dead body to be questioned by a Chief Constable with an air as casual as though she were coming in to tea? —a great deal, psychologists would answer, but Burrows was not a psychologist. He had been reading psychology, which is a vastly different thing.

Without comment, almost eagerly, Ann allowed herself to be fingerprinted, watching the operation with intense interest through her tortoiseshell-rimmed spectacles; Major Blackett thought, however, that he detected a certain tenseness in her bearing when she faced him for questioning.

"You were in this room with your aunt from luncheon until the time the murder was discovered?"

"I was."

"Ah, then you ought to be of great assistance to us."

"I'll do my best, but I don't think there's much I can tell you."

"You were alone with her?"

"Obviously not. Someone must have come in, or she wouldn't have been murdered."

"I quite agree. But surely you must have seen that person and witnessed the crime?"

"If I had, I should have given the alarm at once."

"You were seated facing your aunt, I believe?"

"That is so."

"If you had stretched out your foot you could have kicked her?"

The ghost of a smile wreathed Ann's mouth. "So I could," she agreed.

"And yet she was violently done to death and you knew nothing of it?"

"It sounds odd, I know, but you see, I was reading."

"So I am informed. What was the book?"

"That's it over there on top of the bookcase. *Henry the Fifth*."

"Shakespeare, eh? You have cultivated tastes for one so young."

"Oh, I don't read him as a rule. I fished the book out at random."

"And became so absorbed in it that murder was done almost under your nose and you knew nothing of it?"

"Yes. I'd never realised before that Shakespeare wrote such thumping stuff."

Inspector Burrows breathed hard. "Come, Miss! You're not expecting us to believe that a pretty young lady like you could get so wrapped up in Shakespeare—*Shakespeare!*—as all that?"

Ann turned slightly to regard him with amusement. "Come, Inspector! You're not expecting me to believe that I'm a pretty young lady! I'm not, you know. I'm damned ugly. And even if I *were* pretty, mightn't I still have enough brains to recognise good stuff when I read it—even if Shakespeare wrote it?"

Her eyes travelled from Burrows to the Chief Constable and from the Chief Constable to Burrows.

"I don't know how I can make you understand. You are obviously neither of you keen readers. Well, I am. If a book's any good, I get lost in it. And when I'm lost in a book, I'm oblivious to everything else."

"Then several people might have entered the room without you being aware of them?"

"That is what I have been trying to tell you. I don't suppose I'd have noticed a parade with drums marching through."

"But surely anyone who came in would have spoken to you or your aunt? That would have been the natural thing to do."

"I shouldn't have heard them unless they practically shouted in my ear. I'm like that, you know. And, anyway, Major,"—she glanced up at him shrewdly—"I don't suppose the person who murdered Aunt Octavia went out of his way to attract my attention."

"Oh, quite. But Miss Osborne was not reading, was she? I can't understand how she could have been taken by surprise. Surely, she at least would have seen anyone who entered."

Ann saw the trap. Major Blackett was as good as hinting that only a member of the family, whose entrance would evoke no suspicion in Aunt Octavia's mind, could have taken her by surprise.

"Not necessarily," she replied. "Aunt Octavia was facing me, with her back to the door and the French windows. Anyone could have sneaked in and tiptoed across the room to her without her being aware of it."

"There was a dog in the room," said Inspector Burrows suddenly.

"Wheezy Anna? She never pays attention to anyone but Mother. A burglar wouldn't even make her open her eyes."

"When the doctor was called in," remarked Major Blackett, "he found you trying to unfasten the scarf from your aunt's neck."

If the doctor had told him that, he must also have told him to whom the scarf belonged—

"Certainly," said Ann, without hesitation. "The murderer had used my sister's scarf. If it had been your sister, wouldn't *you* have done the same?"

"That is not the point. You know that nothing should have been touched until the arrival of the police."

"Oh, yes; I read a lot of detective novels, you know. But it was Dorothy's scarf. That made a difference."

"Tell me this, then. Supposing you had seen someone entering the room. Supposing you *had* seen this person murdering your aunt. You have said that in that case you would have given the alarm. But supposing the person was one of your own family; wouldn't that also have made a difference?"

"I am not prepared to suppose all that," replied Ann steadily.

"Was your sister wearing this scarf today?"

"I really don't know. I don't take the faintest interest in clothes."

Looking at her brown jersey, short blue dress and wrinkled brown stockings, Major Blackett could well believe that.

"You are quite young," he said.

"I am nineteen."

"I should have expected a young lady of nineteen to be much more upset over an affair of this nature than you appear to be."

"Age, Major, has nothing to do with it. My sister is twenty-three, but I daresay you'll find her quite cut-up over it all. She's rather sentimental, you see, about death. I'm not. Death is an everyday occurrence."

"But murder isn't!"

"No," agreed Ann. "And I'm struggling between an intense interest in the murder as a murder and a feeling that I ought to be shocked because the victim was my aunt."

"But you aren't shocked?"

"No. I am not a hypocrite. People die horribly every day, but you would not ask me to be morbid about them. Aunt Octavia means no more to me than any name you might pick haphazardly out of a daily newspaper's list of motoring fatalities."

"I see."

Major Blackett looked quizzically at the Inspector. Burrows shook his head.

"That is all for the present, Miss Ann," said the Chief Constable pleasantly.

"Thank you, Major. Good evening."

When the door closed behind her, Major Blackett said softly: "I like that girl."

"Hanged if I do, sir," replied Burrows. "She's a sight too cold-blooded for me."

"You're a sentimentalist, Burrows, and she isn't. I could see her point; and you must admit she's straightforward and candid about her feelings."

"Well, all I can say is she ought to be ashamed of 'em."

"I can see her doing murder, though," mused Major Blackett. "She'd have more stomach for a job like this than her father would."

"D'you suppose the father did it, sir, and she's covering him up?"

"Too early to theorise, Burrows. Let's have in one of the others."

"Which one, sir?"

"Oh, I think—let's see the servant. Perhaps we'll get something out of her."

"Perhaps," said Burrows doubtfully.

Hannah Gale came in and seated herself with a thump. Her arms folded, she gazed at the police officials with a look that said: "Watch your step!" Hostile witness, thought Burrows at once. Hang it, they were *all* hostile!

She firmly declined to have her fingerprints taken. "I've been an honest woman all my life and I know my rights. I don't intend to be treated like a common criminal."

"A mere formality, I assure you," said Major Blackett urbanely. "We have already taken the prints of your master and we have his permission to take from every member of the family."

"Like your sauce!" snapped Hannah. "But if you've taken his, you can take mine."

At the finish of the simple operation, when Sergeant Feathers attempted to wipe her fingers with the petrol-soaked rag, she snatched it out of his hand and wiped them herself.

"Look here," growled Inspector Burrows, his temper thoroughly roused; "if you think we're going to stand your nonsense——"

Hannah fixed him with a steely eye. "You may bully your wife, Sam Burrows, but you can't me. Why, I knew you thirty years ago, when you were propping up lampposts with your back, before ever you joined the force. You always had a swelled head, even before you had a uniform to swell it larger. Don't come the high-and-mighty with me, for——"

Burrows turned purple and glared at the bowed head of Sergeant Feathers, whose shoulders were quivering.

"We won't go into that," said Major Blackett sternly, keeping his face straight with an effort. "Where were you between luncheon and the time the murder was discovered?"

"Where was I? That's a tall order. Mostly in my kitchen, but all over the house. I had my work to do and I went where it took me."

"Did you enter this room before the alarm was given?"

Hannah frowned. Had any of the family admitted entering the room, she wondered? If they had, then so would she. She wasn't going to have one of them singled out for suspicion.

"Perhaps," she said cautiously. "It's more than likely but I don't remember."

"If you were 'all over the house' you must have noticed where the others were?"

"I'm paid to do the housework, not to spy on the family."

"But without spying you would notice the people you encountered?"

"Perhaps I should, perhaps I shouldn't. I'm a hard-working woman and I keep my mind on my work."

"Miss Mimms, for instance, was asleep in her room. You saw her into bed, I believe?"

"That's so. And she couldn't get out. So you needn't go suspecting her."

"She couldn't get out? Why not?"

"The room she has is at the top of the house. It's full of old furniture and the boys keep some of their rubbish in the drawers. I didn't want one of 'em going in and waking her, so I locked her in and took away the key. So she couldn't get out without shinning down the drain-pipe which no one but a copper would consider likely. At half past three I unlocked the door, called her and she went down to her mistress. It was then I heard her screaming."

"And Mr. Osborne? Where was he?"

"In the garden."

"How do you know?"

"I saw him going out."

"How do you know he remained there?"

"If you knew Mr. Osborne you'd know that when he goes out to the garden, he stays there."

"You didn't see him from the windows?"

"I haven't time to stand at windows. He came in when Miss Mimms screamed and made some remark about having been in the garden. That's good enough for me—and it would be good enough for you if you knew him as I do."

"You're very loyal."

"And well I might be. I've worked for the family for twenty-four years and I know 'em inside out. If you knew 'em half as well, you wouldn't be wasting time looking for a murderer in this house!"

"Where were Michael and Dorothy?"

"You'll have to ask them. It isn't my business to keep track of their comings and goings."

"Feeling the way you do about the Osbornes; you were probably incensed when you heard Miss Osborne proposing to cut them out of her will?"

"I could have wrung her wretched old neck!"

There was a pregnant silence, and then—" And someone did do almost that very thing," said Major Blackett quietly.

"Well, you needn't look at me like that. It wasn't me. It wasn't one of the Osbornes, either. None of them would hurt a fly. They always treated her a sight too well and precious little thanks they got for it. If you've any more to ask I'll thank you to ask it and let me go about my business. The younger children will be going to bed soon and they haven't had their warm milk yet."

"It would be too bad for the law to come between them and their warm milk," said Major Blackett smoothly. "That will be all for the present."

"Humph!" Hannah flounced out of the room, muttering something not quite under her breath about the house being 'turned upside down by a pack of—' —a word which Major Blackett hoped he hadn't heard correctly.

"Whew!" murmured Inspector Burrows. "What a wild cat! You were too lenient with her, sir."

Major Blackett smiled. "The world would be a better place if there were more servants of her stamp in it. I could do with one myself. *You* tried severity, Inspector, but I noticed it didn't pay. I wonder what she'd have said to *me* if I'd given her the chance?"

"Who's next, sir?" asked the Inspector stiffly.

"We'd better see Master Peter and Miss Marjory before they retire to bed."

"Very good, sir."

Chapter 13

A FEW MINUTES LATER, the Inspector followed Edith Osborne into the room. He looked sheepishly at his superior. Edith shivered slightly as she passed the draped chair, but when she faced Major Blackett, she was quite composed, although very pale. Her hands were clenched at her sides, as though with a very real physical effort she was trying to keep a grip of herself.

"Inspector Burrows informs me that you wish to question my younger children. I'm afraid I cannot allow that tonight. They are upset and I have sent them to bed."

"I understand," said Major Blackett quietly. "Believe me, I am deeply sorry to add to your cares and anxieties at a time like this, but you will appreciate the necessity for a thorough investigation. After I had sent for Peter and Marjory it occurred to me that it would not be right to question children of their ages in this room. I shall see them later, in less grim surroundings, when they have been soothed by a night's rest. Won't you please sit down?"

Edith seated herself. She looked out of the window with tired haggard eyes. Only now was she beginning to realise what the murder of Octavia Osborne was likely to mean to her family. Her lips trembled as she thought of what might lie before them in consequence of it.

"I am afraid I must ask you to permit your fingerprints to be taken," said Major Blackett gently. "I have already explained the reason to your husband, and he has agreed to the step. And we should like the younger children's prints also—as soon as possible—if you do not object."

"My objections are hardly relevant," said Edith bitterly. "If you will show me how to take them, I will obtain them for you tonight."

"Sergeant Feathers will show you. Tell me, Mrs. Osborne, where did you spend the period between luncheon and the discovery of the murder?"

"Shortly after luncheon I went into the garden to look for my husband. Failing to find him there"—at this Major Blackett and the Inspector exchanged glances—"I concluded that he must have wandered into the fields beyond, a thing he often did when he was worried or perplexed, and I returned to the house and went to my room. I had a splitting headache, so I lay down for a while and did not rise until I heard Miss Mimms screaming."

"Did anyone enter your room while you were lying down?"

"No one. I have no one to prove my alibi, Major, if that is what you mean."

"Mine is an unpleasant job at times, Mrs. Osborne. I have to put many questions which I do not relish asking."

"I appreciate that, Major. Forgive me if I spoke sharply."

"I do not think there is anything more I need ask you for the present. You will let me have the fingerprints?"

"Immediately." Edith took two cards and the inked pad from Sergeant Feathers and left the room.

"The way these people behave," growled Inspector Burrows, "makes me wonder who're the policemen—us or them. They'll have me thinking directly that *I'm* the one who did it."

"Oh, shut up, Burrows," said Major Blackett irritably "I'm sorry, man; but this is the worst job I've ever had to do. I'll see the young lady who owns the scarf next—Miss Dorothy Osborne."

"Very good, sir," snapped Inspector Burrows. "—*if she hasn't drunk her hot milk and gone to bed,*" he added, under his breath.

The way Dorothy reacted to the covered corpse was almost sufficient to console Burrows for the calm poise of her sister. She threw one frightened glance at it and positively darted across the room to the chair by the window. Major Blackett looked at her appreciatively and wished they were meeting in different circumstances. She was quite the most beautiful girl he had ever seen. Surely this divine creature could not be implicated in anything so sordid as a murder?

Sergeant Feathers, also, was gazing at her pensively, but Inspector Burrows maintained a stony exterior. It was all very well for the Chief and Feathers—they were bachelors—but he had been a much-married man for longer than he cared to remember; and even the loveliest woman was only another female to him. Inspector Burrows turned a jaundiced eye on all females.

"Please don't be frightened," said Major Blackett, with his friendliest smile. "I only want to ask you some questions."

Inspector Burrows had the silk scarf in his hand. He held it under her eyes.

"Perhaps you can tell us about this!"

Dorothy gasped and shut her eyes. She swayed. For a moment Major Blackett thought she was going to faint but with a visible effort she regained control of herself.

"It's mine," she whispered hoarsely.

"We know that," retorted the Inspector. "What we want to know is how it came to be about your aunt's neck when she was found dead—and who put it there!"

Terrified the girl stared at him.

"If you'll allow me, Burrows—" said the Chief Constable, caustically.

"Very good, sir," replied the Inspector, with a disgruntled air. Women! Bah! Give 'em looks and they had most men falling over themselves to be nice to 'em.

Someone knocked on the door. Sergeant Feathers went to answer it. He returned carrying the inked pad and the wet fingerprints of Marjory and Peter.

"Did you wear this scarf today, Miss Osborne?" asked the Major, in a kindly tone.

"Yes," shuddered Dorothy. "I wore it this afternoon when I went out after lunch."

"Where did you go?"

"I went over to the Flemings—they live not far from here—to play tennis. But I—I didn't feel like tennis, so I came home in half an hour or so."

"Did you enter this room?"

"No. Or rather, I almost did. I was about to come in through the French windows—I often come in that way in preference to using the front door—but I saw the top of Aunt Octavia's head over the back of her chair and I changed my mind. I went round to the front and up to my room."

"Taking the scarf with you?"

"Oh, no. I am not sure what I did with the scarf—I think I must have dropped it, perhaps in the hall. I didn't have it when I reached my room."

"You are sure of that?"

"Quite sure. I have a habit of dropping things about the house. This afternoon was warm and I wasn't wearing it; I was carrying it over my arm."

"How long did you remain in your room?"

"Until I heard the scream. I lay on my bed for a time"— sobbing bitterly, she might have added, for the scene at lunch had shaken her badly—"and I must have dropped off to sleep."

"I see; then there is little you can tell us. If you don't mind, Sergeant Feathers will take your fingerprints."

"You don't think I—"

"Oh, dear, no. I assure you there's nothing to worry about in having your fingerprints taken. Feathers!"

Sergeant Feathers stepped forward with alacrity. The eyes

of Inspector Burrows were hard and bitter as he watched his subordinate, gently, almost caressingly imprinting Dorothy's fingers on the white card. He noted grimly that the process took considerably longer than usual. A rag, a bone, and a hank of hair, he thought; but how it gets 'em, the poor fools.

"The mother, the daughter, the dead woman's maid," he exclaimed, when Dorothy had gone out; "all in their rooms, all feeling faint. What is this? A sanatorium?"

"I'll see Michael Osborne, Inspector," said Major Blackett curtly.

"Yes, sir," replied Burrows.

"*You spoony old fool,*" he added—but not aloud.

Major Blackett took a liking to Michael at once. Young, dark, slender and very much alive, Michael was exactly the sort of boy the Major had always wanted for a son. That was the devil of it: all these people were so confoundedly likeable.

"You'll hardly need that," said Michael, when Sergeant Feathers approached with the inked pad. He displayed his hands ruefully. They had obviously been washed, but they were rather black. "I never seem to get them quite clean."

"Perhaps you can explain this," said Major Blackett, spreading out the silk scarf.

Michael surveyed the black smears and frowned, wrinkling his nose. "'Fraid I can't. Looks like oil."

"It is. And how would oil get on so dainty an article of feminine wear?"

"Search me. Oh, I say"—the boy reddened—"I wonder if I— You know, I've a beastly trick of wiping oily hands on the first thing I come across. I was working with my motorbike this afternoon"

"That maybe it. Can you remember coming across this scarf?"

"No, I'm afraid I can't."

"Think hard."

Michael thought hard. He shook his head. "I can't remember."

"Did you come into the house during the afternoon?"

"Yes, once. I came in for something I'd left in my room."

"Through the French windows of this room?"

Michael stared. "Lord, no! Aunt was in here. Through the kitchen."

"And through the hall?"

"Yes."

"The scarf may have been lying in the hall. Try to remember whether you saw it there."

Again, Michael wrinkled his nose. "'Fraid I can't."

"You keep your motorcycle in a shed at the side of house? While you were working there, did anyone pass?"

"Yes, Dad did. He was going to the garden."

"Did you see him returning?"

"No, I didn't."

"Did you see anyone else?"

"I don't think so... Oh, wait a bit—I saw Ted Fleming. He spoke to me and went on out to the garden."

"Who is he?"

"Oh, Ted's an old friend of the family. He's spoony on Dorothy." Michael was suddenly conscious of the scratching of Sergeant Feathers' pencil. "I say," he gasped. "Don't take down that last remark."

Major Blackett smiled faintly. "And why was he going to the garden?"

"I didn't ask. He's always been welcome to come and go as he pleases. Old Ted's all right."

The boy glanced over his shoulder at the mantled chair with its gruesome occupant. "I say, I suppose it *was* murder?"

"Definitely."

"Good Lord! I wonder who could have—"

"That," said Major Blackett grimly, "is what we are trying to find out."

"I say!" Michael's eyes widened indignantly. "You don't think one of— Oh, you can't!"

"We are trying to get at the facts." Major Blackett patted the lad's shoulder. "Run along, boy, and don't think about it."

"That's easy to say," replied Michael, as he left the room.

Major Blackett lit a cigarette. He paced the room for a few minutes, with a gloomy frown. "Oh, hell," he said, and tossed the half-smoked cigarette into the grate.

"There's nothing more I can do here tonight, Burrows. I'm going home. Have *that* removed to the mortuary"—he indicated the stark figure of Octavia Osborne—"and arrange for an immediate autopsy. We'd better set the inquest for Monday and get it over with. See that summonses are issued tomorrow to everyone in the house—oh, and you'd better summon this Ted Fleming as well. Report to me at my house some time tomorrow and we'll have a chat. 'Night."

"Goodnight, sir."

*

Sometime later, when Inspector Burrows was leaving the house, the uniformed constable at the gate accosted him.

"There was a woman here a few minutes ago, Inspector, who wanted a few words with you," he said, speaking softly so that the reporters—still waiting impatiently—could not hear. "Said it was about this business."

"Then why the devil didn't you send her in?"

"She wouldn't go in, sir. Said to ask you to drop in on her when you'd finished here. She lives in one of the villas down the road a bit. 'Bide-a-Wee', she said the name was. You're to ask for Miss Whipple."

The reporters were clamouring for the Inspector's attention. He silenced them with a wave of his arm. "If you'll all hang on a little longer," he said, "I'll tell you all you want to know."

He plodded along the dark road to the row of red brick villas. He flashed his light on every gate until he came to the one on which was painted in large Gothic lettering the name Bide a Wee. With a wry grimace, he pushed the gate open and went up a trim path. There was no need to ask for Miss Whipple, for that lady opened the door to him in person.

"You wanted to see me, ma'am?"

Miss Whipple's eyes glistened behind her rimless glasses. "Won't you come in?"

She led the way to a prim drawing-room crowded with bric-a-brac. Seating himself gingerly on a gold-and-red plush chair, Inspector Burrows felt himself being shouldered and jostled by an overwhelming display of china dogs.

"This afternoon, Inspector," said the spinster eagerly, her nose shining, her eyes lit up, "I happened to be sitting at this window and I saw everything that went on over at the Osbornes'. About three I noticed—"

"Half a minute, ma'am," said Inspector Burrows thoughtfully. "You are quite a distance from the Osbornes'. I don't understand how you could see anything very distinctly."

"I have a telescope," retorted Miss Whipple tartly.

Chapter 14

I N THE STILL OF the night Edith Osborne lay awake listening to the fitful breathing of her husband, every breath a long-drawn sigh. He was awake, too; she could feel the tension of his body as he lay beside her. He was suffering—silently, agonisingly—his whole being one vast aching nerve. And there was nothing she could do about it; nothing she could say. Words have their limits which the circumstances far exceeded. It was not as though he were simply mourning the death of his sister; if that were all she could have found a way to comfort him.

But Octavia had not died—she had been killed. And murder makes its victims live. Octavia would never die. The swift tightening about her throat of the gaudy scarf which had ended her life had, at the same time, granted her a terrifying immortality.

No, words were worse than useless. Edith could not say to her husband: "*My dear, I know your sister was murdered in your house; I know the police think one of us did it, and, of course, I see that there is nothing else for them to think. I agree that it is going to root up our whole life and play merry hell with it; but let's not think about it, let's stop worrying and go to sleep.*" She could only stretch out her hand to him and feel him grip it tightly like a frightened child, as though it were the only anchorage in all the world his storm-tossed soul could find.

In the hush of the night the house lived. Its timbers stretched themselves, groaning and creaking; faint whispers rustled through dark passages and empty rooms, and behind the wainscot ran an odd gurgling, like the funny rumbling noise human intestines sometimes make. The clock on the dining-room mantelpiece whirred and clicked before striking a deep, sonorous chime that hung upon the still night air, swelling like the circles that widen on the placid breast of a pool when a stone is thrown into it. It whirred and clicked again before bringing up another swelling note from its cavernous interior. It shouldn't whirr and click like that, thought Edith; but it always has since Michael knocked it over.

Through the house a cry echoed. Edith thought she had imagined it until she heard it again. Stephen sat up.

"That's Peter," he whispered hoarsely. "Sounds like a nightmare."

He slid his feet out of bed and fumbled for his slippers. Edith let him go. Comforting his son might do him good. Stephen padded along the gloomy corridor and went into the room where the boys slept. He could dimly see the limp form of Michael, sunk deep in slumber; and the small white form of Peter, sitting up in the other bed, quaking with terror.

Stephen put his arms round the boy and held him tightly, feeling with pity the spasmodic shudders that ran through the slim body. "It's all right, son, nothing's going to hurt you. Daddy's here."

Gradually, Peter allowed himself to be soothed. The tears stopped coursing down his wet cheeks, and the shuddering ceased except for an occasional tremor.

"Oh, Daddy," he whimpered brokenly, "it was awful. I th—thought Aunt Oc—Octavia was in the room."

"Hush, boy, hush! You'll waken the others. It was only a dream, Peter, only a dream."

"Bob D—Dowell told me once that when people die th—that way their ghosts haunt the places where they were killed for ever and e—ever."

"Bob was talking nonsense, son. There's no such things as ghosts."

The boy was silent for a moment, and then—"Daddy," he muttered, "what happens when you die?"

Stephen's arm tightened on the narrow shoulders. It hurt to know that death had suddenly become a very grim reality to his child. "I don't know, dear. No one knows."

"One day I'll die," said the boy, in a hushed tone.

"You're only twelve, Peter," his father answered, trying hard to talk lightly. "That's very young to think of dying."

"Aunt Octavia didn't die because she was old. Anyone could die the way she did, no matter how young they were."

An icy grip tightened on Stephen's heart. What could he say to dispel the shadow of Octavia's death from Peter's mind? He could find no words that would do it. Like Edith, he realised the utter futility of words in the present circumstances. The wound was there, cut deeply into the sensitive young brain, and only time could heal it. Even if it healed there would always be a scar, puckered and ugly.

Kicking off his slippers, Stephen pushed back the bedclothes and slipped in beside the boy. Peter put two slender arms about his neck and nestled close to him. Stephen stroked the boy's hair and murmured soothingly in his ear.

"You won't leave me, Daddy? You'll stay all night?"

"Yes, son, I'll stay."

"I'm glad."

"Good night, Peter."

"Good night, Daddy."

At five in the morning Stephen gently extricated himself from his sleeping child's clinging arms and tiptoed downstairs. He opened the backdoor and went out to the garden. He had forgotten his slippers and the dew was cool and refreshing to his bare feet. It was a lovely morning, the sky clear and blue, the air sweet and fresh. A bird chirped in the branches of a tree above his head and far away a cock crowed a shrill challenge to the sun.

Yesterday dawned like this, he thought; and yesterday was the most dreadful day of my life. What will today bring?

His roses were coming on. Every day more blooms opened out to their full splendour. An hour later, when Edith came downstairs, she found her husband staring at a rose as though it were a crystal ball. He was still in pyjamas and bare feet. Horrified, she made him go and dress.

Hannah was up, and a fragrant odour of coffee began to pervade the house. The normal Sunday morning breakfast hour was half-past nine, but Edith and her husband breakfasted alone at seven. Edith had decided to let the children sleep until they wakened of their own accord. At eight a boy came clattering up the gravel path and deposited the Sunday papers on the doorstep. Stephen was looking out of a window and the boy gave him a curious stare. He had seen Stephen at least a hundred times in the past year, but he gaped at him as though he were an oddity he was seeing for the first time.

Stephen went out to bring in the papers. He stooped to pick them up and the glaring headline which was spread across the top of the front page of the uppermost paper struck him like a physical blow:

WOMAN MURDERED
WHILE NIECE READS SHAKESPEARE

With shaking hands, he lifted the paper. He leaned back against the portico, weak with horror, and read the subheadings and the columns of type beneath them:

GIRL'S SCARF USED IN CRIME
POLICE QUESTION FAMILY
DEATH FOLLOWS QUARREL OVER WILL

Saturday. Tragedy entered a quiet home in a sleepy Midland village this afternoon when Octavia Osborne aged 71, a wealthy spinster, of Sloane Square, London S.W.1, was strangled with a silk scarf while sitting in the drawing-room of her brother's house in Gay Ladies, a peaceful Blankshire hamlet. An odd feature of the crime is that a niece of the murdered woman was actually reading a book in the room at the time Miss Osborne was done to death. She stated to the police that she heard nothing until her aunt's companion entered the room and gave the alarm...local resident, whose name the police have decided for the present to withhold, has come forward to say that although she was overlooking the house practically all afternoon from the window at which she was sitting, she saw no one enter it except members of the family and Mr. Edward Fleming, 25 year old son of a prominent Brancaster lawyer, who is locally reputed to be engaged to the eldest daughter... scarf which was found knotted tightly about the neck of the murdered woman belonged to Dorothy Osborne, one of her nieces...visit was cut short by a serious family quarrel which arose when Miss Osborne announced the terms of a will she intended to make, disinheriting her brother...draft of new will was found partially burned in a fireplace...had the misfortune to be discharged from his employment the previous day... questioned various members of the family and took a set of fingerprints from each...scouted the possibility that a tramp might have entered and committed the crime...declared that lack of motive rendered such a solution out of the question...

With haggard eyes, Stephen read to the bottom of the page down two closely-printed columns and found the injunction to 'turn to page 16'. Descriptions of the individual Osbornes, further details of the crime, and veiled hints that no outsider could have been responsible for it occupied most of page 16. There was a photograph of the house, taken from the fields behind, in which the drawing-room French windows were marked with an x; a photograph of Major Blackett entering the gate, with the police car in the background; and one of an awe-struck crowd in the roadway outside, under which ran the caption: 'Shocked villagers jostle for glimpse of bereaved family.'

It was damnable. Almost in so many words—but cunningly enough to avoid an action for libel—the newspaper was saying to its readers: 'There are seven members of the Osborne family and one of them must have done it. Take your choice.' The insinuations were plain. No reader could doubt what they were intended to convey: That Octavia Osborne was murdered by her own flesh-and-blood. All over the country at this moment millions of people were poring over their Sunday papers and exclaiming: "*Isn't it awful! Murdering an old woman for her money! I wonder which of them did it? If you ask me, the husband—*"

"*Well, I don't know. I can't quite swallow that yarn about the niece reading while it was done. I shouldn't wonder if she—*"

Stephen could visualise George Bramwell's avid red face in the train on Monday morning as he eagerly swapped speculations with the other men in the compartment and could almost hear him saying: "*D'you know, I travelled down with Osborne only the other evening. He looked precious seedy, I can tell you. Give you five to one he did it. It stands to reason; he had lost his job and was ripe for murder when the old girl refused to help him. Wonder if he'll swing for it?*"

With a groan Stephen tore the paper to shreds and crumpled it into a mangled ball. He snatched up the other paper and crushed them together. As he turned to go down the garden to burn them in the incinerator he saw three young farm labourers, garbed in their Sunday best, lounging in the lane with expressions of morbid gloating on their scrubbed pink faces. They nudged each other and one of them whispered something which made the others burst into loud guffaws.

Sometime later Edith came to him while he was savagely stirring the ashes in the incinerator.

"Time to change for church, Stephen."

He stared at her. "Church? Edith, are you mad? We can't go to church! If you'd seen the papers! The faces of those louts staring in the lane! They'll all be gossiping about us—everyone in the village—if we go out, they'll nudge each other and point. '*They killed an old woman for her money!*' Can't you hear them? We can't face it, Edith. It's too much to be borne."

"I know how you feel, Stephen, my dear, but we've got to face it, sooner or later. We can't show the white feather. We've got to carry on as though nothing has happened. Every Sunday morning since we've been in this house we've gone to church, and we must go today, of all days. Peter and Marjory can stay at home, but the older children must come with us. Don't you see, we'll be letting ourselves down if we shrink from facing our neighbours. If they stare, let them. We'll show them we're not ashamed, whatever they think."

How he lived through the walk to church, the seemingly endless ceremony, and the walk back to the house, Stephen never knew. Staring faces. Goggling eyes. Gloating whispers. A village with a scandal to gnaw on is hell on earth, and the murder of Octavia Osborne was such a scandal as Gay Ladies had never before known.

A camera clicked as Stephen entered the church and he started as though he were shot. When they were leaving, they ran into the Flemings. The distance from the solicitor's house to the church was so short that he and his wife and son almost invariably covered it on foot, but this morning their Daimler was waiting. Mr. and Mrs. Fleming acknowledged their neighbours with the most distant of bows as they climbed into the car. Ted Fleming hung back and spoke urgently to Dorothy.

"Meet me in the orchard behind our garden at four this afternoon. I've a lot to discuss with you—*darling.*"

Mrs. Fleming leaned forward and looked out of the open window of the Daimler.

"Edward! We're waiting."

Someone tittered in the group about the church door.

"*Ow, Edward!*" cried a mocking falsetto. "Don't keep dear Mamma waiting! Mamma will spank!"

There was a roar of coarse laughter. Red with embarrassment, Ted ducked into the car and it glided majestically away.

All the way back to the house Stephen could hear footsteps trudging behind; the footsteps of a giggling cluster of curiosity-seekers, following eagerly to swell the gaping crowds at his garden gate.

Chapter 15

A T A QUARTER TO four that afternoon Dorothy left the house and started down the path to the gate. Halfway she halted in dismay.

There were now hundreds of people pushing and jostling in the narrow road, and long lines of cars parked under the hedges on either side. The village policeman was doing his best to keep the crowd under control but he could not be everywhere at once; and while he marched along one of the garden walls, sternly ordering down those who had climbed up to obtain a better view of the house in which Octavia Osborne had been murdered, a dozen others would swarm up on the other wall.

Some of them had cameras and were taking snapshots of the house. Three or four clicks as Dorothy hesitated told her that she had been 'bagged' by as many murder fans. From the roof of a car a cameraman from one of the newsreel companies was filming the crowd. He swang the camera to take in Dorothy.

The girl averted her face and hurried into the house. She went out by the back door, through the kitchen garden, and into the field behind. Here there were other curiosity-seekers, but not in the numbers that eddied to and fro at the front. Her face grimly set, her head down she hastened through the field into a lane which joined the road a few hundred yards from the house. At the foot of the lane, she paused and looked right and left like a hunted animal. The road in her immediate vicinity was clear. With a thankful gasp, she ran across into the larch coppice on the other side, which skirted the orchard at the foot of the Flemings' garden.

In the orchard she flung herself on the grass and covered her face. She could still feel the cruel scrutiny of those morbid eyes.

It had been like one of those awful nightmares in which you are walking along a crowded street completely naked. Those eyes! Horrible, beastly eyes; the eyes of human animals who revelled in the downfall of their fellows. What had she done that they should look at her like that?—as though she were something in a cage.

They had taken her photograph. In their homes they would hand the prints about, delighted to have such mementoes to exhibit to their friends. They would say: "*That's Dorothy Osborne. You know, one of the family that murdered the rich aunt. Yes, we drove over to see the house and she came out to the garden as bold as brass.*" In a thousand picture theatres she would be thrown on the screen for callous cinema-goers to gape at and wonder whether she was the one who 'did it.'

For a long time, she lay on the friendly earth, clinging to it as though to a consoling mother. When at last she sat up and looked at her watch she was dismayed to find that it was twenty past four. Where was Ted? She stood up and took a few paces down an avenue of trees.

"Ted?" she called softly. "Ted!"

No answer.

Someone was coming. Dorothy heard brisk footsteps on the springy turf and hurried in the direction from which they came, but stopped dead when she saw that the person who was approaching was not Ted, but a trim maidservant in a black dress and snowy cap and apron.

"Miss Osborne? Mrs. Fleming sent me to look for you."

"*Mrs.* Fleming sent you?"

"Yes, Miss"—the girl eyed her covertly from beneath lowered lids—"she told me to ask you to have tea with her. She is on the terrace."

"Oh." Dorothy hesitated. "Alone?" she asked, and could have bitten off her tongue as soon as the question was uttered.

"Yes, miss, alone," replied the girl, with a faint smile.

"Say to Mrs. Fleming that I am not feeling well and wish her to excu— No, wait, please. I'll come."

Mrs. Fleming was not on the terrace, but on the smooth stretch of shaven lawn below it. A tea-table had been laid in the shade of a spreading old elm, and there were two basket chairs placed beside it, in one of which sat Mrs. Fleming. A tall woman in the late forties, with a pale face, she was beautiful in a serene, impersonal fashion.

Her features were delicately formed, almost doll-like with the exception of the nose, which was long and thin and disconcertingly sharp. Her blue-black hair was drawn smoothly down from the forehead and gathered at the nape of her neck, forming a frame for the perfect oval of her face. She looked younger than her age; and yet, older than time. Her make-up was so adeptly applied that it was admirable for its own sake as well as for the added beauty it lent her. Exquisitely gowned, completely mistress of herself, she made Dorothy feel very young and entirely unsophisticated.

"Sit down, my dear," she smiled. "It's nice to see you."

"Thank you," said Dorothy nervously.

"You take sugar and cream, I think? Lucky girl! I daren't touch either. I envy you young things who don't have to worry about your figures. White bread or brown?"

"Neither, thank you. I'm not hungry."

"Oh, but you must eat something. Some strawberries? I assure you they are delightful. I'd simply wolf them myself if I dared."

"No, really."

"A cigarette, then?" Mrs. Fleming opened a silver box and extended it to Dorothy.

"No, thanks."

"I think I shall." Mrs. Fleming tapped a cigarette on

a lacquered fingernail and lit it at the tapering flame of an enamelled lighter. "I seem to live on cigarettes and tea." They regarded each other over the teacups and Dorothy began to feel limp and weak. How could she hope to be a match for this cold, calm woman?

"Oh, by the way," said Mrs. Fleming, as casually as though the matter had only that instant occurred to her, "I have a message for you from Edward. He asked me to say goodbye to you on his behalf and make his apologies for not saying it in person. He wanted to come and see you before he went, but the poor boy was in such a rush that he had hardly time to say goodbye to *me!*"

"Goodbye!" echoed Dorothy, white to the lips. "I—I don't understand."

"No, you'd hardly have heard, would you? It was all so sudden. You see, Mr. Fleming's firm is carrying through some negotiations with a French company in Paris on behalf of one of the big Brancaster cotton manufacturers—some new artificial silk process is involved, I believe—and since Edward has newly joined the firm, his father thought it would be good experience for him to assist in the negotiations."

"Oh!" Crushed and subdued, that murmured "Oh!"

"He left for London directly after luncheon and is crossing to France tomorrow."

"It—it's terribly sudden."

"Sudden? Well, yes."

"How long will he be gone?"

"I really don't know, my dear. Not less than six months. Possibly a year. It isn't certain that he will come home when he leaves Paris. There is a possibility that he will be attached to the staff of his father's London agents for a few years, for the sake of experience."

"I see."

Mrs. Fleming leaned forward and placed a cool hand on the girl's arm. "I know it must be a shock to you, my dear, to find that your childhood playmate has grown up and gone away, but none of us stay children for ever, you know, and men have work in the world to do. I shall always be grateful to you and your family for taking him into your games as a child and making him one of you. I know he regards you all almost as brothers and sisters. An only child can be very lonely and you have done more for him than I can say—but he is not a child any longer and his world has grown far beyond the limits of this sleepy village."

"Why do you harp on the word 'child'?" asked Dorothy unsteadily. "Ted is twenty-five and I am twenty-three. Neither of us have been children for quite a long time."

Before replying, Mrs. Fleming took time to pour fresh tea.

"You are both very young and inexperienced," she said at last. "Charmingly young and inexperienced. You are a nice girl and Edward is a nice boy. You are fond of each other. If you have imagined that your feelings were deeper that is not surprising. You have spent a great deal of time in each other's company, and it is only natural that love should enter into the relationship. But young love is calf-love and although calf-love is very charming and delightful it seldom endures. I expect you will both fall in and out of love many times before either of you chooses a permanent mate. That is half the charm of youth: the inconsequence with which it passes from one love affair to another like a butterfly flitting from flower to flower."

Rising to her feet, Dorothy put a hand inside the neck of her dress and drew up a thin gold chain. She detached from it a gold seal ring, which she placed on the table.

"Ted gave me this," she said dryly, lifelessly. "He asked me to keep it until he could replace it with a proper engagement ring. Will you please return it to him?"

She turned to go but Mrs. Fleming called her back. "Don't think too harshly of me, my dear. Ted is my only child and his well-being is very dear to me. Please don't misunderstand me: I have nothing against you personally. You are a sweet girl; the kind of girl, indeed, I have always hoped Ted would choose for his wife and the mother of his children. But don't you see——"

"Yes," said Dorothy, "I see. Yesterday my aunt was murdered in my father's house and today the papers are full of it. Today I'm one of the notorious family. You don't care about my feelings—you'll trample over them roughshod—as long as your son is freed from what I suppose you would call an 'entanglement'."

"I am his mother. My son must come first with me. This is a matter that concerns his whole future."

"And mine," murmured Dorothy, with a sob in her voice.

"I know, my dear, I know; and believe me, I am sorry for you. I am afraid you are in for a terrible time. There will be a great deal of mud thrown at your family and some of it will inevitably stick. Life will be made unbearable for you. I have an idea. An old friend of mine winters every year in the South of France and last time she wrote me she said that she was looking for a companion for her daughter, who is a little younger than you. I am sure if I wrote and suggested you, she would be only too glad to take you. You would be away from all the unpleasantness which is sure to surround your family. On the Riviera with my friend, no one would dream of connecting you with this terrible affair."

"You are very kind," said Dorothy; "but—no thanks. Just now you said that it is your duty to think of your son. It is equally my duty to think of my family. At a time of trouble—terrible trouble—my place is with them."

"I feel quite sure your mother would rather you were out of it all."

"I know she would, but that is not the point. If my father and mother, my brothers and sisters, are to be crucified by the public, I shall be crucified with them." In the stress of her emotion Dorothy forgot the sensation-seeking pack outside her home. Her eyes misty with tears she came out of the Flemings' gate, turned right along the road, and ran straight into it. She almost had to fight her way through the surging mob which shoved and scrambled for a glimpse of her.

"*Look! There she is!*"

"*That's the eldest girl.*"

"*It was her scarf the murder was done with—*"

"*Look! She's crying!*"

Blinded by the tears which coursed down her cheeks Dorothy stumbled into the house. She went into the dining-room and collapsed on an old leather couch in the corner. There Ann and Michael found her, quivering with pain, torn from head to foot by great shuddering sobs

"Dorothy!" cried Ann, very panic-stricken. "Dorothy *darling!*"

"What is it?" gasped Michael. "Those swine in the road, I suppose? God, I'd like to kill 'em all!"

"It isn't only them," wept Dorothy. "It's Ted as well."

"Ted?" frowned Michael. "What's he done?"

"He's gone away."

"The *worm!*" declared Ann, with vitriol in her tone. "Don't say that. It isn't true."

"Only a worm would give you the chuck at a time like this."

"His parents made him."

"The beasts!" cried Ann.

"No, they're not beasts," said Dorothy, more calmly. "They aren't deliberately doing this to hurt me. It's only that they've got to think of their son; he comes first."

"If Ted were half a man, he'd have told them to go to hell," growled Michael. "Chucking you because they're afraid of the scandal! Oh, it's all so unfair! It isn't as though you'd done anything. It isn't as though any of us had done anything."

"Isn't it?" said Ann quietly.

They stared at her. "What do you mean?"

"You don't think an outsider killed Aunt Octavia, do you?" asked Ann, calmly.

"Ann! How can you talk like that?"

"Look here, Ann, don't gabble such utter bilge!"

"Use your heads, my children. No one had the opportunity of killing her except us Osbornes, Hannah Gale, and Miss Mimms. You don't think Mimms would kill her, and do herself out of a thousand a year for life, do you?—even if she had the guts, which she hasn't. That leaves us Osbornes—and Hannah. Well, Hannah's one of the family. If we knew definitely that *she* did it we'd stand by her just as we'd stand by Daddy.

"The police are playing a game of 'Who's got the Button?' with us. They know one of us did it and they're going to move heaven and earth to find out which. Are we going to help them? Of course not. We've got to do our best to baulk them. When they ask questions, we've got to play stupid and tell 'em nothing."

"But, Ann—"

"It's a question of someone's life. The life of one of us. Father, Mother, Marjory, Peter, Hannah, you, Dorothy, you, Michael—and me. Does it matter which? Do we care which of us did it? Do we? Would we raise a finger to help hang the guilty one?"

"Good God, no!" shuddered Michael.

"Very well, then."

"Ann!" gasped Dorothy suddenly. "It wasn't— You didn't—"

"That," said Ann very earnestly, "is a question none us must ask another."

Chapter 16

MONDAY MORNING. A bell shrilled imperatively in the dusty
staff room at the head office of the Blankshire County
Police, which is situated in the market town of Brestock, eight
miles from Gay Ladies and roughly the same distance from
Brancaster. It sounded again.

"Two rings," said Sergeant Feathers, looking up from his
desk. "That's for you, Inspector."

"I've got ears, my lad."

Inspector Burrows rose ponderously and left the room. He
plodded along a whitewashed passage and tapped on a door.
He cocked his head and listened. "Come in!" said a voice, curt,
impatient. Inspector Burrows shook his head gloomily. It was
as he feared; the Chief was in no good humour this bright and
sunny morning. He turned the handle and walked in.

The Chief Constable's room was more like a study than an
office. The floor was covered by a fawn carpet, tailored to fit
snugly the angles and eccentricities of the skirting boards. On
the hearth lay a magnificent Alsatian dog which pricked its
ears, half rose, and growled softly at the Inspector's entrance.
Major Blackett spoke sharply and it lay down again, stretching
full length on a Persian rug, its black eyes fixed unblinkingly
on Inspector Burrow's face. To right and left of the fireplace
stood two shabby armchairs, invitingly plump, upholstered in
hide. On the mantelpiece was an array of silver cups, ranging
from one Major Blackett had won for running at his prep school
forty years before to one awarded for coming first in the main
jumping event at the Blankshire Horse Show of the current
year; and above hung the snarling head of a tiger, a souvenir of
his long service in Bengal.

Round the walls, which were papered in dark green, hung a collection of sporting prints; and in a corner stood a cabinet which combined the offices of humidor and cellarette. In the centre of the room stood a walnut desk, on which a morning newspaper was spread out. Inspector Burrows flinched slightly as his eyes lighted on it.

"'Morning, Burrows," said Major Blackett coldly. He was standing straddle-legged, with his back to the empty grate.

"Good morning, sir."

"Seen the papers?"

"One or two of 'em, sir."

"Well?"

"Well, sir"—the Inspector shifted uncomfortably— "they seem to agree pretty generally with my—with our theory."

"And our theory is?"

"Well, sir, we know almost to a certainty that one of the family committed the murder."

"We know that, do we? And how do you suppose the papers came to know as much as we do?"

"I told them, sir," replied Inspector Burrows, squaring his shoulders.

"Took them completely into your confidence, didn't you? You did not consult me before taking that step."

"Well, sir, the idea did not occur to me while I was in your company."

"Laying our whole hand on the table for the benefit of the Press is not our customary policy."

"No, sir. And in most cases it would be a stupid thing to do. It is usually wise to keep the extent of our knowledge to ourselves. There is generally nothing be gained and a great deal to be lost by letting a criminal know how far you've got in your pursuit of him. But this case is different, sir. We're up against a funny proposition. We've got to pick our man—or woman—out of a field of seven or eight possibles and the only way we can do it is to put the wind up him in the hope that he'll make some move which will give him away."

"And supposing the murderer lies low and says nothing?"

"In that event, sir, I'm afraid the case will never be settled. We can't put eight people on trial, and we can't choose one by picking a paper out of a hat. There's another advantage to giving full publicity to all the known facts of this case, sir. Newspaper stories make gossip and when folk gossip, things often come out. There's no saying what will come to light if the old women of the village put their heads together. I told you yesterday what I've got already from one of 'em—Miss Whipple."

"Then I'm to understand, Burrows, that you want to go on feeding these sensational stories to the Press?"

"With your permission, sir."

"I don't like it, man. I don't like it. It's not—not quite— Oh well, if you think it will get results, go ahead. What luck with the fingerprints?"

"We found ten different sets in the room, sir, and checked them with those we had taken from the family and the servants. Nine of them agreed with those of the parents, the five children, Miss Mimms, and Hannah Gale. The tenth, which was taken from the frame of the French windows, were those of an outsider."

"Ah!" said Major Blackett.

"I had a hunch about the tenth set, sir, so I had Sergeant Feathers call at a certain house in the village and take fingerprints from the handle of a tennis racquet which he found there. The racquet belongs to Mr. Edward Fleming—and the prints on it matched the tenth set."

"Did they, by Jove!"

"Sergeant Feathers has devoted some time to the study of fingerprints, sir, and he assures me that those on the frame of the French windows had been recently made—not later, in his opinion, than the afternoon of the murder."

"And Fleming was seen in the garden about three o'clock! H'm... Have you interviewed the young man?"

"I called at his house twice on Sunday, sir, but he was not at home. On my second visit I left a summons for him to attend the inquest this morning.

"We have made another important fingerprint discovery, sir. A thumbprint on the scorched draft of the will has been identified as that of Hannah Gale."

"Oho! Then Hannah was the one who attempted to burn it! Have you taxed her with this?"

"No, sir. I thought it better to spring it on her at the inquest."

"Psychological effect, eh?"

"Yes, sir."

Inspector Burrows coughed and glanced at his superior. "Are there any private directions you wish me convey to the coroner before the inquest starts, sir?"

"I don't think so. Why?"

"I should suggest giving Doctor Heffers his head, sir. The coroner's court is less bound up in red tape than we are and he can put questions we daren't even frame. When he gets going, Doctor Heffers can be a regular terror."

"Yes—poor devils!—he'll tear 'em to pieces. Well, rather him than me."

*

All Gay Ladies and the greater part of Brestock turned out for the inquest on Octavia Osborne. It was the greatest free show in years and nobody wanted to miss it. Loungers forsook their lamp-posts; tradesmen left their shops in charge of grumbling assistants; schoolboys played truant; housewives stacked their unwashed breakfast dishes in their kitchen sinks, took their toddlers by the hand and went to see the fun; the reading-room of the public library, haunt of old age pensioners, was deserted.

An hour before the inquest was due to begin the coroner's court was packed to suffocation and the overflow jammed the street, surging to and fro like an ocean gone mad. It was every man for himself. A murmur rose:

"*There they are! Look! That's Stephen Osborne, the tall man trying to push his way to the door. That's his wife, close behind!*" and the rabble pressed forward like sheep, thrusting and shoving for a glimpse of the relations who were suspected of having strangled the dead woman for her money. In the crazy scramble several women fainted and one of them had two ribs trampled in before she could be dragged from under the heels of the mob.

"*I couldn't see 'em!*" wailed a voice. "*Did you see 'em, Kate? What did they look like?*" "*'Twasn't them. They ain't turned up yet.*" "*Late, ain't they?*" "*Maybe they've done a bunk.*" "*I don't blame 'em if they have. I'd do a bunk, too, if the cops was after me for murder!*"

Shortly after ten, word that the Osbornes had been smuggled into court by a back door spread through the crowd like wildfire and many angry voices were raised in disgruntled protests. It was, they all agreed, a dirty trick. "*After us waiting all this time!*" There followed a wild rush down an alley which led to the rear of the court and in the battle that ensued when a thousand temporary maniacs fought to be the first to enter a passage that could accommodate at the most only three abreast, a section of the mob was barged through a plate glass window. No fatalities resulted, but nearly all of them had deep cuts to show for it; and one man was so badly injured that his right leg had later to be severed above the knee.

*

The coroner, Doctor Nicholas Heffers, was a twisted little man with a curved back and hunched shoulders which together with his bald head and hooked nose, gave him a remarkable resemblance to a parrot. Inspector Burrows had warned him that the majority of the witnesses were likely to be stubborn; and he was ready for them. It was his boast that he could take the starch out of the most stubborn witness in two minutes flat.

It took him no more than that to reduce Stephen to pulp; but in Ann and Hannah Gale he found foemen worthy of his steel. He had one passage-at-arms with Ann which almost took the starch out of *him*; and several of Hannah's tart replies evoked appreciative titters from the audience.

The day wore on while he dealt with the Osbornes one by one. He ranted, railed, sneered; going over the same point time and time again; hammering at every answer until it was battered out of shape. There was a short break for lunch and then he started on them again. It was four o'clock in the afternoon before Peter, the last of the family to testify, was allowed to stand down, in a flood of tears. Doctor Heffers leaned back with a malignant scowl at the bench on which the Osbornes were seated, and wiped beads of perspiration from his narrow forehead.

He dealt more gently with the dead woman's former companion, but poor Miss Mimms was in a state of panic before she started to give evidence. There was an electric tension in the court when the coroner said:

"Call Agnes Alicia Whipple."

Miss Whipple rose with alacrity and came forward clasping her handbag and umbrella to her skimpy bosom with one hand and adjusting her pince-nez with the other. There was on her pinched face an avid look and in her peering eyes a glint of jubilation. She bore herself with an air which made it quite clear that she did not doubt the importance of the role she was about to play.

"On Sunday last, between half-past two and four o'clock in the afternoon, you were seated at your drawing-room window looking out?"

Miss Whipple inclined her head gravely. "I was."

Doctor Nicholas Heffers fumbled with the papers on his desk, selected one, and glanced at it.

"You were examining the surrounding countryside through a telescope?"

A gust of laughter caused Miss Whipple to redden. "That is so," she said stiffly.

"Did you at any time have the house of Stephen Osborne under observation?"

"I did. Practically all the time. Not," she added hastily, "that I was in any sense of the word spying on the Osbornes. Inquisitiveness, I am happy to say, is not one of my failings. But across the road from the house in which the Osbornes live is a larch coppice in which dwells a large colony of birds, and it is my delight on bright, sunny days to watch the comings and goings of our little feathered brethren through my telescope. I am also interested in astronomy; that is my principal reason for owning the instrument."

"And quite frequently the Osborne house came into the range of your lens?"

"Quite frequently, yes."

"Did you see any stranger approaching the house?"

"I did not."

"Did you see anyone approaching?"

"I did."

"Whom did you see?" Miss Whipple straightened her shoulders and glanced meaningfully at the jury.

"I saw Mr. Edward Fleming, junior. It was about three o'clock. He pushed open the gate and went up the garden path. In his hand"— her voice rose dramatically—"*was a coloured silk scarf!*"

"He was carrying a coloured silk scarf?" the coroner repeated with emphasis.

"He was," said the spinster firmly.

"Did you see it clearly enough to be able to recognise again?"

A hush so pregnant that it was almost audible fell upon the crowded courtroom.

"I did."

"Is this it?" Doctor Heffers held up the scarf with which Octavia Osborne had been murdered.

"It is," replied Miss Whipple clearly.

"*Ah!*" For a moment the coroner looked disconcertingly like the desiccated harpy he was questioning. "Did this young man go to the front door of the house?"

"He did not. In what I can only describe as a furtive manner he went stealthily round the side of the house."

"Did you see him again?"

"Yes. I had been struck by the oddness of his manner and I kept the house under observation until he reappeared."

"When was that?"

"In about five minutes. He returned the way he had come, but this time he was hurrying, almost running."

"And then?"

"I saw nothing more," said the spinster regretfully, "until one of the Osborne children came running out of the house and darted down the road to Doctor Denham's villa."

"Thank you, Miss Whipple. May I commend you for the clear and straightforward manner in which you have given your testimony? That will be all."

Miss Whipple sailed back to her place, her head held high.

"Call Edward Fleming, junior."

There was an expectant murmuring, much turning of heads and craning of necks.

"Call Edward Fleming, junior."

A rustle of whispers ran through the court like wind through a field of standing corn. A grey-haired man rose with dignity and faced the coroner.

"I am Edward Fleming, senior, of the firm of Harden and Fleming, solicitors, of Brancaster," he said in a dry, precise tone. "I am here to represent my son, who is unable to attend in person."

Doctor Heffers put on a pair of horn-rimmed spectacles and scowled through them at the lawyer.

"Your son has been summoned to attend this hearing. Where is he?"

"He is on his way to Paris on business."

"When did he leave?"

"Early yesterday afternoon."

The coroner squinted in the direction of Inspector Burrows. "Was not a summons to attend served on the young man yesterday morning?"

Inspector Burrows stood up. "It was, sir."

"Then why is he not here?" Doctor Heffers' scathing gaze shifted to Mr. Fleming.

"It was necessary for my son to be in Paris for a conference on Tuesday. All arrangements had been made—"

"This won't do," snapped the coroner, shaking his head. "It won't do at all. I am aware of the various attacks on the dignity of the ancient office of coroner which have been made in the popular press from time to time, but your son is gravely in error if he imagines that office is to be flouted in this manner with impunity. I shall have to consider what steps are to be—"

"At the time my son left for London," replied the lawyer soberly, "it was my understanding that he had no evidence to give which would be of material assistance in this inquiry. The testimony of the previous witness has made it clear that I was wrong. I shall get in touch with my son immediately and request him to return at once for the purpose of making a statement."

Inspector Burrows made his way to the coroner's side and whispered urgently in his ear. Doctor Heffers nodded.

"It is imperative that he return at once," he said aloud. "He may make his statement to the police officials in charge of the case since it is doubtful when the next hearing of this inquest will be held. I intend to adjourn it indefinitely to give the police an opportunity of pursuing a certain line of inquiry."

Clearing his throat self-importantly, the coroner turned to the jury. His office permitted him to indulge his love of mud-throwing without fear of consequences, and he intended to take full advantage of it.

"At this time, I consider it my duty to say that never in all my experience have I known a case in which the majority of the witnesses were so unsatisfactory as they are in this one. You have listened today to a succession of evasions, almost deliberate prevarications, as one member of the dead woman's family after another has been brought forward to testify. You will have noticed with what reluctance they permitted the smallest admission to be drawn out of them. You will have marked the long pauses between questions and answers; pauses which would not have been necessary, you will doubtless feel, if a desire to tell the truth had been all that inspired the witnesses. Perhaps you have come to the conclusion which I, myself, have reached, that there is here a strong presumption of a deliberate conspiracy to defeat the ends of justice by the withholding of vital information. To put it even more forcibly, I feel…"

*

When the end of the hearing came at last it was found to be utterly impossible for the Osbornes to leave the way they had come. The crowd at the rear of the building was even more closely packed than that at the front. A cordon of burly policemen drove a flying wedge through the surging mob at the front and the Osbornes, their heads down, their faces averted, were rushed through the middle of it. In spite of their muscular escort, they were forced to run the gauntlet of yells and jeers, which were to ring in their ears for many a long day.

*

Edith had pressed Miss Mimms to stay with them until she found a new post, but she had pleaded that a change of environment was her only chance of forgetting her terrible experience, and Edith could not help agreeing with her. That evening she departed to spend a short time at a seaside boarding-house which Edith recommended as quiet and cheap. She had enough money, she assured them, to last her for months to come. Stephen made her promise to write him if she needed more.

"Whatever happens," he told her, at parting, "I am going to do my utmost to see that you receive the legacy my sister intended you to have."

Chapter 17

A T HALF-PAST SEVEN the following morning, a young man in a battered felt hat and soiled raincoat walked stealthily up the garden path to the back door of the Osborne's house. He looked through a window and saw on the kitchen table six pairs of gleaming shoes of various sizes. Hannah Gale, in a blue print dress and white apron, with her sleeves rolled above the elbows, was vigorously brushing a seventh pair. The young man tapped on the window and Hannah looked up. He beckoned and she opened the door and regarded him dourly. "And who might you be?"

"I might be anyone, Hannah," he answered cheerily "but for your private information, I'm a reporter from the *London Morning Globe*."

"And by what right do you make so free with my Christian name! I'm Miss Gale to you, you saucy young cub. Be off with you; we want no reporters here!"

"Oh, come," he smiled. "That's no way to talk to a chap who only wants a few words with you."

"Any words you get from me will be short and sharp! I've nothing to say to you or the likes of you, young man!"

"That's only your modesty, Miss Gale. I'm sure there are a lot of interesting things you could tell me if—"

"Well, I don't intend to, so take yourself off before I take my broom to you!"

"I'll give you five pounds for an exclusive interview. Five pounds, Miss Gale! All you need to do is tell me your own personal story of the murder and give me a few intimate little details about the family. You'll never earn a fiver easier if you live to be— Hey! Look out! What are you doing?'

"You young blaggard!"

The chilly contents of a bucket of water with which Hannah had lately washed the front steps drenched him from head to foot. Hannah slammed the door in his spluttering face. She put down the bucket and took up the pair of shoes she had been cleaning when he knocked; and buffeted them with the brush as though she were pounding the hides of all the newspaper men in the country.

Edith came downstairs a little later and was surprised to find the letterbox crammed full of correspondence. Frowning, she took out the thick wad of letters and skimmed through them, glancing at the envelopes. Some of them were typewritten and the rest were addressed in unfamiliar hands. She went into the dining-room and sat by the fire with the letters on her lap. The topmost one was addressed to: 'The Osborne Family'. Her face turned very pale and her lips tightened when she read the lines: *'You are a lot of cowardly rats you ought to be hanged every one of you for killing an old woman for her money…'*

The vindictive scrawl was unsigned. Without reading further Edith tore it into shreds and threw it in the fire. She opened another at random. It too, was anonymous:

'I read about your case in the paper and I thought I'd just write and tell you I don't blame you for what you done, no matter what the world may say. I have a rich old aunt too and my word she is a mean old beast…'

It, too, went into the fire. With trembling hands, Edith opened another and glanced at it briefly. It was in the same scurrilously abusing tone as the first. She could bear no more. She tore up the remaining envelopes unopened and consigned them to the flames.

"How beastly!" she exclaimed bitterly. "How incredibly vile!"

Breakfast was a silent meal. No one ate much. It was as

though the dead aunt were seated at the table with them. Stephen glanced at the morning paper and his face clouded over. A sprawling headline ran across the top of the front page: 'Coroner Rebukes Inquest Witnesses'; and almost the entire page was devoted to an account of the evidence given the previous day. In the centre of the page was a photograph of the Osborne family, huddled together like sheep, passing through the crowd of gaping spectators outside the Brestock Town Hall.

Stephen quietly folded the paper and did not look at it again. After breakfast Edith burned it. She gave Hannah orders that in future the morning paper must be submitted to her for inspection before her husband saw it.

At about ten Ann was going upstairs to make the beds when she heard the doorbell ringing. She turned to come down but when she was a few steps from the bottom Marjory opened the door. Miss Whipple glided over the threshold and sailed into the hall.

"Is your mother in, dear?" she asked brightly.

Marjory hesitated, but before she could reply Ann came running down.

"I'm afraid Mother cannot see you, Miss Whipple," she said icily. "She isn't at all well. She isn't seeing anyone."

"Poor dear, I can quite understand that. She has my sympathy. This awful business must be a sore trial to her. You look quite upset yourself, my child, and no wonder; it must have been a terrible shock to look up from your book and see your poor aunt sitting there dead! I should simply have expired on the spot, I know I should. You must forgive me for running in on you so early in the day, but I wanted to lose no time in expressing to your dear mother my deep sorrow over the whole sad affair. Perhaps you will be so good as to convey to her—"

While she was talking Miss Whipple gradually edged her way along the hall and through the door of the drawing-room.

She stared about her in ghoulish fascination as though she had never seen the room before. Behind her rimless glasses her myopic eyes shone with excitement. On tiptoe she crossed the room to the chair in which Octavia Osborne had been murdered. She eyed it with a shiver of delicious horror.

"The poor thing was actually sitting in this chair when it happened, wasn't she?" she asked in a sepulchral whisper.

Before Ann could stop her, Miss Whipple sat down in the chair and rose again quickly, with a squeal of mock-terror. Ann clenched her fists and started forward.

"You ghoul!" she cried. "You disgusting, prying wretch! Get out of this house before I throw you out!"

"*Oh!*" gasped Miss Whipple. In her agitation her glasses fell off and hung suspended like some grotesque ear-ornament, from a thin gold chain attached to her ear. "How dare you? How dare you speak to me like that? I—I—"

"Get out!"

She sidled to the door, with Ann close behind her. Ann slammed the front door viciously on her indignant back and the spinster, red to the ears, hurried down the garden path, consoling herself with the reflection that at least she had a story to tell which would make her welcome in the drawing-rooms and kitchens of the village for many days to come. She had sat in the very chair in which the poor dead woman had been so brutally murdered! The very self-same chair!

At the garden gate she paused eagerly to pose for the Press photographer and the following morning her sharp features and meagre figure appeared in several newspapers over the caption: '*An old friend leaves after consoling with the bereaved family...*'

Hardly had she gone than Ernie Piper arrived with a telegram for Stephen. Edith took it to her husband and he tore open the buff envelope.

"It's from Octavia's solicitor. The police have given permission for the funeral and she's to be buried at Brancaster this afternoon. He wants to know if I care to attend."

"You shan't go, of course?"

He bit his lip.

"I ought to."

"In other circumstances, certainly; but there is sure to be a crowd. They'd stare at you and you'd hate it."

"Lord, yes. You're right, Edith. I'll wire him that I shan't attend."

Stephen's haggard face and pitiful eyes touched Edith's heart. She put a hand on his arm. "Stephen."

"My dear?"

"Stephen—"

Edith struggled to find words. "Stephen, you—you would never feel that there was anything—anything, Stephen—that you could not tell me?"

He stared at her in horror. "Good God, Edith," he exclaimed.

"I'm sorry, Stephen. Forgive me," she said gently and turned away.

Chapter 18

"ALL RIGHT, HANNAH, I'll answer it!" Ann went to the front door, her face set in hard, uncompromising lines. The doorbell had been ringing at intervals all morning and most of the callers had been unwelcome. Half of them had been reporters, who bore out the reputation of their craft as far as persistence, at least, was concerned. Ann opened the door, prepared to be rude.

Mrs. Fleming was standing on the step.

"Oh," said Ann, momentarily at a loss. "It's you."

"May I see your sister Dorothy?"

"Dorothy isn't well. I don't think she'll see you."

"Please. It's very important."

"After her last interview with you I gathered there was nothing more to be said," Ann replied cuttingly.

"I know. I must have hurt her dreadfully."

"She came home crying. She didn't deserve to be treated like that. She's never hurt a living soul in her life. If you're going to make her cry again——"

"I assure you I've nothing unkind to say to her. Won't you at least tell her I'm here?"

"Well——" Ann hesitated. Weakening at sight of the woman's obvious distress, she said: "Come in. I'll find out if she'll see you. Will you wait in the dining-room, please?"

Mrs. Fleming went into the dining-room and agitatedly paced the floor. Her autocratic face was softened by an expression of great anxiety and her gloved hands were clasping and unclasping spasmodically. She turned eagerly when Dorothy entered the room.

"Where is he?" she cried. "Where is he? Oh, you must tell me."

"Where is he?" Dorothy repeated. "What on earth do you mean?"

"Where is Ted? Where is my son?"

"Ted?" Dorothy stared. "You told me he had left for Paris."

"Then you don't know where he is? I had so hoped you might. He did not go to Paris. He has not even arrived in London. Oh, what am I to do?"

Dorothy's face became even paler. "He hasn't arrived in London? Sit down and tell me about it."

"There's very little to tell. We haven't been able to find out anything, except that he's missing. He left for London on Sunday. He was to spend Monday with his father's London agents before proceeding to Paris. At the inquest on Monday, as you know, the coroner insisted that he be summoned to return. Directly after the inquest my husband telephoned his London agents with the intention of telling Ted to come back at once. But he wasn't there. My husband has been in constant telephonic communication with his agents ever since, but there is no word of Ted. We cabled Paris, but he hasn't turned up there either."

"But where can he have gone?"

"That is what I would give anything to know." Mrs. Fleming looked sharply at Dorothy. "He hasn't written you?"

"Not a line."

"I can't understand it. Why should he disappear? Why?" Mrs. Fleming wrung her hands. "Last night my husband was forced to inform the police that Ted could not be found, and he could tell by the manner in which they received the news that they suspect—suspect—"

"What nonsense!" cried Dorothy. "What on earth could they suspect? Ted hasn't done anything."

"Mr. Fleming thinks they may— Oh, it's so difficult to explain: On the afternoon of the murder, you told Ted, didn't you, that there had been a scene at luncheon and that your aunt had decided to cut your father out of her will?"

"I told him that, yes, but I don't see—"

"Oh, it's perfectly heinous of those wretched police, but Mr. Fleming fears they may think—they may think that Ted, knowing that his father and I would not welcome his marriage with a penniless girl, may have k—killed your aunt to prevent her making the new will."

"But that's absurd! It's ridiculous. I never heard anything so utterly stupid!"

"I know it is, perfectly absurd. But the police aren't reasonable beings. They suspect the most preposterous things of the most impossible people. Ted was seen in your garden at about the time the murder must have been committed. He had your scarf in his hand. I am told his fingerprints have been found on the frame of your drawing-room windows—"

"Well, why not? Ted always came and went freely like one of ourselves. And I've no doubt Miss Whipple imagined the scarf. You know what she is."

"Mr. Fleming has explained that to the police, time and again, but they keep on looking down their noses at him. And, of course, by disappearing Ted has given them genuine grounds for suspicion."

"Then he must be found and brought back without delay."

"That's easy to say. But where is he?"

Dorothy shook her head hopelessly. "I haven't the faintest idea."

"This is awful! The papers are sure to find out about it, and our name will be splashed all over the front page."

"Your name!" said Dorothy, with a sudden burst of anger. "Your name! Is that all you can think of at a time like this? Isn't Ted of more importance than a few messy headlines in a beastly scandal sheet?"

"Nothing is so important to me as my son."

"I'm sorry," said Dorothy. "My nerves are on edge."

"He will write to you."

"Do you think so?"

"I feel sure of it. He is deeply in love with you, my dear."

"Calf-love," said Dorothy bitterly.

Mrs. Fleming shook her head. "Don't quote my own words at me. I have been hard, I know, but I felt I had to be. This changes everything. He will write to you, I know he will. When he does, promise you'll tell me where he is?"

Dorothy frowned. "Supposing he asks me not to tell anyone?"

"But I am his mother. Surely——"

"Yes, I know, but——I'll promise you this: if he does write, I'll do my best to bring him back. If he asks me not to tell where he is, I shan't tell; but I'll try to persuade him to get in touch with you."

"I'm afraid," whimpered Mrs. Fleming. "Oh, Dorothy, I'm so afraid."

Dorothy put her arms about the older woman and held her tightly.

*

Later that afternoon Peter came in and announced that a press cameraman had offered him a shilling to pose for a photograph.

"But you didn't, Peter?" said his mother quickly.

The boy opened a grubby fist and displayed a bright new coin.

"Oh, Peter, how *could* you!" cried Ann.

Peter grinned. "A bob's a bob! But it's all right. They won't print the picture. I spoiled it. When he was taking it, I put out my tongue!"

The following morning, Peter's photograph with his tongue out appeared in newspapers all over the country.

*

There were over four thousand sightseers at Octavia Osborne's funeral. Milling for a view of the coffin and the clay plot which was to be the murdered woman's final resting place, they trampled over graves, trod down the flowers that were on them, and smashed several head stones.

They were incensed by the non-appearance of Miss Osborne's near relations. By absenting himself from his sister's funeral, they agreed, Stephen Osborne had betrayed a sad lack of proper feelings...

Chapter 19

ALTHOUGH INSPECTOR Burrows made an excellent breakfast in record time the following Wednesday morning, attention did not stray for an instant from the newspaper which was propped against the marmalade dish slightly the right of his right elbow. He ate with a mechanical efficiency that was fascinating to watch. Without looking at his plate he cut a sausage in half and thrust the prongs of his fork through it, impaling a square of fried bread; and over all he spread the running yellow of a fried egg. He put the heaped fork in his mouth which opened wide to receive it and withdrew it a moment later, cleaned of every vestige of food. The tip of his tongue came out and lick away a smear of yolk which had adhered to his lips. His jaws munched steadily while the fork collected another gargantuan mouthful. The column on which his eyes were riveted was headed:

SURPRISE DEVELOPMENTS IN VILLAGE MURDER

POLICE SEEK MISSING WITNESSES

WHERE IS EDWARD FLEMING?

There was a photograph of the missing young man the centre of the page. Mrs. Burrows leaned over her husband's shoulder and inspected it approvingly. "Looks like a film star."

"You'll find plenty of film star faces in the rogues' gallery these days, my girl."

"He won't be missing long with his picture in the *Daily Post*. Got two million readers, the *Post* has. One of 'em is sure to spot him."

"More likely the whole two million. Bet you he's 'seen' in a hundred different places, hundreds of miles apart before the day's out. Our job would be a sight easier if folks had less imagination."

"Why d'you suppose he's disappeared?"

"Use your head, girl," mumbled her husband, through a mouthful of sausage-and-egg. "Why do people mixed up in a murder generally disappear?"

"Oh, but that nice young fellow couldn't have done it. More likely he knows something—something that affects someone he loves—and he's run away rather than be forced to tell it."

"Now, that's not a half-bad idea—coming from you," said the Inspector grudgingly.

"Oh, I don't use my head for a hat-rack, like some people I could mention," said his spouse good-naturedly.

When the Inspector arrived at police headquarters, he found Sergeant Feathers poring over a sheet of violet-tinted notepaper.

"Any word of young Fleming?" Burrows asked.

"Not yet, sir."

The Inspector stood by the window picking his teeth. "Shouldn't be surprised, you know," he said with a sapient air, "if he ran away because he knows something he doesn't want to tell; something that might incriminate one of the family—maybe the girl he's supposed to be in love with."

"I can't see that girl as a murderess, sir. Otherwise, the idea seems sound."

"Oh, I don't use my head for a hat-rack like some people I could mention," said Inspector Burrows caustically. "Anything fresh this morning?"

"Only an anonymous letter from Miss Whipple."

The Inspector stared. "What do you mean, an anonymous letter from Miss Whipple? If it's *anonymous*, how do you know who it's from?"

"Well, sir, first time I saw the lady I summed her up as the anonymous letter-writing type, so I took the precaution of obtaining a sample of her fist. It is identical with the handwriting of the note that came this morning."

"If you get much sharper, my lad, you'll be cutting yourself. Give it here." Inspector Burrows frowned as he read the letter:

To the police,

Simon Osborne, Stephen Osborne's cousin, is supposed to have left Gay Ladies before noon on the day Miss Osborne arrived. But he did not leave by train or bus. Did he leave at all? He is a low character and was on unfriendly terms with the dead woman. He is known to have sponged on his cousin for years. Did he kill Miss Osborne hoping that his cousin would inherit her money and that he would be able to sponge on him to a far greater extent that before?

One Who Knows.

Scratching his head over the epistle, Inspector Burrow went to consult his Chief. In a short while he returned.

"The Major says when you've finished those odd jobs I gave you, you'd better go over to Gay Ladies and check up on this. Find out for sure whether Simon Osborne left the village by train or bus on the day of the murder. If he didn't you are to go on to London and see him. See his housekeeper as well. And watch your step, my lad. From all accounts this Simon Osborne is a wily old bird. Don't let him put anything over on you. Draw on the cashier for expense money—although I hardly need tell you that drawing expense money is about all some of you young fellows think about."

It was almost twelve before Sergeant Feathers was able to leave for Gay Ladies. At the village station he interviewed a sleepy-looking porter.

"Know Mr. Simon Osborne?" repeated that worthy. "I should say I do! Wish I had a quid for all the pints I've had in his company in the bar of the 'Wheatsheaf'."

"Do you remember him taking a train from here on the tenth?"

"No, I don't—and why? 'Cause he didn't, that's why. You're not the first that's asked me that. A certain nosy old girl was asking me the same question only the other day. Don't tell me you cops are after the old gent?"

Sergeant Feathers ignored the question.

"You're perfectly sure he didn't leave the village by train?"

"Take my oath on it."

"Well, don't forget, because you may be called upon to do so."

The Sergeant walked through the village to the green where the buses stopped. There was no bus in sight and an ancient with a long white beard informed him that none was likely to come along for a good half hour. While Feathers waited, he saw Miss Whipple coming out of a house. She lingered on the doorstep for several minutes, talking volubly, before departing with the high air of one who has spent a most enjoyable morning. Sergeant Feathers hurried after her and raised his hat.

"Good morning, Miss Whipple. We got your letter all right."

The spinster looked daggers at him but did not deny having written the anonymous screed.

"What makes you so sure that Simon Osborne did not leave the village by bus?"

"I asked all the conductors, that's what," she snapped.

"Then you've saved me a job. Thanks very much. Good morning."

Walking towards her house, Miss Whipple ran into Ann Osborne, who was coming the other way. The spinster stopped and smiled graciously.

"I've just met Sergeant Feathers, my dear, and what do you think? He asked me some questions about your Uncle Simon. Now I wonder why the police are interested in *him*?"

Ann scornfully eyed her up and down and walked on. But she could not help being startled by the spinster's news. The police and Uncle Simon! Surely...Words flew chillingly through her brain; words Uncle Simon had uttered on the morning of the murder: '*Not a bad idea...cutting Octavia's throat...your father would inherit her money and I'd be able to touch him regularly for the rest of my life...I've a jolly good mind to do it myself!*'

*

At half-past five that evening Sergeant Feathers ascended the muddy front steps of Simon Osborne's house in Battersea and knocked portentously on the scarred door. There was no answer. He took a firm grip of the knocker and rapped again, loudly, imperatively, the summons of one who would not be denied. Still there was no answer. He had an uncomfortable feeling that he was being watched. Turning suddenly, he had a brief glimpse of pair of beady eyes and the tip of a red nose through a gap in the dingy curtains of a ground floor room, before the curtains were hastily drawn together. Leaning over, he rapped sharply on the window pane. After a lengthy pause he heard the shuffle of slovenly feet on uncarpeted floorboards, the front door opened slightly, and a head showed itself.

The head was covered with tangled grey hair which fell untidily down both sides of the face. The nose was redder than he had thought and a drip of moisture hung on the pointed tip of it. A scattering of bad teeth like the decaying posts of a collapsed fence were displayed in an open mouth which had the shape and expression of that of a misanthropic cod. Two cunning little eyes stared up at him.

"'E ain't in," said an angry whine, and the nostrils of Sergeant Feathers were assailed by a powerful smell of whisky.

"You are Mr. Osborne's housekeeper, I presume?"

"'Oo I am ain't 'ere nor there. 'E ain't in, that's the point!"

She made a move to close the door but Sergeant Feathers prevented her from doing so by shoving out a large foot.

"If it's the gas," snapped the woman raspingly, "'e said 'e'd be settlin' next week."

"It isn't the gas."

"If it's the rent—"

"It's not the rent, either," snapped Feathers. "I am attached to the Blankshire Police—"

At that, to his surprise, she opened the door wider and came out with a smirk on her face.

"*Ho!*" she said. "*Ho!* I thought you'd be comin' sooner or later. It's about the murder, or I miss my guess."

"Yes, it's about the murder. But how did you know?"

"I know the old stinker I work for. And if I was a cop and someone was croaked and the old stinker was in the neighbour'ood, I'd want to know wot 'e was up to at the time."

"But he wasn't in the vicinity of Gay Ladies at the time of the murder. He returned to London that day by an early train."

"*Ho*, did 'e? 'Oo says so?"

"Well, didn't he?"

"No, me young cock sparrer, 'e didn't. At any rate, 'e didn't show 'is nose 'ere till the Monday, w'ich was two days later!"

A wave of not unnatural jubilation swept over Sergeant Feathers. This was the first big chance he had ever had and things were shaping nicely for him. If it should turn out that

Simon Osborne was guilty, there would certainly be promotion in store for the bright young officer who unmasked him.

"You're sure of that? He couldn't have returned without you being aware of it?"

"Maybe 'e could—but 'e didn't. I wasn't takin' much notice of what went on Sat'day and Sunday; I was feelin' a bit queer, like, and kept to my bed. But before I turned in, I locked the front door *and* bolted it *and* put the chain up, and all the other doors were locked and 'e 'asn't got a key to 'em. They stayed locked from Sat'day arternoon til Monday mornin', so if 'e come in 'e must be 'Oudini."

"He might have been in London and not come home.'

"Not 'im. Where would 'e get the money to sleep elsewhere for two nights? 'E's always on the rocks. No, if 'e was in London 'e'd 'ave 'ammered on the door till I let 'im in. Take it from me, Monday mornin' was when 'e come 'ome. I popped out for a quick 'un about eleven and ran into 'im."

"Your name, please?" said Feathers, producing a note book.

"Cissy Glott."

"You'll hear more of this later, Miss Glott."

"Mrs. Glott," she corrected him sharply, and added: "You keep on the old stinker's track, young man, 'e's the bloke you're after."

"You sound as though you'd be glad if he were hanged."

"I wouldn't shed no tears, you can bet your life on that. The fuss 'e makes if I take a drop of whisky for me rheumatism you really wouldn't believe. I never knoo it to fail: the bad 'uns is mean and the mean 'uns is bad—and the old stinker is mean as 'ell. You can 'ang 'im and welcome."

"Have you any idea when he'll be home?"

"'E'll be 'ome w'en the pubs shut, if 'e can walk. Good afternoon!"

Chapter 20

S ERGEANT FEATHERS walked away, determined to return later and interview Simon Osborne even if it meant missing his last train home, but when he rounded the corner into the next street, he heard someone shouting: *"Mr. Osborne! Hi! I want a word with you!"* Stopping short he turned and saw a hatless man running out of a tobacconist's shop and hurrying after a middle-aged individual who was heading straight for a public-house on the nearest corner. The middle-aged individual was apparently oblivious to the shouts, for he carried straight on with a nonchalant air, but when the tobacconist caught up with him and grabbed his arm he looked round with a start and a broad beam creased his face.

"My dear fellow! I've been meaning for days to drop in on you. How are you? And your wife? Don't tell me she's still got that old bronchial trouble?"

"Look here, Mr. Osborne," said the exasperated tobacconist, "I want my money. It's over a year since the goods were supplied and you haven't—"

"My dear fellow," replied Simon soothingly, "I'm terribly sorry, but—well, in strict confidence, as one of my old and valued friends, I'll tell you the candid truth. It's like this..."

The rest escaped Feathers for Simon lowered his voice to a confidential whisper, but shortly after the tobacconist reluctantly went back to his shop—having obtained no satisfaction whatever—and his shameless debtor, with a bland and princely air, continued in the direction of the public-house. Sergeant Feathers touched his shoulder as he reached out to push open the door.

"Mr. Simon Osborne?"

Before replying, Simon eyed him from head to foot. Not

to be outdone, Feathers boldly returned the appraising glance. He saw a short, rotund figure with a flowing green tie, and egg-stained waistcoat, baggy trousers, and a loose, shapeless jacket on which the stains were too numerous and varied to be catalogued. He saw a round face which closely resembled that of a dissolute cherub, fringed at the temples with fluffy white hair.

Simon frowned. "You don't look like a process server," he said.

"I'm not. I am Sergeant Feathers of the Blankshire County Constabulary."

"And a fine body of men they are, I have no doubt," said Simon cordially, shaking his hand warmly. "Charmed to meet you. I am about to partake of a livener. Won't you join me?"

Sergeant Feathers hesitated. He was an abstemious young man, almost a teetotaller, and he knew it was not considered ethical for a police officer to drink with a man he might later arrest. On the other hand, was it not likely that in the disarmingly cosy atmosphere of a pub and under the influence of drink, Simon Osborne might let slip some vital information which at a more business-like interview he would not dream of divulging?

"Thanks," he said, "don't mind if I do."

They passed through the door of the *Hare and Hounds* together.

"Mine's a double Scotch," said Simon jovially. "What'll you have?"

Excellent! thought Sergeant Feathers. He knew what double Scotches could do. Under the influence of only two at a New Year's Eve party some years before he had thrown discretion to the winds, kissed all the girls, insulted all the men, and insisted on telling his life story to all and sundry, whether they wanted to hear it or not. The more double Scotches Simon Osborne drank, the better for certain the bright young officer's chances of promotion!

"What'll you have?" repeated Simon. "Whisky? No? Then why not try a 'Stinger'?"

"A 'Stinger'?" said Feathers doubtfully. "What's that? Never heard of it."

"Oh, it's a sort of barley wine. Very pleasant, they tell me. Never touch it myself. Too innocuous for an old soak like me."

A sort of barley wine…It sounded harmless enough. Yes, Feathers decided, a 'Stinger' would suit him admirably. He would spin it out, make it last a long time. He would need a clear head to steer Simon Osborne's unguarded tongue in the right direction when it had been lubricated by a succession of double Scotches.

While the barman was pouring the drinks, Feathers took stock of his surroundings. They were in a small private bar, snug and cosy and so dimly lit that the fire made dancing reflections on the mahogany panelled walls. A shabby leather couch flanked the fireplace and beside it was grouped a table and some chairs. Sporting prints hung round the walls and above the mantelpiece frowned the many-antlered head of a stag. There was a solid, old-fashioned air about the place. The bar itself was of solid mahogany and above it rose the four hefty mahogany handles, ribbed with brass, of the beer engines. The barman had a rosy, round face and a way with bottles that was enchanting to watch.

"I've had a few words with your housekeeper," Feather remarked casually, watching Simon's face out of the corner of his eye.

"Have you, indeed?" said Simon equably. "Drunken old sloven," he added, draining his double expanse of Scotch at a gulp. "Same again, Sam," he said to the barman. "You don't want to pay any attention to what *she* says, young man. *I* never do. '*In vino veritas*' they say, but it's been my experience that you never get the truth out of these habitual drunkards. It's a wonder the woman can speak at all. Drinks like a fish. Spends her whole life in a coma. I went down to Gay Ladies for a brief holiday a fortnight or so ago, leaving behind an almost untouched case of Johnny Walker. Silly of me, knowing what she is, but I have to order it by the case, me boy; they won't supply single bottles on credit. Would you believe it—? When I returned there wasn't a drop left. She'd scoffed the lot. Must have been unconscious half the time."

"Drink up, me boy," he added, "you're getting behind."

Feathers looked down and saw three 'Stingers' lined up in front of him. Knowing Simon, the barman had filled the old gentleman's glass as soon as it was emptied and each time he had poured a 'Stinger' for Sergeant Feathers. With the benevolent eyes of Simon upon him, Feathers gulped down his first drink and took a cautious sip of the second.

The door swung open and several people came in at once. They all knew Simon, and greeted him familiarly. "*Hello, Nunky! How's every little thing?*" "*Well, you old soak, you still dodging the bums?*" "*'Ow's the bookie's friend? Lucky I didn't put my shirt on that nag in the two-thirty like you told me to do, or I'd be walking abaht in me undervest tonight!*" They crowded the far end of the bar and Simon turned towards them, exchanging back chat amiably.

Feathers felt out of it. He took another sip from his second glass and tugged Simon's sleeve. Simon turned his head. "Yes, me boy?"

"Er . . . What'll you have?"

The flow of banter ceased and all the faces at the end of the bar turned in Feather's direction. He felt slightly disconcerted by this joint scrutiny, but the faces relaxed in smiles, and one or two of them thanked him warmly. He did not understand for what they were thanking him until the barman arrayed half-a-dozen foaming glasses and a double Scotch on the counter and, looking pleasantly at Feathers, said that that would be three and four-pence-halfpenny, please. A little dazed by this general acceptance of his invitation to Simon, he paid up and relapsed into silence.

"Scroungers," said a doleful voice in his ear. "Born scroungers, all of 'em."

Feathers looked round and saw a lugubrious-faced little man in a dusty bowler hat standing at his elbow. He had come in just too late to avail himself of the Sergeant's unintentional hospitality.

"Free beer, that's all they think of," said the newcomer sadly. "You can 'ardly take a deep breath wivout arf of 'em saying: 'Thanks, old chap, I don't mind if I do.' Cadgers, that's what they are. *I'm* not like that, thank 'eaven," he said, his gloomy eyes fixed steadily on Feather's face. "I believe in waiting till I'm arsked."

They looked into each other's eyes. There was a long silence, then—"What's yours?" asked Feathers weakly.

"Well, now, that's very kind of you, old man. I'll 'ave a pint of old-and-mild, since you're so good as to arsk me.

"Feathers, me boy," said Simon genially, patting the Sergeant on the back. "I want you to meet some dear old pals of mine. Alf, Bill, George, Harry; meet my old friend Feathers. And last but not least, Feathers, me boy, allow me to present you to the charming Miss Dolly Deane, one of the brightest ornaments of the variety stage."

Dolly Deane was a large woman with an immense bosom, a good-natured face as lined as a railway map, and a piled-up mass of hennaed hair. She squeezed Feathers' hand and did bewildering things with her eyes.

"Don't pay no attention to Nunky," she said hoarsely. "It's been a few years since I tripped the boards—although I can still kick a leg with the best of 'em."

"And an enchanting leg it is, too," declared Simon. "You can take my word for that, Feathers, me boy."

"Better than you'll ever see again, you nasty old man, you," responded Miss Deane coyly. "What are you drinking, Mr. Feathers? It's my round."

"Not for me, thanks," said the Sergeant awkwardly. "I've still got a full one and a bit."

"Naughty! Naughty! Mustn't get behind. Drink 'em up, ducky, and 'ave one with Dolly. Up and over and down the hatch with it. That's the ticket. Now the other one. No heel taps. That's the boy! Drinks all round, Sam."

The party gravitated to the couch beside the fire and Feathers found himself seated in intimate proximity to Dolly Deane.

"Don't listen to a word he says, Dolly," cried Simon, from the far end of the couch. "He's a heartbreaker."

"Is that true?" asked Dolly, snuggling closer. "I'll bet it is. I'll bet you're a devil with the girls. Oh, you needn't tell me. *I* know. A man with a dimple in his chin is never to be trusted."

Feathers giggled. He took another drink from his glass, which he had emptied a moment before, but which was now miraculously full again.

"Well, it's a short life and a merry one," said Dolly comfortably. "You have your fun while you're young, ducky. If I were twenty years younger, I'd be making eyes at you myself."

"Twenty years younger!" protested Feathers gallantly. "But that would make you a mere child."

"You *are* a tease!" cried Dolly, giving him a playful buffet. "No, but *reely*, how old do you think I am!"

Feathers regarded her solemnly. "Thirty?"

Dolly simpered. "Thirty-five," she said, deducting ten years on principle and a few more for good measure.

She whispered confidingly in his ear and Feathers shook with laughter. He couldn't hear a word she was saying but it tickled. Three drinks later, Dolly read the sergeant's hand, declaring herself shocked at what she saw there, and then he pretended to read hers and warned her to beware of a tall man with a dimple in his chin. After another drink, they frankly held hands, and Dolly began to sing in a gin-husky soprano:

> *One of the ruins Cromwell knocked abaht a bit,*
> *One of the ruins Cromwell knocked abaht a bit,*
> *Outside the 'Cromwell Arms, larst Sat'day night'*
> *I was one of the ruins Cromwell knocked abaht a bit.*

"'Ere!" protested Sam, the barman, with a glance at the curtained doorway leading to the saloon bar, where the landlord was in charge, "'Ere, pipe dahn a bit, Dolly. You'll 'ave the guv'nor on your tail."

"Go on with you, Sam, we're only 'avin' a bit of fun.

> *Don't 'ave any more, Mrs. Moore,*
> *Mrs. Moore, please don't 'ave any more,*
> *The more you 'ave the more you'll want, they siy*
> *And enough is as good as a feast, any diy—*

A stern face appeared at the curtained doorway. "That's enough of that. You ain't no canary bird. If you want to sing, go outside."

"Garn, Sourpuss," retorted Dolly, hiccoughing on the P.

There was a burst of laughter and the face withdrew.

"Don't pay no attention to 'im, Dolly," said one of the men. "'E's only the landlord."

"What's the world comin' to if we can't 'ave a bit of a song when we're 'appy?" said Dolly.

Feathers giggled again. This was fun. He liked it. "'Nother

lil' drink won't do us any harm," he chanted, burying his nose in his glass. He looked about him expansively and was grieved to find that the party was becoming subdued. It needed livening.

He lifted up his voice:

> *When I gro-o-ow too o-o-old to dre-e-eam,*
> *I'll have yo-o-ou to remember—*

The landlord poked his head through the curtains. "I shan't speak to you again!" he declared ominously.

Feathers wavered over to the bar and put his empty glass down after three perilous attempts. "Drinsh all round," he stuttered.

"You've 'ad enough, sir," said the barman good-naturedly. "I shouldn't 'ave any more, if I were you."

"*Don't 'ave any more, Mrs. Moore—*" sang Feathers in a wobbly tenor.

The landlord appeared with his sleeves rolled up on the public side of the bar. "I warned you," he said.

Feathers felt himself rushing forward under the propulsion of a large hand on his neck and before he realised what was happening, he collided with a lamppost at the edge of the pavement outside. The door swung to behind him and he was left alone in the cold and the dark. He clenched his fists.

"Oh," he muttered. "*Oh!* Wants to fight, does he?"

He staggered towards the public house door, swinging his arms, but before he reached it the fight drained out him and he felt weak and tired. Wobbling to the lamppost, he wrapped both arms about it and was very sick.

*

The next he knew was when he awoke at noon the following day with a blinding headache. He was lying in his underwear on a frowsty bed in an unfamiliar room. His clothes were jumbled together on a chair beside the bed. He sat up with a groan and stared about him wildly.

The door opened and Simon came in. "Well, young man, how are you this morning?"

"Where am I?" Feathers demanded.

"In my spare bedroom. Don't you remember? I brought you home with me last night."

Feathers groaned again and buried his head in his hands. "Drink this," said Simon, holding under his nose a glass containing a reddish fluid in which floated a raw egg. The soul-shaken young police officer pushed it away, but Simon insisted. After he had drunk it he felt considerably better.

When he dressed, he found that his notebook, which contained a summary of all his investigations into the Osborne Murder Case, was in a different pocket to that in which he habitually kept it. He took it out and looked suspiciously at Simon.

"It's a funny thing," said Simon pleasantly, "but I can never get to sleep without reading in bed for a while. Last night I was very nearly stumped. There wasn't a thing to read in the house—except your notebook. And very interesting reading it made, too. I had no idea there was so much in the Osborne Murder Case that hadn't found its way into the papers. And I'd never before known that Mrs. Glott's first name is Cissy. Cissy! My boy, I ask you!"

"You—you—"

Simon sat on the bed and eyed Feathers benignly. "By the way, what did she tell you? You haven't yet entered it in the book and I'd rather like to know."

"She said you didn't return to London until Monday," exploded Feathers.

"Her error," smiled Simon. "I didn't come home until Monday, but I was in London on Saturday evening."

"You did not leave Gay Ladies by train or bus."

"True. You see, my boy, I left Gay Ladies in a state of pecuniary embarrassment. Bluntly, I had not got the fare. I could not touch my cousin, for he had just lost his job. But for a kindly motorist who gave me a lift to Brancaster and another who carried me on to London, I should have been forced to walk, a thought that makes me shudder."

"Where did you spend Saturday and Sunday nights?"

"That's rather a delicate question, my boy. If you press me, I must admit that it—it affects the honour of a lady. A very charming lady. You had the pleasure of meeting her last night."

"You mean— You *don't* mean that henna-haired—"

"The same, my boy, the same. In any other circumstances, wild horses would not have dragged the admission from me, but when the law insists— You need not take my word for it. You can ask the lady herself, although the question, I admit, would be an awkward one to put. Still, I have no doubt she would be delighted to meet you again. She took a particular fancy to you last night. She is to be found every evening in the bar of the *Hare and Hounds* if you care to—"

Feathers shuddered. On the whole, he decided, he preferred to accept Simon's word, unsatisfactory though it was.

"What is the name of the stuff I was drinking last night? That—that barley wine?"

"You want to know what to ask for next time, eh?"

"No," groaned Feathers bitterly. "I want to know what to avoid!"

Chapter 21

A ND QUITE THE gentleman, too, remarked Mrs. Hedges reflectively. "If you ask me—"

Her husband glowered at her over the top of his paper. "If you ask *me*, it'd pay you to mind your own business for a change. Paid 'is rent in advance, 'asn't 'e?"

"I never said 'e 'adn't."

"Paid well, too."

"I never said 'e didn't."

"Then wot are you chewing the fat about? You've no quarrel with 'im as a lodger, so w'y not be content to mind your own business? You've plenty of affairs of your own to 'tend to, if time 'angs 'eavy on your 'ands. Take a look at these, f'r instance—"

Mr. Hedges displayed the pink nakedness of his big toes, both of which protruded through large holes in his socks. "And they're the best I could find in the drawer. Some of 'em look like fishing nets."

"If you'd find a job, instead of sittin' about on your backside all day and all night reading the paper, it might put some 'eart in me to do things for you."

"Don't I go out looking for work every morning, rain or shine? Is it *my* fault if there ain't any?"

"I notice you always go out looking for work a few minutes before the pubs open."

Mr. Hedges took refuge behind his paper. "All right! All right! You win!"

"It ain't natural," mused his spouse, "spending all day in 'is room, walking up and down—wearing out the linoleum—and arguing with 'isself like a madman. And why come to the seaside for an 'oliday and then only go out after dark? 'E's a mystery, that young man is. Calls 'isself George 'Arrison—but all 'is things is marked E.F. plain as can be."

"One of these days 'e's going to come in unexpected and catch you rummaging in 'is bag. Then you won't arf cop it."

They heard footsteps descending the stairs and a hush fell on the kitchen. The footsteps passed through the hall overhead. The front door slammed. Mrs. Hedges listened to the swift tread on the pavement outside until it passed out of earshot, then she rose.

"I'm going next door to 'ave a word with Mrs. Pearcey."

Mrs. Hedges' neighbour led her into a musty-smelling parlour, apologising as she did so.

"My old man's in the kitchen, and you know what 'e's like when I'm chatting with another lady. 'E can't abide gossip."

"I wonder you puts up with 'is nonsense, Flo. If he was mine, I'd—"

"Oh, it don't 'urt me to humour 'im. You remember me telling you, Gladys, that I was sure I'd seen your young man lodger's face before? Well, I took a notion this afternoon and searched through some old newspapers in the cellar, and what do you think I found?"

"I'm sure I can't imagine."

Raising one of the cushions which were placed at prim angles on the sofa, Mrs. Pearcey produced a folded newspaper which had been hidden under it. "If there's a reward, I shall expect you to bear in mind 'oo gave you the tip."

"You know me, Flo. What is it? Let me see."

Mrs. Pearcey flattened the paper on a table and pointed to a photograph on the front page. Her neighbour bent over and stared at it.

"*And all 'is things are marked E.F.!*" she breathed.

*

That night when the lodger returned, he was met on the steps by a burly policeman in a glistening cape who flashed a light in his face. Another policeman came across the street and stood impassively behind the young man.

"You are Edward Fleming?" asked the first.

The young man looked from one dark forbidding shape to the other. "Yes," he admitted.

"I shall have to ask you to accompany us to the police station."

"And if I refuse?"

"That would be a pity, sir," said the constable imperturbably, "but we should take you there in any case."

"On what charge?"

"On suspicion of being concerned in the murder of Octavia Osborne at a house in the village of Gay Ladies on the afternoon of August the tenth."

*

That night a police car rushed Ted to Brestock where he was lodged in a detention room at the headquarters of the county constabulary. Early the following morning his father came to see him. The solicitor wore a long face and he looked at his son with mingled affection and anxiety.

"Well, my boy, this is a terrible business."

"I know, Dad," said Ted nervously, running his fingers through his tousled hair. "But it isn't as bad as it looks. I've been an infernal idiot, but that's the strength of it."

"I hope so, my boy. I sincerely hope so." Mr. Fleming placed hat, gloves, and brief-case on the iron bed and paced up and down the narrow cell. He sighed.

"You've given your mother and me an exceedingly trying

time. I'm prepared to endorse your statement that you've been an infernal idiot. Whatever you were up against, running away was the worst thing you could do. However— Let me hear the whole story."

When the story was told, Mr. Fleming took off his spectacles and polished them vigorously. He put them on again.

"Thank heaven it's no worse," he said, patting his son's shoulder. "I can't tell you what I had feared. Now we are going upstairs to see the Chief Constable and I want you to tell him exactly what you've told me. No—on second thoughts, let me do the telling, as far as possible.'

He sighed again and glanced oddly at Ted over the top of his spectacles. "Your mother's a masterful woman, a very masterful woman. I've let her have her own way, more or less; I'm afraid I lack the necessary stamina to stand up to her. In my case it's worked out fairly well on the whole, but if you let her run your life, she'll almost certainly make a damnable mess of it. Have a little gumption, my boy. Oh well, it's your affair."

He rapped on the door and a constable came to let then out and conduct them upstairs. Major Blackett and Inspector Burrows were awaiting them in the Chief Constable's comfortable office. Mr. Fleming greeted both officials pleasantly. Ted looked sheepish.

"'The mountain laboured and brought forth a mouse.'" quoted the solicitor, dropping into a chair and hitching up the knees of his trousers. "When you've heard my son's story, I think you'll agree he has behaved like an ass—but not a criminal ass."

"We'll reserve judgment on that point, Mr. Fleming," said Major Blackett non-committedly, "until we've heard the story."

He looked searchingly at Ted. "Well, young man?"

Ted cleared his throat and glanced uneasily at his father.

"The suggestion that my son should leave for Paris the day following the murder," said the lawyer smoothly, "originally emanated from his mother. You don't know my wife, Major? Well, to be perfectly frank, Mrs. Fleming has a habit of getting her own way. She is a fond mother, perhaps over-fond, entirely devoted to Ted, who is our only offspring. We first heard of the murder latish on the afternoon on which it was committed, and at dinner that evening Ted announced that he intended to marry the eldest Osborne girl. His mother was horrified. Ted and Miss Osborne had always been the best of friends, but my wife had no idea that attachment was warmer than friendship. She declared that the marriage could not be considered for a moment in view of the scandal in which the girl's whole family had suddenly become involved.

"Ted put up a fight, but I think I said—did I not? —that his mother has a habit of getting her own way. Against my better judgment I permitted myself to be enlisted on her side and we coerced Ted by every means in our power. After a heated discussion that lasted well into the night, Ted reluctantly agreed to go to Paris for a few months. His understanding was that by the time he returned the scandal would have blown over and the marriage would then be more feasible. His mother's intention was to put a stop to the affair for good, by fair means or foul, while he was gone.

"The following day, Sunday, my son left for London en route for Paris. On the train between Gay Ladies and Brancaster he thought over the whole position and decided that in yielding to his parents he was being unfair to the girl he loved. He decided to take the next train home, but when it came to the point, he found that he could not do that. His mother had put it to him that unless he broke with Miss Osborne for the time being at least, he would be estranged from us for good. Quite naturally, he felt that was a prospect not to be faced lightly.

"He could not make up his mind what to do. His parents

and his future—or the girl he loved? No easy choice, gentlemen. There was a train leaving for the seaside resort where he was apprehended last night, and, on a sudden whim, he took it. He wanted time to think, to make up his mind in peace."

"You stayed there for over a week, although you knew we were looking for you?" said Inspector Burrows sharply, scowling at Ted.

"I knew so little about the murder—and it was vital for me to settle my own problem—"

"You've put us to considerable trouble and expense, young man," growled the Inspector. "And made the case against you a lot blacker than it was."

"Come, Inspector," said Mr. Fleming blandly, "you won't go so far as to say that there's a case against him? Isn't that pitching it rather strongly?"

"He was seen approaching the Osbornes' house in a furtive manner half an hour before the murder was discovered, carrying in his hand the silk scarf with which the murder was committed. If all those facts don't constitute a pretty stiff case against him," grunted Burrows, "I'll eat a pair of regulation boots, nails and all."

"Yes, I did go to the house about three that afternoon," Ted admitted, "but to say that my manner was furtive is utter tosh. I may have been a little nervous. You see, I was going to ask Mr. Osborne for permission to marry his daughter, and at a time like that a chap naturally feels—"

"Quite," agreed Major Blackett, "but if you went to see Mr. Osborne I should have thought your obvious course would be to ring the front doorbell and ask for him."

"But I knew I'd most probably find him in the garden."

"And did you?"

"No. He wasn't there."

"So, you entered the house through the drawing-room French

windows," murmured Inspector Burrows casually—a little too casually.

Ted stared. "You're quite wrong. I didn't enter the house at all. I meant to go in that way, in fact I was on the point of doing so when I noticed the old lady sitting there and changed my mind."

"What about the scarf?" Burrows demanded fiercely. "You were carrying it when you approached the house and half an hour later it was knotted tightly about the old lady's neck!"

The young man turned pale. "I don't know how it got there. Dorothy came over to my house to play tennis shortly after lunch, but she went home in a little while, pleading a headache. She left the scarf on a seat beside the court and when I went over to see her father, I took it with me with the intention of returning it."

"What did you do with it?"

"When I turned away from the drawing-room French windows I decided to go home and come back to see Mr. Osborne later. As I walked past the side of the house, I noticed that a window which opens into the hall was ajar. I put my hand through and dropped the scarf on the hallstand."

There was some further questioning, after which the Flemings were permitted to depart, but Ted was cautioned that he must not attempt to leave the neighbourhood again without permission from the police. When father and son had gone, Major Blackett looked at his subordinate with raised eyebrows. "Well?"

"I think he's lying, sir. Trying to protect his prospective father-in-law. There was more on his mind the week he was away than the problem of defying his parents, or he'd have come to a decision sooner. He knows more than he's told, I'll be bound. I think he met Stephen Osborne in the garden and gave him the scarf to restore to Dorothy..."

Chapter 22

O N THE JOURNEY from Brestock to Gay Ladies after leaving
the Chief Constable's office, Ted drove his father's Daimler
and in his burning impatience kept the speedometer needle
quivering between the sixty and seventy marks. At his parents'
house he brought the big car to a sudden halt and his father
climbed out.

"You'd better come in for a minute, Ted," said Mr. Fleming
quietly. "Your mother will want to see with her own eyes that
you are all right."

"I'll be home later," Ted called back over his shoulder.

He drove on and soon was standing on the doorstep of Stephen
Osborne's house, furiously ringing the bell. The door opened and
Hannah Gale's face appeared in the aperture. Dour and forbidding, it was the face with which she had greeted most callers of
late; and few of them had been sufficiently bold to attempt to pass
it. Her expression relaxed at sight of Ted. She almost beamed.

"Master Ted! Well, I *am* pleased to see you, sir. This will be
a big load off Miss Dorothy's mind. Come in, sir, Come in. I'll
tell her you're here."

"Thanks, Hannah. You're a gem."

To Hannah's mind the occasion called for something more
dramatic than a formal announcement of a caller. She went to
the foot of the stairs and in a stentorian voice bellowed:

"Miss Dorothy! It's Master Ted! Master Ted's here, Miss
Dorothy!"

A door opened on the upper landing and Dorothy came
running downstairs. "Ted! Then you're alright? The police have
let you go? I was so afraid when your father let us know last
night that they'd found you!"

"I'm alright, darling. They let me go this morning after I'd answered a few questions."

"Oh, I'm so glad!"

Hannah discreetly withdrew and Ted made a move to take Dorothy in his arms, but she drew back and the joyous light died out of her eyes. In an altered tone she said: "Your mother will be pleased. She has been very worried."

"I know. I've been a fool. But it isn't Mother I'm thinking of. It's you, Dorothy, I'm terribly ashamed myself. I—"

"Ted, *please*. Let's not go into that."

"But I want to make you see what I was up against; why I went away. I couldn't think straight, Dorothy. I was at my wits' end. I had too much to decide. But I've made up my mind now. I can't live without you, Dorothy, and I've come to tell you so."

Dorothy was silent for a moment. When she looked up there were tears in her eyes. "It's too late, Ted. Nothing can ever be the same again for us after that Sunday when I waited for you in the orchard and you didn't come."

"But, don't you see, darling, I—"

"I see you didn't love me the way I wanted to be loved. The way Father loved Mother. Nothing could have kept him from her. Nothing. Marrying her meant that he would be penniless, but he did not hesitate for a moment. You did. You were afraid I'd cost you your career and you took a whole week to make up your mind whether I was worth it. Oh, I'm not blaming you. I'm not the woman Mother is. She's ever so much finer than I shall ever be. But whether I was worthy of it or not, I wanted the ungrudging love she had, and you couldn't give it. I wanted everything—or nothing. I'm sorry, Ted, terribly sorry." With a sob, she darted up to her room.

To the Osbornes, the weeks that followed were like a long drawn-out nightmare. Peter was glad when the holidays ended and the first day of a new school term dawned. The once cheerful atmosphere of his home had changed completely. Tempers were on edge, everyone wanted to be alone, no one would play with him, not even Marjory. He had spent most of his waking time for weeks moping about the house, feeling thoroughly miserable, and it was with a light heart that he started for school.

He went to the Grammar School in Brancaster and by taking an early train he was able to be in the playground a full half-hour before classes began. Usually, this half-hour was passed swiftly in a game with the other early birds, but this morning when Peter arrived, bursting with eagerness to see his friends again, he found the boys clustered near the gate, talking so excitedly that they were not aware of his approach.

"We ought to get up a round robin," he heard one of them say, "and take it to the Head."

"Hello, you fellows," said Peter cheerily. "What's a round robin, young Brooks?"

There was an uncomfortable silence. The boys looked at him so oddly that Peter flushed red.

"I say! What's up?"

"It's like your beastly cheek, turning up this morning," retorted Brooks. "I told you he would, you fellows."

"What on earth are you talking about?" stammered Peter. "Why shouldn't I turn up? What's wrong with all of you?"

"I'll tell you what! My father says it isn't fair to expect boys from decent families to mix with you—so now you know!"

"My family's as good as yours—and a jolly sight better!"

"Oh, is it! Well, your father killed your aunt for money!"

For an awful moment Peter thought he was going to be sick. There seemed to be nothing at all where his stomach ought to be. He began to tremble at the knees. The mocking faces of the other boys seemed to melt into each other, to waver dizzily before his eyes.

"You dirty liar!" he cried, his lips trembling.

"It's true! I saw it in the paper."

"So did I!" shouted another boy.

"Your father's a murderer," sneered Brooks, encouraged by this support. "A dirty murderer, that's what he is!"

"Take that back!" gasped Peter, clenching his fists, "or I'll—"

"Yah! What'll you do? Strangle me with a scarf I s'pose? Go on, cry-baby! Look, you chaps, he's crying!"

Peter hit him squarely on the mouth and a trickle of blood ran down Brook's chin. A delighted shout rose from the other boys: "a fight! a fight!" and they crowded in see the fun.

"Sock him, Brooks!"

"Give him a hiding, Brooksy!"

"I'll bet he killed the old woman himself!"

With a sob, Peter flung himself on his tormentors lashing out right and left at their gloating faces. For a moment they stood their ground and then an unreasoning terror gripped them, inspired by Peter's wild eyes and grinding teeth, and they fled in all directions. Brooks ran as quickly as any of them, but he tripped and fell and Peter sprawled on top of him, pummelling him with all his might. Nothing was left in Peter's frenzied mind but the desire to hurt, to hurt. He had Brooks by the throat and was banging his head on the ground when a master appeared on the scene, grabbed him by the collar, and dragged him, kicking and struggling, off his howling victim.

Peter could give no coherent account of what had happened, and the other boys lied. He came home in the middle of the morning, his face streaked with tears and livid with still-bubbling anger. He brought a note addressed to his father in which his headmaster politely regretted that it had been found necessary to suspend him for a term 'in consequence of a savage and unwarranted attack on another boy.'

At dusk that evening Hannah came to her mistress with a troubled look on her homely face.

"It's Miss Marjory, ma'am," she said anxiously. "The child's just come home and when I opened the door to her, she ran straight upstairs to her room with tears streaming down her cheeks. I followed her to find out what's wrong, but she won't tell me anything. She's lying on her bed, poor lamb, sobbing as though her heart's breaking."

When Edith went up, Marjory threw herself upon her and clutched her tightly as though never could she bear to let her go. The girl's slim body was shaking convulsively, wracked from head to foot by great shuddering sobs.

"Oh, Mummy!" she gasped. "Oh, Mummy!"

Edith had to bite her lips until she drew blood to keep back her own tears. She drew Marjory on to her lap and nursed and petted her as she had not done for many years.

"Oh, Mummy, the girls—If you could have heard them—"

"Sh! my darling. Sh! It's over now. You shan't go back. You'll never have to see them again."

Gently, Edith undressed the trembling child and put her to bed. She sat on the bed, stroking Marjory's forehead, until the girl was lulled to sleep. When Edith tiptoed out of the room, she met Hannah on the landing.

"Master Peter's been sick, ma'am."

"Hannah, Hannah, what am I to do?"

"The Lord only knows, ma'am. I'd like to get my hands on those murdering little blaggards. I'd learn 'em to go teasing the life out of the boy with their wicked lies and sneers."

"They were only boys like Peter, Hannah. That's the strange thing about it all. Those people who are hurting us, they're—they're just people, people like ourselves. They're not wicked, only very thoughtless. Something in our plight seems to have thrown them back to the animals from which we sprang."

Stephen was waiting for Edith in the hall. There were deep lines of worry under his eyes. "Michael is in the dining-room," he said in a low tone. "He has something to say to me. I thought you'd better hear it as well."

Edith's heart sank. More trouble. She ought to have expected it, she realised bitterly; she ought to have known better than to imagine that her children could take up their lives again as though nothing had happened. Dear God! What a curse had been laid on her unhappy family!

She squeezed her husband's arm. "Cheer up, Stephen."

Michael was pacing the dining-room floor like a caged animal. He wheeled round when they entered the room and for a moment his face softened, then it became hard and determined again.

"I can't stand it any longer, Mother," he said flatly. "I've been through hell today for the last time."

"I understand, son," said Edith quietly. "Sending you back to school was a mistake. We ought to have foreseen what would happen. You had better study at home for a few months. When all this blows over, you can go to another school. If you put your back into it, you'll soon make up for lost time."

"That won't do, Mother. I'm not going back to school—any school—ever again."

"But, Michael, you've always wanted to be a doctor—"

"What I've always wanted doesn't matter now. I'm not the person I was at the end of last term. Then I was just one of the fellows in the upper fifth. Now I am Michael Osborne, one of the suspects in the notorious Osborne Murder Case. I can't go to school. I can't become a doctor. I can't do any of the things I could have done before." His voice rose, a little wildly;

"Oh, it isn't only school. It's—it's everything. The blighters in the village—the newspapers—the staring eyes—the pointing fingers—the damned sneaking feeling I've got even when I'm with my own family; especially when I'm with my own family! I can't stand it any longer. I've got to get out of it all, I tell you! I've got to get away."

For a while, Edith was at a loss. She looked at her husband, who was slumped in a chair with his face buried in his hands. There was no help for her from that quarter.

"I'm thinking of asking a relation to take Peter and Marjory for a time," she said, as calmly as she could manage. "He might be willing to—"

The boy shook his head vehemently.

"Going to relations would be as bad as staying here. I want to change my name and go away where no one knows me—as far away as possible."

"But, Son, we can't afford to—"

There was a suspicion of moisture in Michael's dark eyes. He gulped and laid a hand on his mother's arm.

"I'm not quite such a rotter as all that. I don't want you to give me the money. I have a few pounds saved out of the money I earned helping Doctor Denham with his car."

"A few pounds won't last long, dear," said Edith with a tremulous smile.

"Before it's gone, I'll find a job. Don't worry, I shan't starve, I may not be a qualified mechanic, but I know enough about cars to be worth my keep to a garage."

The following morning Michael strapped a suitcase to the carrier of his motorcycle and started off, his small savings in an inner pocket that was fastened with a safety pin. His mother looked after him until he was far out of sight, and then she went up to her room and remained there alone for a long time. When she came down her eyes were sunk in hollows, but there was a smile on her lips. Someone had to smile, to keep up the family morale, and that someone had to be Edith.

A few days later a reply came to a letter Edith had written to her cousin, a clergyman at Morecambe, who wrote that after much prayerful deliberation he had decided that it was his duty to have the two youngest of 'her unfortunate family' to stay with him for a month or so. Peter and Marjory left by train for Morecambe that afternoon, in a state of growing excitement at the prospect of a holiday by the sea, away from what had become the hateful village of Gay Ladies. Edith suggested that sufficient funds might be spared to send Dorothy and Ann to some quiet resort for a few weeks, but her daughters flatly refused to consider it.

"And leave you and Dad to fight it out alone?" cried Ann. "Not likely!"

"Our place is with you, Mother," said Dorothy quietly.

"But I should feel happier if you were out of all this."

"Well, we shouldn't!" retorted Ann, kissing her mother. "So that's that."

No one ever knew what the ensuing week meant to Edith. Never before had she been parted from any of the children for so much as a single night.

And then a wire from Morecambe plunged the depleted household into a state of nervous anxiety. It read:

Children missing beds not slept in last night have consulted police no accidents reported diligent search under way.

*

When the flurry created by the telegram was at its height, Peter and Marjory walked in, grubby and hungry, but in the best of spirits. The previous evening when the rest of the clergyman's household was asleep, they had packed their things in silence and stealthily crept out of the house. A friendly lorry driver, bound for Brancaster, had come miles out of his way to bring them home.

"We've never had such a rotten time before in all our lives!" declared Marjory. "I hate to say it about one of your relations, Mother, but the Reverend was an awful prune. He kept trying to pump us about the murder."

"And all the time he'd roll his eyes and say: '*dear, dear, what a shocking calamity!*'" added Peter. "But he loved hearing about it, just the same. And he wanted us to pray for Aunt Octavia."

"I told him you wanted us to forget about Aunt Octavia," said Marjory, "and he said you weren't bringing us up properly."

The following evening, when the family was seated at supper, Michael came home. He put his motorcycle in the shed, dumped his suitcase in the kitchen, slapped Hannah on the back, strode into the dining-room, and dropped casually into a chair.

"Hello, Mother," he said. "Hello, Dad."

For the moment his swagger deserted him and he had a rather touching small-boy air. "Golly," he said, "it's good to be home again."

Stephen held out his hand across the table. "It's good to have you home, Son."

They shook hands solemnly; and then Michael grinned up at Hannah, who was coming into the room with a laden tray. "Buck up, Hannah, old girl. I'm as hungry as a hunter."

That night he squatted on the end of Ann's bed and talked for half an hour with hardly a pause for breath. On his second day away from home, he had found a job as a helper in a garage at

Carlisle. He had given his name as Jimmy Milligan and told the proprietor he was an orphan. At first, he had been fairly happy, although he had missed everyone at home like blazes— "even you, old Funny Face!"—and, Lord, what a relief it had been to be no one in particular once more! To walk down a street and not have that beastly feeling that people were craning their necks to look after you! To be treated naturally, easily, like a normal human being, instead of a bally freak in blessed sideshow! Yes, there had been a lot of advantages to being Jimmy Milligan, the orphaned garage hand.

"But this morning a bloke drove in in a big saloon and, while I was under the car draining the sump, I heard him yarning with the boss about the Osborne Murder Case. I kept telling myself that the Osborne Murder Case was no concern of mine, that I was Jimmy Milligan and didn't care two pins what anyone said about the murder of an old lady in an obscure Blankshire village. But it didn't work. I was all ears. My face was red under its coating of oil. Couldn't help it.

"And then the bloke said: 'As a matter of fact I understand the police are satisfied that Stephen Osborne did it, but they can't produce sufficient evidence to satisfy a jury, so they are delaying the arrest and hoping that fresh evidence will turn up.'

"When I heard that, I was all burned up inside. I slid out from beneath the car and stood up.

"'I am Michael Osborne', I said, 'and Stephen Osborne is my father. And *you* are a damned liar!' With that, I punched him on the nose!"

Ann clapped her hands. "Good for you, Mike! What did he do then?"

"For a moment I thought he was going to hit me back, and he could have crumpled me up with one punch. Gosh, he looked as big as a house. But I didn't care. I wanted him to hit me. Oh, it wasn't that I was trying to play the giddy hero, it was something deep inside me, something I don't understand, something I can't explain. I wanted him to hit back and I didn't care if he killed me.

"But he didn't. He stood looking at me for a while, rubbing his nose, and then he said: 'You're right, Sonny, I'm a damned liar. What's more, I'm a damned fool as well. I was just talking, that's all. I'm sorry.'"

"'That's all right.'" I said.

"It was then I realised that I'd let myself down by running away and changing my name. I went across to the corner of the garage where my bike was standing, started it up—and headed for home."

Chapter 23

WITH HANDS THAT trembled slightly, Stephen filled the blackened bowl of a favourite briar with Latakia and fumbled for matches in the pockets of his shabby tweed jacket. He was frowning as he strolled down a winding path to his rose garden. He stood staring at the last blossoms of the season for some minutes, his forehead wrinkled, his teeth clamped tightly on the chewed mouthpiece of the pipe, his thoughts far away; and then, from an inside pocket he drew a letter which had come in the morning post and read it for the third time.

PARFITT, MARIN & PARFITT, SOLICITORS
7, Royal Exchange,
Midland Square,
Brancaster

STEPHEN OSBORNE, ESQ.
Gay Ladies, Blankshire.

29th September, 1936

Dear Sir,

Miss Octavia Osborne's Trust

As we informed you in our letter of August 30th, of which we have not yet received an acknowledgment, you and your five children are the residuary legatees under a will made by your sister in May, 1924: which is, to the best of our knowledge, Miss Osborne's last will and testament. Under the terms of the will the entire estate, with the exception of a few minor bequests, is to be held on trust on your behalf during your lifetime, and you are to receive the income from it. After your death the capital is to be divided equally among your children, on their attaining 25 years of age. While we are not yet in a position to provide you with an exact statement, it is probable that the residue will be in the region of one hundred and eighty thousand pounds.

We regret that there is little likelihood of the estate being settled in the near future, since the deceased's affairs are unusually involved.

Yours truly,

PARFITT, MAKIN & PARFITT

Stephen had tried not to think of what his sister's death would mean to him financially, Edith and he had not discussed it. They had studiously avoided the subject, fearing that the barest mention of it would invoke the spectre they were trying to exorcise. Octavia had been murdered to prevent her leaving the money to charity, and to talk about the money was to bring up the question Stephen and his wife were trying to ignore, the question that haunted them, nevertheless, every waking hour, the awful question of the identity of the murderer.

It was not surprising that a previous letter from the solicitors had gone unanswered. Stephen had not received it. During August and early September, scurrilous anonymous communications had been coming in their hundreds by every post and after the shock of reading a few of the initial batch Edith had burned each day's correspondence unopened.

It was the last sentence of the letter that caused Stephen to frown and chew nervously on the stem of his pipe. '...*there is little likelihood of the estate being settled in the near future, since the deceased's affairs are unusually involved...*' Having known Octavia, Stephen could not swallow the explanation. Octavia's affairs involved? Impossible! Her judgment had been shrewd, her business sense admirable, her love of order almost a mania. No, in death her affairs would be as orderly as her prim person had been in life. There was another reason for the delay, and Stephen did not need to be told what it was. Messrs. Parfitt, Makin & Parfitt were playing for time. They were waiting to see whether the police would take the first step towards eliminating Stephen from the position of heir to his sister's fortune by arresting him for her murder.

His train of thought reminded him that funds were running low. Only a few pounds were left to his credit at the bank. It was urgent that he obtain more money within a few days. But from what source could it be obtained? To approach Octavia's solicitors was out of the question. Knowing all the time that they were thinking that to obtain money he had committed murder, the interview would be unbearable. They were probably expecting him to come to them, and making up their minds what answer to give him.

His bank? He had had an account with it for twenty-four years and in all that time he had not once been overdrawn. The manager had always been friendly, he seemed to appreciate the straightforwardness of his small affairs. Surely, he would be willing to allow him an overdraft of a reasonable amount

The matter was urgent, so, early that afternoon, Stephen went to Brancaster and called upon the branch that carried his account. He was shown into the private room of the manager, who expressed the formal hope that all Stephen family were well, and condoled with him on the death of his sister. When Stephen ventured to broach the subject of his visit, the manager gave him no help. He put his fingertips together and listened in silence with a blank face to his client's halting request. After Stephen had managed to blurt it out, the manager still made no remark for what seemed to his client an interminable period. He frowned and adjusted his spectacles.

"An overdraft of one hundred pounds," he said at last in a dry, impersonal tone. "You have not stated what security you propose to offer."

"I can offer no security," said Stephen, reddening "But—er—"

He passed the solicitors' letter across the desk and the manager read it with raised eyebrows. "I am afraid," he said, "the bank could not consider advancing such a sum without security unless you could find some person of substance to guarantee the advance."

"That is out of the question. There is no one I could ask."

"You have a daughter who is of age, have you not?"

"Dorothy? Yes, she is twenty-three. But"—Stephen smiled, slightly—"I am afraid Dorothy is not a person of substance. You will hardly be likely to regard her as a suitable guarantor for a loan of a hundred pounds."

The bank manager coughed. With one hand he stroked his chin and with the other he drummed lightly on the desk-top.

"She is—er—a residuary legatee under the will of your sister."

For some moments Stephen did not comprehend what the bank manager was getting at. When realisation dawned, he gasped and his face turned very pale. His mouth opened, but he did not speak. With a visible effort he stumbled to his feet. He put out a shaking hand which groped all over the desk before it found the letter. In trying to fold the letter, he made a ragged tear in it. The bank manager said something in an apologetic tone, but Stephen did not hear it. He turned and went blindly out of the room.

It was not until late that night that Stephen could bring himself to show the letter to Edith and tell her of his interview at the bank. Edith took his haggard face in her two hands and looked at it lovingly for a long time, and then she pressed a kiss on each of his burning eyes. She cradled his head on her bosom and soothed him as though he were a little child.

"Don't think about it anymore, Stephen, my darling. And don't worry about money. I knew we should need some and I've arranged to sell the Consols Mother left me. Five hundred pounds will last us a long time."

"But—Edith!" he protested. "That is your own little nest egg. We agreed never to touch it—"

"There is no 'mine' and 'thine' in family life, Stephen, my dear. We need the money, and that's all there is to it."

After a pause, Edith said: "Stephen, there's something I've been meaning to speak to you about. We ought to move. It isn't only us the curiosity-seekers flock here to see, it's the house in which the murder was done, as much as anything. Well, let them have the house—we'll find another."

"Yes, we ought to move," agreed Stephen hoarsely. "We shall never be happy here again. Sometimes I think we shall never be happy again anywhere."

The following day they began house-hunting. They chose a quiet suburb of Brancaster, on the far side of that sprawling city from that on which Gay Ladies was situated. In the afternoon they found a medium-sized house with a pleasant garden which seemed reasonably suited to their requirements. They returned to the agent from whom they had obtained the keys and inquired about the rent. It was higher than their present rent, but not too high.

"I think we'll take it," said Edith, after a consultation with her husband.

"You are very wise, madam," said the agent with professional enthusiasm. "It's a good solid residence, built at a time when houses *were* built, not thrown together and held up by the wallpaper. Thoroughly modernised, too, with every convenience you could reasonably ask for. And the neighbourhood's good. I live in it myself. Up-to-date shops. A fine park. Good schools. You didn't say whether you have a family, Mr.—Mr.—"

The agent glanced at Stephen's card and his face changed. His gaze travelled from the card to Stephen and from Stephen to Edith. There was an uncomfortable pause.

"I—er—will you excuse me for a moment?"

He was gone for a few minutes and when he returned, he was frowning and shaking his head.

"This is very unfortunate, very unfortunate indeed. I must apologise, Mr. Osborne, a stupid blunder has been made. My clerk—careless of him, incredibly careless—I'm afraid he sent you on a fool's errand. That particular house was let only the other day."

"But the board is still up!"

"No doubt, sir. Probably my workman has not yet found time to take it down. You know what these fellows are."

"I see."

Stephen bit his lip and looked at Edith.

"There is a card in your window advertising a house in Eden Road which might suit," she said.

"Eden Road.... Let me see. Oh, *that!* That house is in rather bad repair. And the landlord positively refuses to do anything to it. You'd have to spend hundreds to make it decently habitable." The agent rubbed his chin doubtfully. "As a matter of fact, I don't think there's a house on my books at the moment that would suit your requirements."

Suddenly the truth dawned upon Stephen. "What you really mean is that you won't rent me a house because I am involved in a murder."

"You put it bluntly, sir. I hesitated to say so, but that's about the size of it. It isn't *me*. I'm sure I have nothing against you personally, sir, nothing whatever. It's the owners of the properties.

They wouldn't have it. People talk, you know. If you moved into one of the houses on my books everyone in the neighbourhood would know about it within twenty-four hours. It would never do, it really wouldn't. Your lives would be made unbearable; and it would harm the property."

"Surely—if—if we changed our name—"

"It wouldn't work, sir. They'd find out soon enough who you were. They'd say"—he coughed apologetically—"they'd say there must be something in the newspaper stories, or you wouldn't change your name—if you see what I mean. If you'll allow me to advise you, sir, you'll stick it out where you are."

Chapter 24

"I still think Stephen Osborne did it. He had lost his job and was desperate when she refused to help him. He owed her a grudge for having done him out of his inheritance all those years. He claims to have been in the garden at the time of the murder but we have only his word for that: no one saw him there. Besides, it's only a step from the garden to the drawing-room through the French windows and he could have done it in a matter of seconds—"

"Let's not overlook the point that there was oil on the scarf. It seems to me that that is a feature of the case to which none of us have paid sufficient attention. It's agreed, more or less, that the oil must have got on the scarf from Michael's hands, but I think we've accepted his explanation too readily. No normal lad is going to absent-mindedly wipe his oily hands on an expensive silk scarf. I think this is what happened; Michael, coming in from the shed where he kept his motor-bike, looked in through the open drawing-room door and saw his aunt sitting there with her back to him. At the same time, he noticed the scarf on the hall-stand. At Michael's age, a boy wants terribly to be a man. Michael had heard his aunt abusing his father at luncheon and threatening to cut him out of her will. In some twisted way he must have felt that to avenge the insults and prevent her from disinheriting his father by ending her existence would be a justifiable, even manly action. He picked up the scarf and—"

"We mustn't lose sight of the fact that the dead woman would have been out of the house an hour and a half before the time of the murder had not Edith Osborne persuaded her to remain until four. To my mind, that's significant. She hated the old woman, who had been the cause of a terrible scene. It would be natural to want to get rid of her as quickly as possible. And yet, she coaxed her to remain a little longer. Why? Edith Osborne is a strong-minded woman and devoted to her family. There's probably nothing she wouldn't do for the sake of her husband and the children—"

"Talking about strong-minded women, what price the maid? She, too, hated the dead woman: and not even the mother is more devoted to the family than she. Murder would not readily occur to a lady like Edith Osborne, but Hannah Gale is of the type that goes in for direct action, the type that thinks with their hands. A whole-hogger, utterly devoted to her employers, utterly ruthless in her hatred of anyone who would harm them—"

"If it's a ruthless type we're looking for, let's consider Ann. There's a cold-blooded young lady, if you like. Not a nerve in her body. Reading Shakespeare when the murder was committed if you swallow her story—I'm damned if I can!"

"What about young Fleming? Oh, I know he isn't the likeliest suspect, but he's got to be considered. The silk scarf was in his possession at three o'clock. He may be lying about what he did with it. He's very much in love with the eldest girl, and young men in love don't stop to think. He was in the garden alone half an hour before the murder was discovered. He could have entered through the French windows and killed the old woman. Motive? Well, hearing from Dorothy that the old woman was to disinherit her father—knowing that his parents would jibe at their only son marrying a penniless girl—"

"If we're considering Fleming, let's not forget the younger children. Doctor Denham says that no particular strength was exerted in the commission of the crime. A child could have done it. I'm told young Peter recently made a murderous attack on another boy at his school—"

"It's my opinion that we ought to concentrate our attention

on Simon Osborne. To my mind he's the likeliest of the lot. A drunken waster, with no moral code and not the ghost of a conscience, he stood to gain considerably by the old woman's death and he'd think no more of it than of treading on a beetle. He sponged shamelessly on his cousin when Stephen was poor. He could look forward to limitless easy pickings if the timely death of Octavia made Stephen rich. His alibi for the time of the murder is weak. I wouldn't mind betting that Simon's our man!"

*

The ashtrays were overflowing with spent matches, ash and cigarette and cigar stubs. The atmosphere was hazy with smoke. Down both sides of the long table in the Chief Constable's room six men were seated in the informal postures of those who have been sitting in talk on hard seats until the sittable portions of their anatomies are tired. They were weary of the discussion, which had gone on for hours. '...*about it and about, but evermore came out at the same door wherein I went...*' The six men were Inspector Burrows, Sergeant Feathers, an official representing Scotland Yard, a local solicitor, the coroner, and the Chief Constable—who was stifling a yawn.

Major Blackett rose.

"Gentlemen," he said, "we're getting nowhere. This is the twenty-first of our weekly conferences on the Osborne Case and we are simply going over old ground week after week. None of us has a fresh idea to put forward. There isn't an avenue of speculation that hasn't been explored time and time again. The fact that we can make out a reasonable case against any individual member of the family is nullified by the fact that we can make out as good a case against every member of the family.

We can't put 'em all on trial, nor can we settle it by drawing a name out of a hat.

"Gentlemen, this is the last conference on the Osborne Case that we shall hold. Unless further evidence comes to light, the Osborne case is closed!"

*

In this decision the Chief Constable was following rather belatedly on the heels of the press. For lack of fresh material, the newspapers had dropped the case a number of weeks ago. The public was tired of it. People were beginning to forget who the Osbornes were. In the village of Gay Ladies, they still remembered and goggled at the Osbornes every time they went out, but villages have long memories for their own scandals. To the world at large, the Osbornes were becoming just another family.

Chapter 25

Edith was humming to herself as she came downstairs early one morning in November. She felt more cheerful than she had done since the awful day in August when Octavia was murdered. Life was becoming bearable again now that they were no longer living in the full glare of publicity. Now that they were no longer stared at and pointed out wherever they went the children were beginning to forget, to laugh and be happy, to take up the normal pursuits of healthy young people. Michael, Peter and Marjory were at new schools and finding that they were no longer regarded as freaks for having had an aunt who was murdered. Ann was trying to write a novel and appearing at meals with her spectacles askew, her hair standing up on end, and ink all over her fingers.

Oh, life was good again. Not as sweet as it had been—Edith knew that the old feeling of peace and security in the bosom of her family was gone, never to return—but good, nevertheless. The only fly in the ointment was Stephen. Poor Stephen. Stephen did not forget. He hardly ever went out. Edith could not remember the last time she had seen him smile. His hair was whitening, he was growing old before her eyes. Something must be done about Stephen. She would speak to the children, make them see how much their father needed them. If anything could raise him from the awful depths of morbid brooding into which he had sunk, they could do it.

Edith went out on the front steps and brought in the morning newspaper. She scanned the front page briefly and turned to the Women's Page. Suddenly she put a hand to her heart and uttered a bitter cry. "*Not again! Oh, they can't start it all over again—*" She was staring an advertisement which occupied almost half the page:

THE FAMILY THAT CAN'T FORGET!

ONCE HAPPY, NOW PLUNGED IN GLOOM
BY MEMORY OF MURDERED AUNT

In the *Sunday World* next week will be told for the first time the
inside story of the Osbornes, the tragic family which figures
in the most engrossing unsolved mystery of recent years. An
absorbing human narrative of normal, everyday family life;
shattered forever by a sudden and cruel death which brought
the father a fortune, but destroyed the happiness of his loved
ones. This story, told by an intimate friend and illustrated
by exclusive pictures, will touch the hearts of all who read it.

Exclusive to the
SUNDAY WORLD
OVER 3,000,000 NET SALES!

"They can't do it! They can't do it! That's over! They can't start
it all again!"

Hannah came into the hall and stared at her mistress's white,
strained face. "What is it, Ma'am? Is anything wrong?"

Edith tore out the page and folded it. "Don't ask me any
questions, Hannah. I've got to go to London at once. I'll be
back tonight. I know I can rely on you to see to things while
I'm gone."

"Of course, Ma'am."

During the four-and-a-half hour's journey from Gay Ladies
to London, via Brancaster, Edith's mind kept saying: "They
can't do it. They can't start it all over again. Why won't they let
people forget us? There can't be any news in a story that's been
told so often. They've squeezed it dry."

The *Sunday World* building was a tall white structure in a

turning off Fleet Street. On the roof stood an enormous board with the clamouring legend:

SUNDAY WORLD
OVER 3,000,000 NET SALES!

In the entrance hall a burly commissionaire, his chest covered with ribbons, smiled pityingly at Edith when she asked to see the editor. "Have you an appointment, Ma'am?"

Edith shook her head.

The commissionaire made a clucking noise with his tongue and teeth. "If you'll fill in this form, Ma'am, stating your name and the nature of your business, I'll send it up." His expression seemed to add: "*but a fat lot of good that'll do you!*"

Edith wrote her name on the form but left blank the space provided for an explanation of the nature of her business. The commissionaire took it and shook his head, but summoned a boy who took the slip of paper upstairs. It seemed hours before the boy came back. Looking at the clock, Edith was startled to discover that only five minutes had elapsed. The boy said something to the commissionaire and handed him the form Edith had filled in. The man approached her, twisting the paper in his thick fingers.

"I'm sorry, Ma'am, but the editor is rather busy this morning…"

Edith took the form from him and wrote: 'from Gay Ladies' under her name. "Will you be so good as to send it up again?" she asked.

The commissionaire glanced at what she had written and his eyebrows rose. He stared at Edith, who returned his gaze steadily. "Certainly, Madam," he said with alacrity. "Boy!"

Before long the messenger was back. This time he walked up

to Edith, clicked his heels, and said: "Mr, Snaith will see you at once, Madam. Please follow me."

Mr. Snaith was a dapper little man of about thirty-five who bore a strong resemblance to a canary. He had very sleek yellow hair, sharp features, and bright birdlike little eyes. He was smoking a cigarette in a long amber holder. When Edith entered, he bobbed up to shake hands with her and bobbed down again all in one motion.

"Good day, Mrs. Osborne. Won't you sit down? May I offer you a cigarette? No? You won't mind if I smoke? Thanks. Now, what can I do for you?"

Edith took the advertisement from her handbag and passed it across the desk to him. "I came about this."

Mr. Snaith raised his eyebrows. "Yes?"

"You must not print that article."

"No? But I'm afraid I must. We've advertised it extensively. Our readers will be looking for it. We can't let them down."

"If you print it," said Edith unsteadily, "I shall sue you for libel."

"I don't think you will, Mrs. Osborne. We are very careful, you know. Our solicitors have been over every word and they assure us that the story offers no grounds for an action. Would you care to see it? I have a proof here."

From a drawer he took a sheet of paper the size of a newspaper page and placed it before Edith, who looked at it with eyes that grew more and more haggard. It was worse, far worse, than she had feared. It was actually illustrated by photographs of her children from babyhood to their present ages; photographs she had loved and cherished, which no one but close family friends had ever possessed. They must have been obtained from someone to whom she had personally had given them in the glowing pride of motherhood.

The letterpress was an intimate study of her family life and touched on things no one but an intimate friend—or one who had been an intimate friend—could have known. And suddenly she knew who must have written it, Simon Osborne. The 'Uncle' Simon her children adored...

"You see, Mrs. Osborne," said the editor smoothly, "there isn't a word that could be considered actionable. It is merely a simple record of family life and of a tragedy which entered into it. Sympathetically treated, I'm sure you will agree?"

"It's damnable," said Edith in a hushed tone. "It rips away the last shreds of privacy that were left to us. It is as though your three million readers were marching into our house and watching us eating—sleeping—brushing our teeth."

"You think so? I am inclined to agree. As a matter of fact, that is why I bought it. Nothing pleases the public more than a good human interest story and this one is really rather well done. Human interest, Mrs. Osborne, is what has gained this newspaper its enormous circulation."

"Mr. Snaith, I—I am appealing to your better nature. Don't print this article. Don't! Can't you see what it will do to my family? We've suffered so much already. We've been through such a lot. Now people are beginning to forget. This will start it all over again."

"Mrs. Osborne, I'm an employee of this paper and it is my duty to do my best for it. I've been a newspaperman for almost twenty years and I assure you I've never printed a story with a wider appeal than this one. To kill it would be a crime. I'm sorry, but I cannot do it."

"But the murder of my sister-in-law is not news. It is an old story."

"But a story of which the public is not likely to tire, Mrs. Osborne; and this approaches it from a new angle. There is nothing so absorbing, you know, as a murder. And an unsolved murder!—that's a winner every time. Most murders die on us with startling abruptness as soon as the murderer is tried and hanged. There is something final about a hanging; it leaves us with nothing more to say. But an unsolved murder—that's always a story, offers endless grounds for speculation. The public loves it."

"Am I to understand, then, that this is not a single isolated article? Do you mean to go on raking up the scandal indefinitely?"

"Not the *Sunday World*, Mrs. Osborne. We'd soon lose our readers if we harped on the same string too long. No, this story will finish the case for us for a time at least, but some other paper is sure to re-hash it again before long. It was a meaty murder, you know—too meaty to be dropped. Next time a murder is committed and the culprit isn't caught every paper in the country will dig up the Osborne case, together with all the other unsolved murders of the past decade, and link them together in an editorial on the inefficiency of the police. I believe there's a man writing a novel based on the case. He's calling it. 'Murder in The Family', I'm told. I don't suppose his will be the only book the case will inspire. Unsolved murders have a way of popping up again in print—again and again."

"So that even after I am dead, and my children are grown men and women, this awful business will still haunt them, souring their lives?"

"When you die, Mrs. Osborne, the Osborne Murder Case will feature in your obituary notice. When one of your daughters marries, the papers will remind their readers that she is a niece of a murdered woman whose murder never was solved. If one of your sons distinguishes himself—"

"Stop! For God's sake, stop!" cried Edith, ashen to the lips. "I can't bear it."

"I am sorry, Mrs. Osborne. I was trying to make you see my point. I can't kill this story. It's too full of interest."

"Forever and ever. On and on. Always this curse on my unhappy family—"

"Unless, of course, the police discover the murderer. As I said, hanging is final in more ways than one."

Mr. Snaith lit a fresh cigarette with rather more care than was necessary. He studied his fingernails for a time. At last, he looked up.

"I hesitate to suggest this, but since the publicity is inevitable, there seems no reason why you shouldn't benefit in some way from it. Why don't you write me a story giving your own angle of the case? Our readers would lap it up. I can offer you—say— five hundred pounds—"

Edith did not answer. She only looked at him, that was all. It was enough.

"Sorry," he said uncomfortably. "Thought I'd just mention the offer."

As she left the *Sunday World* building Edith was mocked by an array of placards on the opposite wall. With pitiless monotony they read:

READ

THE FAMILY THAT CANNOT FORGET

AN ABSORBING HUMAN DOCUMENT

IN NEXT WEEK'S

SUNDAY WORLD

OVER 3,000,000 NET SALES

The placards were repeated on each of a long row of motor-vans ranked outside the building. The words hammered in her brain: '...*the family that cannot forget...an absorbing human document…the family that cannot forget…three million net sale…an absorbing human document…the family that…has three million readers…'*

Numb, miserable, she sat in a tea-shop so long that the waitresses began to discuss her among themselves. "*Gives me the creeps she does.*" "*Looks as though she's seen a ghost.*" "*Seen a ghost? Looks like a ghost 'erself if you ask me!*"

The pot of tea she had ordered as an excuse for sitting down grew stone cold, untouched.

Chapter 26

L UNCH WAS OVER, the dishes were washed and dried, and for half an hour no pressing duty called Hannah's attention, she collected the silver from the dining-room and began to polish it. She put all her brawn into the task. Hannah was a firm believer in elbow-grease. While she rubbed and buffeted, her mind was as busy as her tireless arms.

There was something wrong, she knew. It was not merely the brooding shadow which had hung over the household for long months. That had begun to abate. This was something tense and terrible, something that had only evinced itself within the past twenty-eight hours, something that had plunged her mistress back into the gloom from which she had gradually emerged.

It had been late last night when her mistress had returned from London and gone straight to bed with a headache. There had been no need for her to say that she had a headache, it had been written in the grey pallor of her face. This morning, for the first time in many years, she had remained in bed. She had refused food and answered Hannah's anxious inquiries in dry, toneless monosyllables. The master had been up and down stairs all morning like a broody hen, and every time he had come down his expression had been more unhappy than before. Now he was mooning about in the garden among his precious roses.

Oh, something was wrong, there was no doubt about that, and Hannah, who would have cut off her right hand to aid any of the Osbornes, was powerless to do anything about it. That hurt. Hannah vented her frustration on the silver. She rubbed until it dazzled the eyes, and went on rubbing.

Stephen came into the kitchen and stood by the door undecided, stroking his hair nervously.

"I suppose— Your mistress— She hasn't rung for you, Hannah? Or—or anything?"

"No, sir, she has not. And—taking a liberty—if I were you, sir, I should let her be. She doesn't want to be disturbed."

"I—I expect you're right," he said huskily.

He went through the hall and Hannah heard him wearily mounting the stairs. She shook her head. The master's fretting and fussing was doing the mistress no good. There he was, going up to gloom at her again, when he knew perfectly well, she'd be better left alone. Rub. Rub. Rub. In her abstraction, Hannah put fresh polish on silver she had already shone to perfection.

What was that? It sounded like a cry. No, not a cry, more a hoarse growl. Hannah pushed open the kitchen door and listened. The house was still—she shivered—still as the grave. She stood listening, and after a time she heard dragging footsteps crossing the floor overhead. Back and forward they went, two or three times, and then she heard a door opening and the steps came out to the upper floor landing.

The first Hannah saw of her master as he started to descend the stairs was his feet. Her mouth opened and remained like that. His feet seemed to fumble their way down as though he had lost all power to guide them. They made her scalp prickle. It seemed an age before his legs followed and then his body. Hannah saw his face; his staring eyes. His eyes—oh, God! —all the horror of Death and Damnation was in his wide, stricken eyes. His mouth was slack, as though some terrible blow had shattered the teeth in it and left it pulped.

"Good gracious, sir, what is it? Mr. Osborne! What's wrong, sir?"

Stephen looked at her, trembling as though with the ague.

"The doctor, Hannah..." he muttered hoarsely. "Go quickly... the doctor."

He went through the kitchen, and out of the house. There was something in his hand. Hannah could not see what it was. She looked after him for some moments, and then, with a gasp, she darted upstairs. At the door of Edith Osborne's room, she raised her hand to knock, but some power stronger than habit drove her headlong into the room.

She came to an abrupt halt at the foot of the bed. All the strength drained out of her at what she saw, and she put out a trembling hand and clutched at the bedrail for support. She tried to speak, to stammer out something, but her paralysed tongue would not utter the words. As abruptly as she had entered the room, she hurried out of it and clattered down the stairs. Throwing wide the front door, she ran out of the house and down the garden path.

Hurrying along the road, she was stopped by Miss Whipple, who caught her arm and stared at her with glistening eyes.

"What is wrong, Hannah? Has anything happened?"

Hannah glared like a mad woman.

"Damn you, you vulture!" she cried. "Take your hands off me! Let me go!"

Tearing herself free she ran across the road, threw open the gate of Doctor Denham's garden, and hurried up to the door of the house. She beat a frantic tattoo with the knocker.

"I want the doctor," she panted, to the startled maidservant who opened the door. "The doctor—quickly—oh, for heaven's sake, hurry!"

The commotion brought Doctor Denham from his surgery to the hall. He looked curiously at Hannah's distorted face and dishevelled hair.

"My good woman, whatever—"

"It's the mistress, Doctor, it's the mistress! She's very ill—perhaps dying! Oh, Doctor, come quickly. I'm feared she's dead—"

"I'll come at once."

Doctor Denham went back to his surgery and took his case from the corner. He hesitated, stroking his lower lip thoughtfully. He put out his hand to the telephone on his desk, but withdrew it without lifting the receiver.

"I wonder..." He bit his lip. Suddenly he lifted the receiver and asked for a number.

"County Police Headquarters?" he said, when the call was answered. "This is Doctor Denham of Gay Ladies. I wish to speak to Major Blackett... That you, Major? I—I— Oh look here the Osbornes' maid has just called, in rather an agitated state, to summon me to her mistress. She's afraid Mrs. Osborne may be dead... No, she didn't say anything to suggest foul play, but her manner... Yes, that's what I thought... I wasn't sure, but I imagined you might... You're coming at once? Very well."

The impression of something much worse than serious illness which Doctor Denham had received from Hannah's bearing was confirmed almost as soon as he entered Edith Osborne's room. His lips tightened; his eyes grew stern.

He looked up and met Hannah's horrified gaze. "Is she—is she—"

"Go downstairs," he said quietly, "and fetch me a table-spoonful of mustard in a tumbler of lukewarm water. Hurry, woman, hurry!"

Hannah was gone before the last words were uttered. In an incredibly short time she was back, with the tumbler in her hand. Doctor Denham was bending over her mistress. A hypodermic syringe gleamed in his steady fingers.

"Bring hot water bottles," he said, taking the glass without looking at Hannah, "and all the blankets you can find."

For some minutes the doctor and Hannah were too busy

to think. When at last the doctor stood back from the bed, Hannah clutched his arm desperately.

"Will she live? Oh, Doctor, will she live?"

"I'm afraid not. She has only about one chance in a hundred."

Hannah broke down and wept, her hoarse sobs shaking her great frame.

"For heaven's sake don't do that," the doctor said irritably. "Who else is in the house?"

"Only the master. Oh, but he went out."

"Only your master, eh? H'm..." Doctor Denham took a few paces back and forwards. "You had better go to your kitchen, Hannah. I'll call you when the police arrive."

Hannah gaped at him.

"The police!" she repeated.

"I said the police," snapped Doctor Denham huskily. His hands were beginning to shake. How he wished they would stop! "My good woman, don't make this harder for me than it is already. It isn't my fault, you know. The police have got to be called in—er—cases like this. They will be here presently."

The door opened and Stephen stood on the threshold. Doctor Denham went over to him, preventing him from coming further into the room.

"Doctor! My wife...will she live?"

"I am afraid not."

A sob rose in Stephen's throat.

"There is nothing you can do here, Mr. Osborne," said the doctor quietly. "But you had better remain within call. I may tell you that I have summoned the police."

Stephen gave him a long look and stumbled down the stairs.

*

Hannah sat in her kitchen, all the pulsing life gone out of her, slumped heavily in a chair like a sack dumped in a corner. The doctor paced the bedroom biting his lips. Through the window he kept an eye on the road, and he went downstairs to open the door, when a car drew up at the gate with a squealing of brakes.

Major Blackett came hurrying up the path followed by Inspector Burrows and Sergeant Feathers. The Chief Constable looked inquiringly at Doctor Denham.

"She isn't dead," said the doctor hoarsely. "But I am afraid there is no hope for her. She has taken—or been given—poison. Strychnine."

"There's something else," responded Major Blackett keenly. "I can see it in your face."

"Yes, I am afraid there *is* something else," agreed the doctor shakily. "Some months ago, Stephen Osborne was rundown and I—I prescribed strychnine."

The Chief Constable took the stairs two at a time, followed by the others. He looked at the limp form of Edith Osborne, swathed in blankets, and his expression grew grim. Inspector Burrows prowled about the bed.

"No glass, sir," he said meaningfully.

"That isn't conclusive. She might not have used a glass. Was there a bottle on the bed or the floor, Doctor?"

"That was the first thing I looked for. There was no bottle."

The Inspector crawled under the bed and came out empty-handed. "Nothing doing, sir."

Sergeant Feathers was kneeling by the hearth, rummaging in the fireplace.

"What are you doing, man?" demanded the Major.

The Sergeant stood up and exhibited a heap of burned paper which he had removed from the grate and placed carefully on a handkerchief.

"Might be a clue here, sir," he replied.

Major Blackett nodded. He frowned.

"Can you tell me how long ago the poison was administered?"

"Not more than a few minutes before I was called in, and that was a quarter of an hour ago," said Doctor Denham. "Er—the maid tells me that only she and her master have been at home this afternoon."

"Oh? And where is Osborne now?"

"He was here a few minutes ago. I think he went out to the garden."

From the window Major Blackett noticed a woman in animated conversation with the policeman he had left at the gate.

"That Whipple woman is downstairs," he said irritably. "She seems to want to come in. Run down, Feathers, and find out what's on her mind."

In a few minutes Sergeant Feathers returned.

"She's been using her telescope again, sir," he reported soberly. "Says a while ago she saw Stephen Osborne digging a hole in the far corner of the garden and hiding something in it."

Inspector Burrows uttered a triumphant exclamation. "I've always said Osborne's our—"

"Sergeant Feathers!" said Major Blackett.

"Sir?"

"Go and dig up whatever it was he hid, and bring it to me."

"Very good, sir."

The ensuing ten minutes were a nightmare to Doctor Denham. A peace-loving man who abhorred violence and was kindly disposed to all his neighbours, he dreaded to think where all this was leading. He looked out of the window at the well-ordered garden Stephen Osborne had tended so lovingly, and a lump rose in his throat. A feeling of pity for the poisoned woman and her unfortunate husband were mingled in his perplexed mind.

Sergeant Feathers came back and showed his Chief a small bottle and glass, both of which he was holding with extreme care by a spotless handkerchief.

"Strychnine, Doctor?" asked Major Blackett quietly.

The doctor sniffed the glass. "Strychnine," he agreed.

"There are fingerprints on both, sir," said Sergeant Feathers. "If you'll give me a minute—"

"Go ahead."

The Sergeant dusted black powder on glass and bottle and examined them through a magnifying glass.

"Osborne's, sir," he said at last.

"We'd better find him quickly. You'd better come along, Doctor—in case."

They had not far to look. They came upon Stephen Osborne in the field behind the house, standing beside the chattering stream that wandered merrily through it. There was a razor in his hand, but they did not give him time to use it. After they had overpowered him Inspector Burrows cautioned him that anything he might say would be taken down and might be used in evidence at his trial

Stephen looked at him with the eyes of a dead man. He did not speak.

Chapter 27

NIGHT WAS FALLING: the street lamps of Brestock sprang up like yellow eyes in the gathering dusk. In the Chief Constable's comfortable private room, Doctor Denham paced the floor alone. The shrill voices of children at play floated up to him from the street below and he groaned in acute mental anguish. He lit a cigarette and threw it in the grate after a single puff. The door opened and he turned with relief. "I'm glad you're back, Major. This business has upset me more than I'd realised."

Major Blackett, too, looked troubled. With a sigh, he dropped two typewritten sheets of paper on his desk and reached for a cigarette. He pushed the box toward the other, but Doctor Denham shook his head. "Care for a drink?"

"A little brandy, perhaps," replied the doctor jerkily. "I feel rather shaken."

The Chief Constable selected a square-cut decanter from the tantalus and poured a generous measure of amber liquid which he only slightly diluted with soda, before handing it to his guest. He half-filled a tumbler with neat whisky and swallowed three-fifths of it at a gulp. Over the rims of their glasses the eyes of the two men met.

"He's made a statement?"

Major Blackett nodded. "I have it here. Sit down, and I'll read it to you." He picked up the papers he had dropped on his desk, and read them aloud:

"I, Stephen Osborne, have been duly cautioned and of my own free will have elected to make this statement, which is true in every particular to the best of my knowledge and belief. After the scene at luncheon on the day of the murder of my sister,

I went out to the garden and walked up and down, trying to think. I was desperate. I knew my sister would not relent from her determination to cut me out of her will and I could see in store for me nothing but a lifetime of poverty and humiliation. At fifty, with no aptitude for business, I had little hope of finding a position to replace the one I had lost. I could see myself sponging on my children for the rest of my life and the prospect was not to be borne. The only alternative was to kill Octavia while her will in my favour still stood.

"I went into the house in search of some weapon with which to kill her and in the hall found my eldest daughter's scarf which suggested to me the idea of strangling her. I crept into the drawing-room and was horrified to find that my daughter Ann was also in the room. She was engrossed in a book and was unaware of my presence. I could see, in fact, that she was completely oblivious to her surroundings. Had my brain been functioning properly, I might have abandoned my project, but I was so filled with hatred of my sister that I could think of nothing but the thing I had come to do. After it was over, I left the room without disturbing my daughter.

"Since I did this, I have been desperately unhappy. Somehow or other, my wife guessed the truth and of late it has been torture for me to meet her eyes, knowing that she knew. My family life has been wrecked through my action, and although my wife never reproached me in words, there was in her eyes an everlasting mute reproach. Today I could bear it no longer. There could be no further happiness in life for her or for me, and I decided to end life for us both. I poisoned my wife with strychnine and was about to terminate my own existence when I was apprehended by the police.

"Signed,

"STEPHEN OSBORNE"

"Poor devil!" murmured the doctor sadly. "They were a charming couple, devoted to each other. The 'faithful unto death sort.' Ah, well! I—I suppose he'll hang?"

"Bound to."

"Did you suspect him all along of the first murder?"

Major Blackett frowned at his glass. He drained before replying.

"No," he admitted, "I didn't. Confidentially, I suspected his cousin, Simon Osborne. We all had our pet theories and no two were alike. Only Burrows suspected Stephen Osborne; he did from the start."

The doctor went to the tantalus and recharged his glass. There was a troubled look on his kindly face.

"I suppose you're quite satisfied with this statement?"

"Certainly. Why not?"

"I don't quite know. There's something about it, though, that doesn't ring altogether true." The doctor paced the floor restlessly. "Damn it, I can't conceive of any circumstances in which a man like Osborne would kill his wife. For one thing, killing her meant leaving the children to face this whole ungodly mess alone and he loved them too much to do that to them."

"The fact remains," said Blackett, "that Edith Osborne was poisoned."

"It doesn't make sense. It doesn't fit with what I know of Osborne's character. If he couldn't face his wife, he'd have committed suicide. Why kill her and make the position of his unhappy family a hundred times worse?"

Major Blackett chewed his upper lip. "Confound you, Doctor," he grumbled. "As far as I was concerned, this case was settled. And now you've given me the awkward feeling that there may still be a lot more to it."

There was a knock at the door and Sergeant Feathers put his head into the room.

"Miss Ann Osborne would like to see you, sir."

"Ann Osborne? Oh, hang! I can't see her now. Tell her to go home."

"I don't think she'll go, sir. She's very determined."

"Oh, Lord!" groaned Major Blackett. He looked helplessly at Doctor Denham. "Doctor, you've got to help me with this. Telling the child about her father is going to be the very dickens of a job. All right, Feathers. You may show her in."

Ann came in like a whirlwind.

"I hoped I'd find you here, Doctor," she said in a dry, agonised tone. "I want to know about Mother. Hannah told me you'd had her removed to the County Hospital. I went there, but they wouldn't let me see her, wouldn't tell me anything, except that she is still unconscious. Doctor, will she live?"

"I do not know, my dear. I am afraid there is not much hope."

Ann uttered a stricken cry and her face went a sickly white. For a moment the doctor thought that she was going to faint. She turned to Major Blackett. "What are you doing with my father?"

Doctor Denham stood up, moistening his dry lips nervously. He put a hand on the girl's arm which was warm and trembling like the body of a trapped creature of the woods.

"Ann, my dear, please be brave. Ann, you've got to be brave. What am I going to tell you will come as a great shock. You've got to meet it with courage. Ann, your—your—"

He could not go on. Ann looked at him with anguished but tearless eyes.

"You are trying to tell me that my father has been arrested for murder. But it's all a mistake, a terrible mistake."

"He has made a statement, Ann," said Major Black quietly, "in which he admits having killed your aunt and—and—"

"He made it up from beginning to end. Don't you see, he's doing this to protect me."

"To protect *you!*" exclaimed the Chief Constable.

"Ann! You don't know what you're saying!" cried the Doctor.

Ann laughed harshly. "Oh, yes, I do. *I* killed Aunt Octavia. Why you didn't see through me from the start, heaven only knows. My story was thin enough. I was so engrossed in my book that murder was done right under my nose and I didn't know it! How could a hard-headed policeman believe a yarn like that for an instant? Why, it's too absurd for words. And yet, you swallowed it, hook, line, and sinker!

"Do you really believe I could have settled down calmly to read in the same room as that awful old woman? After the scene she had made a few minutes before? Oh, you can't believe that, it's too impossible. I tried to read. I wanted to show her how little I cared. But I could not concentrate on the book. I was too cold with fury. One thought kept recurring in my brain: Aunt Octavia must not be allowed to make the new will. She must never leave the house alive. After a time, I put down the book and said, very politely: 'Will you excuse me a moment?' I meant to go out to the kitchen and find a sharp knife, but I saw Dorothy's scarf hanging in the hall and decided that it would do quite as well. I stole back to the drawing-room. On tiptoe, scarcely daring to breathe, I approached from the rear the chair in which Aunt Octavia was sitting—"

Now Ann was sobbing, wildly, hysterically. Appalled, Major Blackett stared at her in silence for a time, and then he said:

"But this afternoon you were not in the house when your mother—"

"That was not an attempt at murder. I think I can see what happened. Mother knew I killed Aunt Octavia—I told her a few days ago—and the knowledge must have been too much for her. She must have tried to kill herself because she could not bear to live."

"But your father was seen burying the empty poison bottle! His fingerprints were all over it! He confessed—"

"Do you think Father would acknowledge to the world that Mother committed suicide? He would rather, a thousand times rather, be hanged!"

"You realise," said Major Blackett quietly, "that I shall have to place you under arrest."

"Yes, I realise that. And you'll let my father go?"

"That's the important thing, as far as you're concerned," put in Doctor Denham, "your father's freedom."

"You mean," said the Chief Constable thoughtfully, "that Miss Osborne's whole story may be a tissue of lies, designed to lift the burden of guilt from her father's shoulders?"

"I mean exactly that," said the Doctor.

Ann stared from one of them to the other. "You can't think that. You mustn't think that. It isn't so."

Major Blackett touched a bell-button. In a few moments Sergeant Feathers reappeared.

"Place Miss Osborne in charge of the Matron," said the Chief Constable.

When the girl left the room, Blackett turned to Doctor Denham. "There's a ring of truth about her story," he said.

"You were as ready to accept her father's," the Doctor pointed out.

Chapter 28

THAT NIGHT a professor of chemistry at Brancaster University
spent long hours in his laboratory piecing together the scraps
of burned paper Sergeant Feathers had found in the fireplace of
Edith Osborne's room. First, he sprayed the hundreds of black
fragments with a chemical that made them hard and amenable
to handling without crumbling, then he glued each one to a
sheet of cardboard. He cut them out, spread the thickened pieces
on a table and started methodically to fit them together, like a
jigsaw puzzle. During this process, it soon became obvious that
two separate sheets of paper had been burned. The hour was late
when he finished laying them out in their original shape. He
photographed them by a violet ray process, and on the prints
he took from the developed plates, the writing showed up white
and clear against a black background.

The professor read it and clicked his teeth in surprise. He
put the prints in a drawer and went home to bed.

In the morning, Sergeant Feathers came to the laboratory and
the scientist handed him the prints without comment. Feathers
read them and uttered a startled exclamation.

"Good heavens! This alters everything! The Chief must
see these without delay. I can't tell you how grateful I am,
Professor."

"Only too glad to be of assistance. By the way, how are you
getting on with that book you asked me to lend you?"

Feathers reddened. "Not very quickly, I'm afraid, sir. Bit
too deep for me."

"Keep at it, young man. You won't learn anything worth
knowing without a great deal of solid effort, don't stick to the
book for good; I may want it myself someday."

*

Ann and her father had been detained overnight at police head-quarters. At ten o'clock that morning, Major Blackett and Inspector Burrows held a consultation.

"I'm in favour of confronting Osborne and his daughter and making her repeat her story to him," said the Inspector. "I don't believe a word of it myself, but her father is the only person who is likely to be able to put his fingers on all the flaws in it. If he really murdered his sister, as I'm fully convinced he did, he ought to be able to disprove her story quite easily."

"What if she sticks to it through thick and thin? Where will we be then?"

"In a fine mess," grunted Burrows. "In that case, we'll have a fat chance of convicting either of them. Put the father on trial and the daughter's only got to go into the box and tell this yarn of hers to get him off scot-free. Put the daughter on trial, and the father pulls the same stunt. If we can't prove that one or the other is lying, we're sunk. Unless"—he brightened perceptibly— "unless we can prove that they were in it together."

"I can't see that angle, either," retorted the Chief Constable. "Oh well, let's have 'em up."

In a few minutes Ann was ushered into the room, looking pale and worn after her night in the cells, but still very determined. Stephen was brought in almost on her heels. When he saw his daughter, he started nervously. "Ann! What are you doing here?"

Ann gave him a wan smile and tried to speak, but the words would not come. The sight of him had brought her very close to tears.

Before Stephen could say anything further, Major Blackett motioned them both to chairs which had been placed facing the window. "Mr. Osborne, yesterday evening you made a voluntary statement, admitting to the murder of your sister and the attempted murder of your wife. Later, your daughter Ann came here of her own free will and she also made a statement, one diametrically opposed to yours. I propose to read it to you and then you can tell me exactly what you think of it."

He picked up a sheaf of papers which had been typewritten at Ann's dictation and was about to read from them when there was a knock at the door. With a scowl, Inspector Burrows crossed the room and answered it.

"The Chief Constable can't be disturbed now, my lad. Oh! That's different." He looked back over his shoulder. "Sergeant Feathers, sir. Says it's of vital importance."

"Tell him to come in."

Sergeant Feathers entered and handed the Chief Constable the two prints he had received from the chemistry professor. "Thought you'd like to see these at once, sir."

Major Blackett examined the prints and a low whistle escaped him. He pored over them for a long time, and then he leaned forward and handed them to Stephen.

Stephen glanced at the prints and his eyes widened with horror. He dropped them and with a groan buried his face in his hands.

"Of course," murmured the Chief Constable, "you'd hardly need to read them, Osborne, since it was you who burned the originals."

Ann picked up the prints and read the clear white writing of one of them, which she recognised immediately as her mother's handwriting.

To the Police:
It was I who killed Octavia Osborne. I had thought I could go on concealing my guilt forever, but find I cannot. It weighs too

heavily on my conscience. I cannot face the public shame of a trial for murder and the punishment which would inevitably follow, so I am going to end my life by means of poison which I have taken from my husband's medicine chest, to which I have a key.

Edith Osborne

The second note was not headed, but the wording left no doubt for whom it was intended. It read simply:

Forgive me, if you can. I love you all very dearly.

"I could not bear your mother to be branded a murderess," muttered Stephen brokenly. "So, I destroyed the notes she left and hid the bottle. It would have been easier to die on the scaffold than to live to see that stain upon her name."

With a cry, Ann threw her arms about him and held him tightly, sobbing bitterly. "Oh, Father, Father! And I thought that you—"

With a trembling hand, Stephen stroked his daughter's hair. Over her shoulder his tragic grey eyes looked at the Chief Constable.

"Is there any news of my wife?" he asked, in a whisper thick with emotion. "Will she—will she—"

"Doctor Denham 'phoned me half an hour ago," replied Major Blackett soberly. He frowned at the prints on his desk— Edith Osborne's confession of murder—and added in a low tone: "I am afraid she will live."

"You shan't do anything to her!" cried Stephen. "She didn't know what she was doing when she wrote that confession. I killed Octavia! Do you hear? I did it!"

The desk telephone rang shrilly. Major Blackett lifted the

receiver. "Yes?—*Whom?*—What does he want?—Oh, all right send..." Major Blackett replaced the receiver and frowned at his subordinates. "Simon Osborne," he said. "Now, what the devil can he want?"

In a few moments Simon entered the room.

For once in his life, his bearing was far from jaunty. He had the sagging appearance of a pricked balloon. All the bounce, the braggadocio, the unabashed swagger that usually distinguished him, were missing. His unhappy face lengthened when he saw that Stephen and Ann were present.

"I—I am ashamed to face you, Stephen," he stammered. "This—this ghastly affair is all my fault. I could have prevented it. Until the end of my life I shall be cursing myself for failing to prevent it. Oh, I'm a worthless old waster, Stephen, but, believe me, if I had only foreseen what would happen, I should have spoken out long ago. Tell me, will Edith live?"

Stephen nodded dully.

"Thank God! If she had died it would have been my fault."

"What on earth are you talking about?" Major Blackett demanded.

"The editor of the *Sunday World* told me of Edith's visit to him. He told me what he said to her. When I read in last night's paper that she had been found dying of poisoning, I realised instantly what had happened. She left a note, I suppose, confessing to Octavia's murder?"

"I have it here," said the Chief Constable, "but—"

"Yes, that is what she would do. That was Edith. The editor told her that there would never be any peace for her family as long as the murder was unsolved. Edith loved her children. For them, no sacrifice was too great. So, she wrote her 'confession' and tried to end her life. If I had only foreseen that this would happen—"

"Yes?" said Major Blackett, his voice grown suddenly cold. "If you had foreseen it, what would you have done?"

"I should have revealed the identity of the person who really murdered Octavia."

"Ah!"

"Yes. Almost as soon as I heard about the murder, I knew who did it. It was obvious. There was only one person who *could* have done it. Edith? Stephen? Never. Neither of those two loving parents would have murdered Octavia and left their daughter in the room with the body. They would never have submitted her to the ordeal of looking up and seeing a murdered corpse a few feet from where she sat. Nor would Hannah Gale. Oh, Hannah could kill, but not like that. She loves the children almost as dearly as Edith did.

"Ann? No, not Ann. She would not have committed the crime with Dorothy's scarf. Ann's too loyal for that. And her whole temperament would be utterly opposed to murder by strangulation; if Ann killed, she would use a knife.

"Dorothy? She's too gentle for murder, in her the capacity to hurt is totally lacking. Michael could have done it, but not with a scarf—not with Dorothy's scarf. Peter? Marjory? Not they! Why should they kill Octavia? For her money? Rubbish! They don't know what money is. They're too young for money to have any importance in their eyes. To them, a pound is as big a sum as a million. Oh, the identity of the murderer was obvious."

"Why didn't you reveal it immediately?"

"I thought I was being clever," said Simon pathetically. "You see— You'll think me a disgusting old wretch, and you won't be far wrong. I am writing a book about the crime: 'Murder in The Family'. I wanted to keep the identity of the murderer to myself until the book was finished. I thought that publicly to announce it simultaneously with the publication of the book would be a magnificent publicity stunt."

Simon crossed the room and opened the door. "Come in," he said.

Chapter 29

Miss Mimms came in. During the past months she had aged almost out of recognition. The lined, sallow face was now pitifully emaciated and yellow. She was still dressed in her dead mistress's castoff clothing. Timidly she blinked about her and when she saw Stephen and Ann her eyes filled with tears. She made an uncertain move towards them, but changed her mind and wearily seated herself on the edge of a chair which Simon brought forward for her.

"*You!*" cried Major Blackett, aghast. "You killed Octavia Osborne?"

"I did," she said firmly, although it was only by a supreme effort that she kept her voice from trembling.

"But why? What possible motive had you?"

"I killed her because in this new will she was going to leave me a thousand pounds a year for life."

"But the will had not been made. By killing her when you did you prevented her from making it. You robbed yourself of the legacy."

"The legacy..." Miss Mimms smiled, ever so faintly. "That was only a joke on Miss Osborne's part. A very cruel joke. You see, I have a growth. It—it cannot be cured. In July my doctor warned me that I had not longer than six months to live. Miss Osborne knew that. It amused her to tease me with a legacy I could not possibly live to enjoy."

"Good God!" breathed Major Blackett. "How infernally vile!"

"It *was* cruel of her, wasn't it? But she was like that, you know. I lied to you when you questioned me immediately after her death. I said she was kind to me. She never was. She was cruel, terribly cruel. But I daren't let you see how much I hated her. Making other people suffer was the only real enjoyment she got out of life. She used to treat me like a slave. I never had a minute I could call my own. You'd have thought, wouldn't you, that she'd be a little easier on me after she knew I was dying? But no. When I was wrung with pain, when I would have given my soul to be allowed to go to bed and turn my face to the wall and suffer alone, she would have a 'headache' or an 'attack of indigestion' and I would have to sit up half the night bathing her forehead with eau-de-Cologne, or reading to her. It was all put on. When she thought I was not looking she would squint sideways at me with a malevolent smirk on her face, positively gloating over my suffering. She was a terrible woman. Hard. Bitter. Wicked. I could have forgiven her all that. You get used to putting up with things. But this final ghastly joke at my expense I could not forgive.

"A thousand a year for life—and she knew that I was dying on my feet! It was like smacking the face of a corpse. When I was told, her appalling brutality made me faint, and Hannah took me upstairs and made me lie down. I lay there for a long time, thinking...thinking... I can never tell a living soul what my thoughts were. At half-past three Hannah called me and I went downstairs.

"I noticed a beautiful silk scarf hanging on the hallstand. I love beautiful things, although I have possessed very few. I took it down and fondled it. There were oily smears on the delicate fabric. That was a wicked shame. I wondered whether I could get the stains out with a little bottle of stuff I always carried. I was still holding the scarf in my hand when I looked through the open drawing-room door and saw my mistress sitting beside the fire.

"There she sat. Arrogant. Disdainful. Full of her own importance. Puffed up with pride. Her head fiercely erect, her back as stiff as a poker. I did not notice Miss Ann. Had a hundred people been in the room, I should have had eyes only for my mistress.

"Then and there I knew what I must do. I crept to the back of her chair and looped the scarf about her neck, crossed the ends and pulled them tight with strength I never knew I had. I expected her to struggle. I was bracing myself to hang on like—like grim death. But she did not struggle. She gave one jump, that was all. Before I knew it, she was dead. You wouldn't have thought she'd die as easily as that, would you? So strong, so fierce, yet she died without a struggle. I knotted the scarf and stood back to look at her.

"It was then I realised what an awful thing I had done. I screamed. I could not help it. The horror of finding myself a murderer was shattering. Miss Ann started up and I noticed her for the first time. I thought she must know I had done it, but she didn't. The others came running in, but no one seemed to think for a moment that it might have been me...

"At first, I thought I'd give myself up, but I could not bring myself to do it. I had only a few months at most to live. My savings were sufficient to enable me to live quietly, in peace— such peace as I had not known for long years. No, I could not give myself up. I decided to do that only if one of the Osbornes was arrested for the murder. Then it would be my duty to confess. I see now"—she sighed—"that it was my duty to confess at the beginning. I am sorry, bitterly sorry."

After Miss Mimms had finished speaking there was a long silence. The others stared in stunned bewilderment at this meek little woman in drab grey, who sat so submissively with her gloved hands folded on her lap. Miss Mimms smiled faintly.

"Please do not look so distressed, all of you," she said apologetically. "I am not going to hang."

THE END

THE MONOCLED MAN

WITH A BLAND AIR of triumph Mrs. Throstle played the ace of hearts. Mr. Throstle, who was his wife's partner, and who had already taken the trick with the king, started as though he had been shot. His face turned purple and his eyes bulged with rage. For a moment he was speechless. Then, finding his voice, he 'let himself go' for almost five minutes.

Mrs. Throstle met his fury with an innocent stare, and a smile that was intended to placate, but succeeded merely in infuriating her husband even more.

"Yes dear," she said gently. "I knew it was your king, but I felt that it would be best to make quite sure of the trick."

Her husband choked and spluttered with wrath. Before he had sufficiently recovered to say the things which were forming in his mind, Mrs. Throstle led a diamond quickly, and the game went on.

Their opponents, Mr. and Mrs. Bordell, looked at each other significantly. This was the sort of scene which invariably took place when the Throstles invited the Bordells over for a 'quiet' game of bridge. Mrs. Throstle had no memory, and still less skill at cards, while Mr. Throstle, who took bridge very seriously indeed, had absolutely no control over his temper. The 'quiet' game usually ended by Mr. Throstle throwing his cards across the room and refusing to play anymore.

The game continued in silence for a short while, then Mrs. Throstle broke the silence.

"What are trumps, my dear?" she inquired brightly.

Her husband sneered bitterly. "Spades! Spades! Spades!" he shouted. "You've asked that idiotic question a dozen times tonight already!"

Mrs. Throstle smiled gently. "Yes, my dear, but last time I asked, you said clubs," she remonstrated.

"Of course, I did," snapped her husband. "Clubs were trumps last time you asked."

Mrs. Throstle looked puzzled. "You seem to change about so," she replied. "I can't keep track of the trumps. Wouldn't it be better to settle the question once and for all."

To ward off the apoplectic seizure which seemed about to attack Mr. Throstle, Mrs. Bordell explained to Mrs. Throstle the principles of bidding at bridge, an explanation which she was called upon to make every time they played.

Mrs. Throstle nodded comprehendingly. "I see, my dear, I see," she said. "I'm afraid I'm very stupid. Wouldn't it be better if we played whist?"

Her husband frowned. "It would *not* be better," he said in a loud voice.

Mrs. Throstle smiled apologetically. "All right dear," she murmured. "Only I do seem to know what I'm doing better when we play whist."

The game proceeded almost peacefully for a time, then Mrs. Throstle looked up with an exclamation.

"That's funny!" she said. "There's a red spot on this five of clubs."

Her husband snorted. "Don't be an idiot!" he snapped.

Mrs. Throstle eyed him reproachfully. "I wish you wouldn't address me like that—" she began. Then she glanced down and her expression changed. "Henry! There are two red spots now!"

She threw her cards on the table and, as she did so, a red spot appeared on the back of her hand.

Instinctively, everyone looked up. They gasped with horror when they saw that a circular patch of crimson had appeared in the ceiling. The stain was slowly widening and from the centre of it dripped an occasional drop of something extraordinarily like blood.

For some moments the Bordells and the Throstles sat motionless, staring at the widening stain. Then Mrs. Throstle shivered and stood up suddenly, as another drop fell onto the back of her hand. She upset the chair, which went over with a crash.

The sound broke the spell which had held them in its power. All stared up at once. They stared at each other.

Mr. Bordell was the first to find his voice. "Good Lord, Throstle. What are we going to do?" he demanded.

The host shook his head numbly. His brain felt chilled; he was unable to think.

"The Honourable Ernest Hardcastle has the flat above," whispered Mrs. Throstle in a tone of awe.

Mrs. Bordell screamed suddenly and clutched her husband's arm. "George! Do you suppose he is—" Her voice trailed away. The thought was too horrible to utter.

Her husband was not a sensitive man. "Murdered, you mean?" he queried.

She nodded dumbly.

At the word murdered, Mrs. Throstle gave a piercing shriek, and proceeded to have hysterics for several minutes. The others were busily engaged with smelling salts, vinegar, and ammonia, trying to bring the good lady to her senses.

In the midst of it all the bell rang loudly. It was not the timid sound that visitors usually made but harsh and peremptory, the summons of authority. Mr. Throstle gulped violently, rubbed his forehead frantically with a silk handkerchief, and hurried to the door. He found a burly policeman standing in the hall.

The policeman stared at Mr. Throstle with belligerent eyes. "What's up here?" he demanded. "I was passing and I 'eard a lady scream. What's up?"

Mr. Throstle pointed a shaky finger in the direction of the drawing room. "C-come in," he stammered. "I t-t-think it's m-murder."

The policeman started, then squaring his shoulders, pushed his way past Mr. Throstle and strode to the drawing room. Mr. Throstle closed the door gently, then followed the stalwart figure in blue.

They found the Bordells bending over Mrs. Throstle, who was lying on the sofa. The policeman glared suspiciously at the Bordells.

"Who did it?" he demanded, with a jerk of his thumb toward the inanimate woman.

Mr. Throstle hastily intervened. "That is my wife, constable," he squeaked in a shrill voice. "She has fainted. The murder—if there is one—is in the flat above. Look!"

The policeman's eyes followed the direction of Mr. Throstle's pointing finger, and came to rest upon the crimson stain in the ceiling. He advanced until he stood directly under it and putting out his hand caught one of the red drops that fell. He looked at it closely and sniffed it suspiciously.

"Blood!" he said quite unemotionally.

The others looked at each other uncomfortably. This expert opinion confirmed their own diagnosis. Mr. Throstle pointed a shaky finger at the carpet.

"There's quite a pool on the carpet," he squeaked. "The carpet is ruined. I paid eighty guineas for that carpet. All that blood will simply ruin it. That carpet will never be the same again!"

The policeman glanced down. "Nice carpet," he murmured, then his eyes travelled back to the red spot on his hand. "Blood, all right," he added.

Mrs. Throstle stirred uneasily on the couch and muttered something unintelligible. The policeman jerked his thumb in her direction.

"Better get her out of here," he suggested. "If she come round and sees the blood she'll be off again."

Mr. Throstle nodded. With the aid of Mr. Bordell, who took Mrs. Throstle's head and shoulders, the unconscious woman was carried into her bedroom. Mrs. Bordell brought up the rear, carrying the smelling-salts, ammonia, and vinegar.

The policeman tilted his helmet and scratched the back of his head. Murders were not much in his line.

Mr. Throstle returned to the drawing room. "What are you going to do?" he asked.

"Inform the proper authorities," replied the policeman portentously, "and take charge until they come. Likewise," he added, inspired by an idea. "Likewise, investigate upstairs immediately, in case the victim may still be within human aid. Who did you say lived upstairs?"

"The Honourable Ernest Hardcastle," replied Mr. Throstle impressively.

"The Honourable Ernest Hardcastle?" repeated the constable gravely. "That sounds serious. We'll have the place full of reporters in no time."

"He's a very distinguished man," Mr. Throstle murmured. "He dresses for dinner every night. Not that we don't of course, but he wears tails," he added hurriedly. "He wears a monocle, too!"

The policeman nodded. "There won't 'alf be a to do," he murmured vaguely.

He went to the window, threw it up, and popped his head outside. In a few seconds the sound of his whistle shattered the silence in Portman Square. There was a pause, then Mr. Throstle and the policeman heard heavy footsteps, running.

Another policeman came round the corner puffing with exhaustion. The first policeman attracted his mate's attention with a shout. "Come up here, Bert," he cried.

The other looked up, nodded, then vanished into the doorway of the building. Mr. Throstle hastened to open the door of the flat. In a few moments both policemen were in conference in the drawing-room.

The first policeman pointed to the crimson pool upon the floor. 'Bert' examined it closely.

"Blood!" he proclaimed.

The first policeman nodded. "Blood it is. There's been murder done!"

Bert stared at him. "Who did it?"

"When you've been as long in the force as I have," replied the other with asperity, "you'll learn not to ask foolish questions. How do I know who did it? It was done upstairs."

"Let's go upstairs and see," suggested Bert.

The two policemen proceeded upstairs, with Mr. Throstle at their heels. Most of the occupants of the building were out, and the procession arrived at the flat above without being disturbed by curious tenants.

Bert pressed the bell button with a plump finger. There was no answer. He rang again and again, with no better result. He turned to his mate:

"They don't answer," he said heavily.

Mr. Throstle felt an impulse to point out that murdered men don't usually answer doorbells, but felt that such levity was not in keeping with the solemnity of the occasion.

The policemen stared at each other.

"Why don't you batter in the door?" demanded Mr. Throstle.

Bert nodded. "We'll do it!" he exclaimed.

Together the constables applied their shoulders to the door.

They heaved several times, and the door suddenly opened with a splintering crash.

They found the flat in darkness. One of the policemen turned on his flashlamp and illuminated the hall of the flat with it.

"Hello! Hello!" he cried. "What's up in there?"

There was no answer.

They advanced into the hall, found the electric light switch and turned it on. They went gingerly along the hall to the door of the room which was directly above the Throstles' drawing-room.

Mr. Throstle closed his eyes convulsively as one of the policemen threw open the door of the room. He felt that he did not want to be the first to see the horror that the room contained. He opened his eyes again at an exclamation from one of the policemen.

"Blimey!" said that worthy. "The blinkin' room's empty!"

He found the electric light switch, depressed it, and the room was flooded with light.

Mr. Throstle looked about him. The room was neat and orderly. Apparently, everything was in its place. There was no bruised and battered corpse upon the floor. There was not even a pool of blood!

The policemen stared at each other in wonder.

For a little while the two policemen and Mr. Throstle stared stupidly at each other. They hardly knew what they had expected to find—perhaps a room like a slaughterhouse, with at least one corpse lying in a welter of blood. Certainly not this luxurious, tidy room, with its neat and well-ordered appearance. They felt disappointed and cheated.

Mr. Throstle's owl-like eyes widened suddenly. He pointed to a rug on the floor. "Look!" he stammered. "There's a red stain on that rug!"

One of the policemen strode over and kicked the rug away. Underneath, parts of the bare board of the floor were soaked with blood. The policeman gasped: "There have been queer happenings here tonight!"

Without more ado, he went quickly to the telephone and rang up Scotland Yard. He was instructed to take charge of the flat and to disturb nothing until Inspector Greig arrived.

While one policeman had been telephoning Scotland Yard, the other was examining the room with interest.

Mr. Throstle went poking about the corners of the room looking for clues, until he was angrily told to leave things alone.

In a quarter of an hour Inspector Greig arrived. He was a tall, thin man in a bowler hat and a fawn overcoat. His eyes were bluish-grey and had a sharp look about them; they seemed to bore right through Mr. Throstle.

In a few brief sentences the senior policeman told Inspector Greig all that they knew. The Yard man nodded keenly, and dismissing one of the policemen to return to his beat, he commenced to make his own investigations of the room. He ignored Mr. Throstle, and for once it suited Mr. Throstle to be ignored, for it gave him the opportunity of remaining and watching the detective at work.

Apart from the stain upon the floor, Inspector Greig found nothing which seemed suspicious in the room. Elsewhere in the flat, however, he found plenty to interest him.

The flat consisted of four rooms and a small kitchen and bathroom. Besides the drawing room, there was a dining room and two bedrooms. Both bedrooms were in a state of disorder. The mattresses on the beds were slit open and stuffing strewed about the floor. Drawers were open and their contents were mixed higgledy-piggledy like the wares of a jumble sale. Several suits were cut to ribbons, every part of the lining have been slit open, and the soles and heels of every pair of shoes in the wardrobe had been ripped off.

In one bedroom the window was wide open. Looking out, the inspector found that it led onto a fire escape, which gave access in case of emergency to a dark alley. The detective felt little doubt that someone had entered the flat by that means, and departed again after making a complete mess of both bedrooms.

But where did the bloodstain come in, he wondered. And why did the intruder—or rather intruders, for the work was obviously that of more than one man—leave without searching the dining room and drawing room as they had searched the bedrooms? Obviously, the answer was that they had been disturbed, but by whom? By the occupier of the flat perhaps, but in that case where was he now?

Taking all the facts into consideration, the detective decided that the intruders had been caught in the act by the occupant of the flat, who had been wounded, perhaps even killed. That would account for the bloodstain, and the fact that the intruders had left hurriedly without finishing their search. They had probably taken their dead or unconscious victim with them, to cover up their crime.

Or perhaps they had found the thing for which they had been searching, and had quarrelled over the possession of it. Perhaps one of them had tried to double-cross the other—or others—and in the ensuing argument someone had got hurt.

In the absence of clues to indicate the truth, there was no way to prove Inspector Greig's theories, but he felt that they were both possible theories. They at least gave a basis on which to build.

The point was, what was the thing for which the intruders were searching? They could not have been ordinary burglars, or they would not have taken the trouble to examine the interior of the mattresses and the heels of the shoes. They have been searching for something which they had reason to believe was in the flat; something that was small enough to be hidden in the lining of a suit.

Mr. Throstle had been following the detective from room to room, deeply interested in the investigations. It gave him quite a thrill that he, Henry Throstle, was actually permitted to watch one of the great Scotland Yard detectives at work.

He was a little disappointed that the Inspector had not produced a magnifying glass and studied every inch of the floor with it, or wrapped a cigarette end in his handkerchief with an air of mystery. Nor did the great man, in his bowler hat and neat overcoat, look the least like Sherlock Holmes.

Still, it was thrilling to dog his footsteps round the flat and watch the unravelling of a real mystery. Probably, Henry Throstle reflected, the newspapers would print his photograph, perhaps side by side with that of the detective himself. He could visualise the captions: 'Business Magnate Discovers Murder in Portman Square.'

Mr. Throstle was not quite a business magnate. He was, to

be precise, a wholesale agent for plumbing supplies, but the newspapers always exaggerated these things. If he could only help to solve the murder! That would raise him a cut above all his friends. None of them had achieved anything like that.

If someone had actually been murdered, Mr. Throstle hoped it was the aristocratic Honourable Ernest Hardcastle. Not that he bore any malice toward that gentleman, to whom he had not spoken more than a dozen words, but it would make the whole affair much more important if the Honourable Ernest Hardcastle was the victim.

It wouldn't be like discovering the murder of an ordinary person, a mere 'mister.' Why, an 'honourable' was related to lords; usually a peer's son! The next best thing to having blue blood oneself would be to discover the murder of someone who had, or still better, to discover the murderer!

With that ambition, Mr. Throstle looked carefully for cigarette ends, or pieces of mud to wrap in his handkerchief. He felt that the Scotland Yard man was making a mistake in neglecting such valuable clues. He succeeded in finding a stump of sodden cigar which Inspector Greig had just discarded, and a few lumps of mud which the police had brought into the drawing room on their boots. These he wrapped in his silk handkerchief, feeling that he had stolen a march on the distinguished detective.

Inspector Greig turned to Mr. Throstle suddenly. "Know anything about Hardcastle, the man who occupies this flat?" he demanded.

Mr. Throstle considered the question. "Er, not much," he replied diffidently. "He has not lived here long—just about two months. Before that, I understand he was touring the United States. Quite an important person, my wife says. She invited him to dinner once but he couldn't come. Pressure of social engagements, I suppose. He is always fashionably dressed—plenty of money, I suppose."

The detective nodded. The room was luxuriantly enough furnished to indicate that the tenant was a man of means.

"I wonder!" began Inspector Greig, reflectively.

"What?" demanded Mr. Throstle promptly.

"Oh, nothing."

Actually, Inspector Greig was wondering just what the Honourable Ernest Hardcastle possessed which others coveted so much.

At that moment a key grated in the lock of the flat door and Inspector Greig and Mr. Throstle hurried into the hall. Standing in the doorway they found a tall man who regarded them with amazement.

The newcomer was very thin. He was wearing well-fitting dress clothes and a monocle gleamed in his eye. His dark hair was brushed straight back and gleamed as though it was well polished. At the other extremity his patent leather shoes also gleamed. In one hand he carried a shiny top hat. Mr. Throstle thought, rather absurdly, that the newcomer gleamed far too much. He carried the traditional 'air of polish' to excess. Over one arm was a smart black overcoat.

One of Mr. Throstle's first emotions on seeing the Honourable Ernest Hardcastle standing in the doorway, apparently live and well, was a feeling of disappointment. It was not then the aristocratic Hardcastle who had been murdered. Probably, it was a plain 'mister' after all. Still, a murder was a murder.

The Honourable Ernest Hardcastle entered his flat and closed the door. He glared questioningly from his neighbour to Inspector Greig. "Introduce me, Throstle," he said blandly. "And won't you please explain this visit? At first, I thought I was in the wrong flat, but this *is* my humble abode, isn't it?"

Mr. Throstle struggled to find words but Inspector Greig quickly interposed. "I am Detective Inspector Greig of the C.I.D.," he explained smoothly. "There has been a peculiar happening here tonight, Mr. Hardcastle."

The other's expression did not change. "What kind of peculiar happening?" he asked softly.

"Your bedrooms have been turning into a shambles, for one thing," the detective replied. "And someone has been wounded or killed, for another."

Without a word the man in evening clothes strode past the others and entered his bedroom. When they followed, they found him staring with amazement at the ruin that met his eyes.

"What on earth—" he began.

The Inspector nodded. "That's what *I* want to know. The men who did that were searching for something. Do you know what that something was?"

The other shook his head. "Haven't the foggiest. I don't keep any jewels or money around."

"They weren't looking for money," responded the Inspector. "They were after something small. You can see they've ripped the linings out of all your clothes. They wouldn't have done that if they had been ordinary burglars.

Hardcastle looked blank. "I can't guess what they were after," he reiterated.

"Where were you tonight?" the detective asked.

"At the Apollo Theatre," Hardcastle replied, shooting a keen glance at the detective. "Why?"

Inspector Greig shrugged his shoulders. "You can see the position," he pointed out.

Hardcastle laughed. "I see. You think that they were after something—a stolen idol from a sacred temple in China, or something melodramatic like that—and that I'm in the know, but keeping it dark? Well, you are wrong, quite wrong, old top."

"I suppose that you can prove you were at the theatre?" responded the detective doggedly.

Hardcastle drew a slip of cardboard from his waistcoat pocket and passed it to the detective, who examined it carefully.

"You can see that the date is right," Hardcastle pointed out. "I was alone, and I can't remember seeing anyone I know, but I expect that someone who saw me might remember me. A programme girl or someone of the sort."

The detective nodded and returned the portion of ticket. "What was the name of the play?" he asked.

Hardcastle was amused. "Don't you read the papers?" he parried. "It was the first night of *The Seventh Gong*, a play about China. Horribly mysterious and all that. You should go and see it. It's quite in your line. Chinese crooks, and three murders in the first act."

The detective did not permit himself the ghost of a smile. He started to say something, but the telephone bell interrupted him. "Hello!" he said.

A harsh voice came to him from the other end of the wire. "Is that 'The Dude'?" The voice demanded. "This is Carponi. Say, you poor fish, don't kid yourself. You're fooling with dynamite and you're liable to get hurt any minute now. If you don't 'come across' right now, you'll be sorry. You got 'Squiffy' but we'll get you and get you good."

Having said its say, the voice abruptly ceased talking and there was click as the receiver at the other end was hung up. Inspector Greig impatiently jiggled the hook until the operator answered. She was unable to tell him more than that the call had come from a public telephone about a hundred yards from Portman Square.

The detective hung up the receiver and wheeled round. "Who is 'Squiffy?'" he demanded.

Hardcastle shook his head. "I don't know," he replied. "*I'm* not. I've only had a couple all evening."

INSPECTOR GREIG regarded Hardcastle suspiciously. The object of his gaze removed his monocle and polished it vigorously before replacing it in his eye, and returned the detective's stare with interest.

Greig shrugged his shoulders. "I'll be back in the morning to look around," he remarked, drawing on his gloves. "I want to get to the bottom of this affair."

Hardcastle smiled affably. "Only too pleased to help you, old boy," he responded. "But I haven't the foggiest idea of what it's all about."

Greig nodded noncommittally. He had his own opinion of the affair, and he was certain that Hardcastle knew more of the reason for it than he admitted. He glanced at his watch.

"It's just a quarter to twelve," he said. "I don't expect you'll have any more trouble tonight, but if you should, I'll be at the Yard till one."

Hardcastle laughed. "You don't think that I'm going to spend the night here amongst all this mess?" He responded. "I shall spend the night at the Savoy."

"You are probably wise," agreed the detective. "I'll give you a ring at the Savoy in the morning."

With a curt nod of his head, he left the flat, followed by the constable and Mr. Throstle. In the street he gave instructions to keep an eye on the building during the night, and to delegate that responsibility to the officer who relieved him in the morning.

When he was alone Hardcastle surveyed his tattered suits ruefully. "The fools," he murmured. "Oh, the fools! Well, now they've found me I'll have to move on. Dashed awkward."

Talking to himself he began to pack a suitcase, from which

the lining had been ripped, with shirts and pyjamas, which were the only things in his wardrobe which had not been reduced to ribbons.

At five minutes to twelve, a powerful saloon car purred up to the building and two men got out leaving a girl at the wheel. After a whispered conference, they crossed the pavement to the doorway of the building. A policeman detached himself from the gloom and eyed them suspiciously.

"Live in this building, gentlemen?" he asked.

"What the hell has it got to do with you?" the shorter of the two men demanded, but his companion silenced him by roughly shoving him aside.

"No, constable," he replied, in a harsh voice which tried in vain to sound pleasant. "We don't exactly live in this building. We are calling on a friend."

"That's right," chimed the little man. "A swell pal of ours lives here."

The policeman looked from one to the other dubiously. "I'm afraid I'll have to know more about your business," he began.

He moved across the pavement to examine the license on the car. Before he had reached the car, the taller of the two men barred his way, and at the same time, jabbed a large blue steel automatic into his stomach. Before the policeman realised what was happening, his helmet was knocked over his eyes, and he was struck a stunning blow behind the ear, by a clubbed automatic in the short man's hand. With a groan he dropped to the pavement.

"Good work, Shorty," commented the tall man approvingly. "He ought to be 'out' for twenty minutes. Gimme a hand to dump him in the alley."

They carried the unconscious policeman round the corner and left him propped up against a wall in the lane behind the buildings. Then they returned, and after a reassuring whisper to the girl at the wheel, disappeared into the building.

In estimating that the policeman would be 'out' for twenty minutes, the tall gunman was too sanguine. In less than five minutes the constable opened his eyes with a groan and sat up weakly. His head was throbbing viciously, but with an effort he staggered to his feet. As he did so, his attention was attracted by the sound of a shot and, looking up, he saw a tall man in evening dress clamber through a window of Hardcastle's flat and go clattering up the fire-escape.

A dark shape appeared at the window and an automatic spat its deadly missile after the man in evening clothes. The man on the fire escape stumbled, but righted himself, and kept on climbing. Two men—the two who had attacked the policeman—climbed through the window and pursued the man in evening clothes up the fire escape.

It was time, the policeman decided, to take a hand in the game. First, he blew several loud blasts upon his whistle. Walking unsteadily across the lane, he found that the bottom of the fire-escape, which was old and loose, could be reached by an effort. He seized the bottom rung and dragged the ladder down, then clambered up it.

The men he was following had reached the roof by this time, and a shot rang out, followed by another and then another. When the policeman peered over the edge of the roof, he was greeted by a bullet which chipped a piece off the slate just beneath his nose. He ducked down and blew his whistle again. As he did so, another bullet whizzed over his head.

On the roof a battle royal was in progress. Crouched behind one chimney stack was the Honourable Ernest Hardcastle, with an automatic in his hand, and another on the roof beside him. His eyes were fixed through a crevice in the brickwork, on the opposite side of the roof, where the tall and short gunmen were hiding behind another chimney stack. At the slightest movement he fired, and his shot was answered by two shots which rang out across the roof.

'Shorty' and the other man, who was obviously the leader, had three automatics between them, and they used them with deadly precision. Fortunately for the man they were hunting not even the gleam of an inch of his shirt front gave them a target. They were firing at random, and at the flash of Hardcastle's automatic, and so far, none of their shots had taken effect.

From all over the neighbourhood scores of policemen were running towards Portman Square. Hardcastle realised this. He knew that the whole neighbourhood would be alarmed by the firing and that if he remained on that roof the game would soon be up. He decided to make an attempt to elude his pursuers.

Rising to his feet, he dashed across the sloping roof and clambered over the brickwork on the roof next door. As he ran across the slates, the report of 'Shorty's' automatic rang out. Hardcastle threw up his arms, staggered and fell, and rolled down the slope.

"Got him, chief," exulted 'Shorty.' "Right in the back."

As Hardcastle rolled down the roof he clutched desperately and managed to grab the guttering. For a moment he hung perilously a hundred feet above ground, then his dangling legs touched the drain pipe, and by manoeuvring about, he secured a foothold.

Gingerly he let himself down hand over fist until he found himself within half a yard of a darkened window. Making a supreme effort, he swung himself to the window-ledge and, kicking in the glass, climbed through into the bedroom of a house.

He had made sufficient noise by this time to awaken the occupants of the house, even if they had not already been roused by the battle on the roof above him. He took no precaution, therefore, to prevent his presence being known. He dashed through the room and down the stairs. He met no one on the way. The inmates of the house were awake but they felt that discretion was called for, and they discreetly kept their heads under the bedclothes.

Opening the front door, Hardcastle smoothed his rumpled evening clothes and walked boldly out. The car in which 'Shorty', his chief and the girl had arrived was still standing in the street. It was empty but a tall policeman stood beside it.

Hardcastle advanced boldly. "What's the matter, constable?" he asked. "I was just going to bed when all this racket started."

The policeman eyed him up and down. Hardcastle's smart appearance, and the fact that he had emerged from one of the houses in a perfectly natural manner, reassured him.

"There's something fishy going on up on the roofs, sir," he replied. "There's some fellows up there with revolvers."

Hardcastle's face expressed astonishment. "Good Lord!" he ejaculated. "How extraordinary! Fellows with revolvers in Portman Square! What are we coming to?"

As he spoke, he edged nearer to the policeman and suddenly swung a savage punch which landed neatly on the constable's chin with a resounding smack. The policeman dropped in his tracks as though he had been shot.

Without a glance at his victim, Hardcastle jumped into the car, pressed the self-starter, put her into gear, and drove off down the street, accelerating rapidly. He was in second gear when he reached the corner, and went straight on, oblivious to the shouts that followed him.

At the corner of the next street two policemen appeared in the middle of the road, holding up their hands, and blowing lustily on their whistles. Setting his teeth, he drove straight at one of them. The man stood his ground gamely until the last minute, then leapt with astounding agility for the pavement.

Hardcastle drove straight on, doing over fifty miles an hour. He knew that it was useless to hope that he could get clean away by car, for by this time the Flying Squad would be heading for the neighbourhood. He wanted to get as far away from Portland Square as possible, however, before the trap closed in too tightly.

He ignored the peremptory summons of another police whistle, but this time he was unlucky. As the car flashed past the constable, the latter flung his truncheon, which shattered a side window and struck the steering wheel. Hardcastle lost control. The car swerved across the road, mounted the pavement, and crashed into a shop window.

Badly shaken, but unhurt, Hardcastle climbed out. He looked back and saw three policemen running towards him. Summing up the situation swiftly, he ducked through the shattered window into the shop. At the rear of the shop, he tried the back door desperately. The door was locked and the key gone, but stepping back a pace or two, he sent three shots into the lock which smashed it to pieces. He threw the door open, dashed into the lane behind, and took to his heels.

Meanwhile, the two gunmen had seen Hardcastle fall from the roof. They ran across the slates, and peered down into the street below, expecting to see a crumpled figure in evening clothes lying on the pavement. They saw the car standing at the kerb, empty, but otherwise the street was deserted. From all directions, however, they could hear the sound of police whistles.

"Gee, boss," said 'Shorty', "Sadie's beat it."

"I don't blame her," snorted his chief. "The place will be swarming with cops in a coupla' shakes. Let's get away."

They darted back across the roof. They found the fire-escape blocked by half a dozen policemen, who were mounting steadily to the roof. The constable in advance, the one who had given the alarm, was steadily climbing onto the slates.

'Shorty' raised his automatic to fire, but the other knocked his arm down.

"Nix! You fool, nix!" he hissed. "Don't shoot till you have to. They hang you for shootin' cops in this country."

They doubled on their tracks, and ran like hares across the adjacent roofs. Now and then they turned and fired a shot which was calculated to go wide of any target, but which had the desired effect, that of slowing the pursuit. The men of the Metropolitan Police are not cowards, but it takes more than a brave man—it takes a lunatic—to get too close to the mouth of a Colt which spits death!

So it was that the pursuing police lost the two gunmen in the maze of chimney pots. By the time they found the unfastened skylight through which their quarry had escaped from the roofs, it was too late. 'Shorty' and his chief were already far away, through the police cordon which was rapidly forming around Portman Square.

Chapter 4

ON THE FOLLOWING morning Detective Inspector Greig
sent for Detective Sergeant Peter Martin. He sat drumming
his fingers until that capable young officer arrived.

Peter Martin was twenty-six years old, tall and squarely built.
He had dark hair and keen brown eyes which were set wide
apart. His reputation in Scotland Yard was that of a tenacious
and thorough officer, who knew his job inside out and who only
needed a little more experience to qualify him for promotion
to the rank of inspector.

Greig indicated a chair when Peter came into the room.
He leaned back on his own chair, lit a cigar, and inspected his
junior thoughtfully.

"Know about last night's affair?" he asked. "The battle royal
that went on in Portman Square?"

Peter nodded. "I was there," he replied. "Not in time to join
in but afterwards with a squad car. We scoured the district until
five this morning, then I had a couple of hours sleep, a Turkish
bath, breakfasted, and came down here. I had a feeling you
might want me."

"Good work," responded Greig approvingly. "Look at these."

He pushed a little pile of papers across the desk. Peter
examined them with interest. They were circulars from the
headquarters of the New York police; descriptions of 'wanted'
criminals, in some cases with photographs attached.

The first circular described a gang leader Pete Carponi, who
had a record, literally speaking, as long as his arm. He was
'wanted' in New York, Chicago, Philadelphia, and San Francisco.
The list of his crimes included bank robbery, safe-blowing,
kidnapping and murder.

Of late years, it was understood, he had settled down quietly to bootlegging and assassinating for hire. His photograph showed a face that was cold and merciless, with a scar which ran from his temple to his chin. He was five feet ten inches tall and weighed fourteen stone. His hair was dark, tinged slightly with grey. He was forty-one years old, quite a respectable age for a gunman, whose occupation is not conducive to longevity.

On the same circular, his lieutenant, 'Shorty' Manusco and 'Squiffy' Fields, were described. They each had a record of viciousness which their photographs bore out.

'Shorty' had tiny little eyes and a rat-like visage. He was less than five feet two inches in height. His favourite weapon was a machine gun.

'Squiffy' Fields had a pronounced squint and a face more like an ape than a man.

Under the heading of remarks, it was said of 'Squiffy' that he was 'credited with the murder of three clerks during the robbery of the National Bank of Springfield, Conn'.

Looking at 'Squiffy's' photograph, Peter could quite believe it.

A second circular carried the photograph and description of Edward Hardwick, alias 'The Dude', alias Lord Hardwick, alias The Marquis of Binghampton, alias the Honourable Ernest Hardcastle, and a dozen other aliases. The photograph was of a thin man with a pleasant, dignified face, who wore a monocle in his left eye.

It was not a 'rogues gallery' photograph, for this man of many aliases had not yet fallen into the hands of the police. He was wanted, however, in New York, for the theft of the famous Lavery Diamond from Mrs. Vandergilt-Jennings of Long Island. The diamond was valued at £100,000, and there was reward of £1,000 for its recovery.

The third and last circular described 'Cincinnati Sadie'

Levinsky. Her height was given as five feet seven inches, and her appearance described as 'pleasing'. She was a confidence-woman, a hotel thief and a shoplifter. She was believed to have been an accomplice of 'The Dude', who had fallen out with her, and cheated her of her share in the 'spoils that had resulted from their partnership in crime'. There was no photograph of 'Cincinnati Sadie' available.

Peter returned the papers to his chief with a smile. "Scarcely Salvation Army types," he commented.

Greig shook his head. "Hardly. I believe them to be at the bottom of last night's affair. The American police inform us that Carponi and his gang have joined up with the woman Levinsky, and come over here under assumed names. 'The Dude' is the man who has been masquerading as the Honourable Ernest Hardcastle, and who's flat in Portman Square was the scene of the disturbance last night.

"It isn't hard to figure out what happened. The Levinsky woman and 'The Dude' probably stole the diamond in partnership, and 'The Dude' double-crossed his accomplice and escaped over here with the diamond. The woman enlisted the help of Carponi and his gang, and came over here on 'The Dude's' trail; they found him, and made an effort last night to find the diamond.

"They were turning his flat upside down when 'The Dude' came home and found them at work. In the melee that probably followed, 'Squiffy' was wounded, or killed, and the others escaped. I expect that 'The Dude' disposed of 'Squiffy's' body somewhere, then returned, little suspecting that the alarm had already been given, through 'Squiffy's' blood slipping through the floor into the flat below. Later, Carponi, 'Shorty' and 'Cincinnati Sadie' returned to make another attempt at finding the diamond, and that attempt resulted in a revolver battle on the roof."

Peter Martin nodded reflectively. "You seemed to have summed up the situation pretty accurately, Chief." he agreed. "It all sounds weird and wonderful. A bit of Chicago transported to London."

"That's exactly what it is," replied Inspector Greig. "And our job is to round up that gang as quickly as possible. We've got to show them that 'gunplay' doesn't go in London. It is unfortunate that the affair should happen now. Several of our best men are giving evidence in the Deptford murder case, and Inspector Manning, Reid and Foster are bust rounding up a counterfeiting gang. I've got to place a lot of reliance on you, Martin. I hope you won't fail me."

Peter met Greig's eyes squarely. "Trust me, Inspector," he said eagerly.

"Very good. It's a chance for you to show what you can do. I want you to go to 'The Dude's' flat and make a thorough investigation of every article of clothing and every shred of paper in it. You'll be looking for clues that point to 'The Dude's' present whereabouts. It isn't likely that he's left anything but there's always a chance. He must have known that the woman he cheated would find him in the long run, and he's probably prepared a hiding-place in advance. Your job is to find that hiding-place."

Peter nodded. "What about the car he escaped in," he asked.

"I've looked into that. It was stolen earlier in the evening from a member of the Carlton Club. It was left in front of the building by Carponi. The woman was at the wheel but she disappeared when the shooting started."

After receiving certain other instructions, Peter left Greig's office. Before leaving Scotland Yard, he went to his locker and unearthed his revolver. It was by no means unlikely that he would have need of it before long.

In front of the flat-building in Portman Square quite a crowd was gathered. It consisted of errand boys, governesses with small children and prams, and other curiosity-seekers.

At the entrance to the building stood two stalwart policemen who had been posted to keep unauthorised persons out. Peter displayed his warrant card, which won him the immediate respect of both constables.

"Anyone entered the building this morning?" he asked.

One of the policemen shook his head. "No one but Inspector Greig and the Commissioner, and the reporters, who left with them," he replied. "Oh, and a young lady who was visiting one of the tenants. She seemed alright, so we let her pass."

Peter nodded and went into the building.

He had a skeleton key in his hand when he mounted the stairs to 'The Dude's' flat, but he found that it was not necessary. The door was already open and standing slightly ajar!

Silently he pushed the door wider and tiptoed in. He heard faint sounds coming from one of the bedrooms. Scarcely breathing, he slid his feet carefully over the polished floor and quietly opened the door of the bedroom.

There was a woman inside, who was busily engaged in ransacking one of the drawers. When she straightened up, Peter saw that she was young, dark, and certainly 'pleasing' in appearance. So 'pleasing' was she that for a moment Peter was lost in admiration of her. In that moment the girl turned and saw Peter standing in the doorway. She gasped, and the colour faded out of her cheeks.

"'Cincinnati Sadie'!" Peter exclaimed.

The girl drew back. "No! No! You are making a mistake," she cried, so vehemently that Peter almost believed her. Then he remembered that 'Cincinnati Sadie' was a clever confidence-trickster. He almost laughed at himself for being so nearly gulled.

The girl's eyes never moved from his face. "What are you going to do?" she demanded.

She was more than merely 'pleasing'; she was beautiful as she stood there with her eyes flashing and her breast heaving. But Peter had known more than one beautiful crook.

He fumbled for his handcuffs. "I'm going to take you into custody," he replied grimly.

"You're not! You can't!" she exclaimed fiercely.

Peter's handcuffs were in his hand and he advanced towards her quietly. Suddenly, as though by magic, a tiny but serviceable mother-of-pearl handled revolver appeared in the girl's hand.

"Stand back!" she cried. "Stand back, or I'll shoot!"

Peter halted uncertainly, then started forward, but saw the girl's hand tighten on the trigger, and halted again. His eyes searched her face looking for a sign of weakness but her face was set and grim. He had little doubt that at the first suspicious movement on his part she would fire without hesitation. Under the circumstances, the only thing to do was to keep still. He remained very still with his eyes fixed on her lovely oval face.

Afterwards, if asked to describe her in detail, he could have done so with the greatest of ease. His description would have been something like this: "Nose tilted upward a little, but at a delicately attractive angle; hair, dark and wavy, and with a soft natural lustre; lips, something like Clara Bow's, but much more seductive; eyes, luminous, dark, and appealing; figure, perfection; legs—"

As he stood there, he reddened a little at the thought. "What on earth would the Chief say if I turned in a report like that?" he wondered.

Aloud he said: "Look here, you had better put down that cute little popgun, and come quietly. You can't get away, you know. There are two policemen at the door downstairs and another guarding the fire escape."

She shrugged her shoulders. "I can look after myself," she replied calmly.

His eyes expressed his admiration for her. "By George! I'll bet you can, too!" he exclaimed. "But that's not the point. Be a good girl and put down that toy before it goes off 'pop' and breaks something. We'll take a taxi to Scotland Yard if you don't want to be seen with the bracelets on."

She laughed a silvery laugh. "I'm not going anywhere with the bracelets on," she replied. "Not even in a taxi."

She had a rich American accent which was immensely attractive. Altogether she seemed so charming that Peter had to keep reminding himself that she was a crook, to keep from succumbing.

She glanced round swiftly, keeping her revolver trained on the fourth button of Peter's waistcoat. She nodded towards a cupboard.

Peter was about to refuse, but he saw a dangerous gleam in her eyes, and changed his mind. After all, a dead detective sergeant was of little use to Scotland Yard or anywhere else. Discretion being the better part of valour, he opened the door of the cupboard and stepped inside. The door slammed and he heard the click of the key in the lock, then the girl's retreating footsteps. In a moment or two the door of the flat was shut with a bang.

On the stairs, the girl met a little man, with a drooping grey moustache, and a figure from which time had smoothed all manly grace. He was picking up cigar ends and putting them in a silk handkerchief. The girl sized him up as a likely ally.

"In that flat," she said swiftly, "is one of the slickest crooks in London. I've locked him in a cupboard but he may escape. If he does, please do your best to hold him until I return with the police."

Henry Throstle, our friend who lived in the flat below and felt he'd make a good detective, puffed out his rabbit-like chest.

"You may rely on me," he replied impressively. "But—er—don't be too long."

With a grateful smile the girl disappeared downstairs.

In the darkness of the cupboard Peter Martin fumbled for his revolver. Finding it, he held it by the barrel and battered the door with the butt. The panels were flimsy and a few well-directed smashes knocked one panel out. He put his hand through, found the key, and turned it in the lock. Then, opening the door of the cupboard, he rushed out through the bedroom and into the hall. Opening the door of the flat he found Henry Throstle standing in a belligerent attitude in the corridor outside.

"Where did that girl go to?" Peter demanded.

Without a word Mr. Throstle lowered his head and charged, butting Peter in the stomach. With a muttered 'ouch!' Peter subsided onto the floor.

Mr. Throstle stood over him triumphantly. His triumph was short-lived, however. Before he knew where he was, his legs were jerked from under him and he found himself on the floor with Peter sitting on his chest.

"What the dickens are you up to?" snapped Peter indignantly. "Do you realise you are obstructing an officer in the execution of his duty!"

Henry Throstle gaped with dismay. "She—she said you were the slickest crook in London!" he stammered.

Peter rose from Mr. Throstle's chest. "You fool! You fathead!" he cried. "That girl was 'Cincinnati Sadie'!"

He dashed down the stairs two at a time.

Mr. Throstle sat up and rubbed his chest. "Oh dear!" he wailed. "And she seemed such a nice girl, too!"

Chapter 5

B Y THE TIME Peter reached the street the girl was out of
sight. The policemen on the door informed him that she
had strolled out of the building casually, smiled at each of them
in turn, stepped into a neat two-seater which was parked at the
kerb, and driven away.

Peter reviled them for having permitted her inside the building, but they pointed out that she 'seemed alright', a fact which
Peter was forced to admit.

In his heart he knew perfectly well that had he not found
the girl ransacking one of the bedrooms of the flat, and had
she not 'pulled a gat', he would never have suspected her of
anything worse than powdering her nose. Although Peter was
not normally susceptible, there was something about the girl
which had definitely attracted him.

It was impossible, of course, or so at least he told himself,
for him to fall in love with a feminine crook, no matter how
attractive she might appear, especially a feminine crook with
the unmelodious name of 'Cincinnati Sadie' Levinsky. Still
more remarkable was it to imagine that he could harbour tender
feelings for a girl who had menaced him with an automatic and
locked him in a cupboard, like the merest infant.

Still—there had been something about the angle of that
neat, shingled head, poised on a rounded ivory throat, that he
reviled himself inwardly for being such a fool, and went upstairs.

He found Henry Throstle sitting on the stairs, still nursing
his chest. The little man rose and became pathetically apologetic
over his blunder. The girl, he said, had seemed 'such a nice girl.'
Surely, he was not to be blamed for believing her?

Peter waved his apologies aside. It was perfectly alright, he replied, only next time would Mr. Throstle kindly try not to be such an abject ass? It may be that Peter's feelings were hurt at the readiness with which Mr. Throstle had believed he was the 'slickest crook in London'.

Mr. Throstle was eager to make amends.

"Look here," he whispered. "It's only fair that I should make it up to you in some way. Now *I've* been investigating this affair myself—"

"Yes," murmured Peter patiently.

"Yes! And I've made an important discovery! The murderer smokes La Tirella cigars!"

Peter sighed. "My dear sir," he said wearily, "La Tirella cigars are sold for five pence each. They are smoked by taxi-drivers who take them in tips. They are given away in boxfuls by stockbrokers who smoke Coronas. Every Christmas thousands of unhappy husbands receive La Tirella's from families who know nothing of these matters and eventually the dustman gets them. If our murderer—and by the way we are not at all sure that murder has been done—if our 'murderer' is misguided enough to smoke La Tirella's it proves only that he is a man of low tastes and doesn't help us in the least to find him. There are hundreds and thousands of men of low taste in London you know."

Mr. Throstle looked mysterious. "Ah!" he whispered. "But I haven't told you all. One of his front teeth is broken!"

"How do you know?"

Dramatically, Mr. Throstle produced a silk handkerchief and from it a stump of cigar.

"Look!" he commanded.

Peter looked. He remembered suddenly that Inspector Greig of the Yard had the bad taste to smoke La Tirella cigars. He remembered also that his chief had a broken front tooth. It was with some difficulty that Peter kept a straight face.

"You have made an important discovery," he said impressively. "Far too important to be dealt with by a mere detective sergeant. Next time Inspector Greig is here, show him that stump of cigar. Tell him that the man who smoked it is a murderer. He will be interested."

Mr. Throstle beamed. "Thanks very much. I'll do that!" he responded.

"Just one thing more," Peter continued earnestly. "Don't mention my name. I want you to have all the credit."

"Thank you! Oh, thank you!" said Mr. Throstle gratefully.

"Don't mention it," replied Peter magnanimously.

He turned away quickly, opened the door of Hardcastle's flat, entered, and closed it behind him. The strain of keeping a straight face had been too much for him. He spent a couple of hours examining every nook and corner of the flat, but without success. 'The Dude', as Hardcastle was called by his crooked associates, had not left a single discoverable clue to his present hideout. It was with feelings of disappointment that he left the building. Not only had he failed in his search, but he had actually let 'Cincinnati Sadie' slip through his fingers. What rankled him even more was the fact that she had tricked him with such consummate ease.

He started suddenly. Across the street he noticed 'Nippy the Nark', who was gazing at the flat-building with evident interest. 'Nippy' was a police informer as his nickname implied. He was one of the crooks who lived by betraying their fellows.

Usually, 'Nippy' had an unkempt down-at-the-heels appearance, but today he was dressed in a brand-new suit of somewhat loud design. He wore a collar and tie in place of his customary muffler. His shoes were new and shiny patent leather and instead of a cap he wore a brown bowler at least a size too small.

Evidently 'Nippy' was well in funds, for he was one of those who believe that the proper use of money is to buy beer with it. It would take more than an ordinary windfall to make 'Nippy' extravagant in clothes.

Peter crossed the street and took the informer by the arm. 'Nippy' looked wildly around for a means of escape, but decided that it was wisest not to try any 'funny business.'

"Whence the sudden prosperity, 'Nippy'?" asked Peter.

'Nippy's' ferret like eyes became very cunning.

"I ain't doin' nuthin' Mister Martin," he whined. "I 'eard about the affair last night, an' I was just lookin' at the buildin' same as anyone might do, curious-like."

"Have you tried the British Museum?" Peter inquired genially. "They tell me there's lots to look at there. Out with it, 'Nippy.' You're not watching that building for fun. You weren't made that way. Your fun comes in bottles. Who sent you to look over the place?"

"You're wrong, Mister Martin, dead wrong," 'Nippy' whined. "You know me, I'm always on the square with you fellows. I wouldn't lie to a cop."

Peter laughed heartily. "You should go on the 'halls'," he commented. "You'd be a riot. Tell me, where did you acquire the snappy duds?"

'Nippy' blinked. "A legacy, Mister Martin, a legacy from me uncle," he said earnestly. "Me uncle Sam, what was in the grocery business. 'E left me free 'undred pounds in cash."

Peter's face was expressive of disbelief. "When did poor Uncle Sam die?" he asked.

He saw by the informer's face that he was thinking rapidly. "Two weeks ago, last Wednesday," 'Nippy' replied at last.

Peter looked at the informer's check-suit. "And this is your idea of mourning?" he asked.

'Nippy' shuffled his feet.

"Well, you know how it is, Mister Martin," he replied uncomfortably. "Nice, serviceable piece of goods, this is. Oughter last."

"Unusual for the lawyers to give you your legacy so soon," remarked Peter thoughtfully. "It usually takes several months at least to settle even a small estate."

'Nippy' looked panic-stricken. "There weren't no lawyers in the deal at all, Mister Martin," he said hurriedly. "Me uncle sent for me when he was dying.'Orace' he said—that's me Christian name, 'Orace', he said—"

Peter shook his head sadly. "Did anyone ever tell you what a wretched little liar you are?"

'Nippy' looked hurt. "As sure as I'm standing 'ere—" he began.

"Don't!" retorted Peter. "Why perjure your soul?"

He stared into the informer's eyes. "I wonder if you happen to know Pete Carponi?" he asked.

'Nippy's' eyelids flickered slightly. He quickly assumed an expression of injured innocence.

"Carponi? Carponi? Egyptian name, ain't it?" he murmured. "No, I don't know no one of that name, Mister Martin. There's a bloke wot keeps an ice-cream shop in Camberwell Road—"

Peter shook his head. "No, Carponi isn't an ice-cream man, as you know jolly well," he retorted. "Alright 'Nippy' beat it—but remember, I've got my eye on you."

Like a shot from a gun 'Nippy' started off down the street, as soon as his arm was released. Peter gave him a start to the corner, then followed. He was just in time to see 'Nippy' hail a taxi and climb in. Peter hailed another taxi which was crawling round the square.

"Keep that cab in sight," he directed, displaying his warrant-card, "and try not to let the occupant know that we're following him."

As the taxi picked up speed he leaned back on the cushions and lit a cigarette. His suspicions of 'Nippy' had been confirmed at the sight of him hailing a taxi. 'Nippy' was of a class that habitually ride in buses or walk. The luxury of a taxi suggested more money than the informer could have acquired honestly.

'Nippy' was little different from any other police informer. He knew on which side his bread was buttered, and he could usually be relied upon to turn into police headquarters any useful information which he acquired. He betrayed his acquaintances and quite often those he called his friends without the slightest compunction, on a strictly cash basis.

If 'Nippy' was withholding information on this occasion it must be that he was being better paid to keep his mouth shut. Possibly he had stumbled across Carponi and his gang and had been well paid to fall in with the scheme which the gang had in hand. Even a fractional share in a diamond worth £100,000 would be enough to buy 'Nippy' body and soul. If his suspicions were correct, it would be well worthwhile for Peter to keep the informer in sight.

By expert driving and a considerable amount of luck, Peter's taxi managed to keep pace right across the city with the one which contained 'Nippy'. The only fly in the ointment was that 'Nippy' was too shrewd to have overlooked the taxi that kept always a little behind his. The informer must be well aware that he was being shadowed—and yet he kept on going, without any attempt to shake off pursuit.

Peter was watching for the slightest suspicious movement in the taxi ahead. He half-expected 'Nippy' to dodge out at a traffic jam and take to his heels, but the informer remained in his taxi. Peter guessed correctly that the crook was playing for time, trying to work out a fool proof means of escape.

Finally, 'Nippy's' taxi drew up outside a dingy, dilapidated restaurant in Whitechapel. Peter's driver stopped a hundred yards behind. 'Nippy' dodged out of his vehicle, paid the driver, and hurried into the restaurant. Peter did likewise. By the time he had covered the hundred yards to the restaurant 'Nippy' had disappeared.

The place consisted of one large room, which held a dozen tables covered with oilcloth, and perhaps four times as many chairs. The dining room was deserted. As Peter entered, the proprietor, a greasy-looking individual, came through a curtained doorway at the rear.

"Vat d'you vant?" he asked suspiciously.

Peter brushed past him, and found himself in a filthy kitchen, which completed the premises. There was a single large cupboard in the kitchen which Peter found innocent of anything more questionable than tins of soup and other provisions. Apart from the cupboard there was evidently no place for anyone to hide. The proprietor had followed Peter and now faced him menacingly.

"I ask vat you vant!" he said angrily. "Vat d'you vant?"

Peter seized his arm and shook it roughly. "The man who came in here—where did he go?"

The other shook his head. "How should I know?" he retorted. "I tink he was crazy. He ran in the front door and out again at the back, vidout saying a word. I tink you are crazy, too. I'm too busy to be boddered with such crazy fellers. Go avay, or I'll call a policeman."

Peter waited no longer. He plunged out of the back door, leaving the man talking angrily to himself. He found himself in a lane that was littered with boxes and refuse. There was no sign of 'Nippy'.

He ran to the end of the lane and down a side street onto the main road again but the informer had vanished.

Coming down the street, however, was a figure that looked

260 Stories of Crime & Detection

familiar. It was the figure of a girl of slightly more than average height for a woman—a comely, attractive figure. He started forward and grasped her arm, then realised his mistake. Although at the distance this girl had seemed so familiar, a second look told him that he had been mistaken in recognising her as the girl in the flat.

They might almost have been sisters, so amazing was the resemblance. This girl's hair was darker, her nose a trifle longer, her lips a little fuller. Her eyes were almost black, instead of hazel. In build, the two girls were much the same.

Peter raised his hat apologetically. "I'm awfully sorry," he said. "I thought I knew you."

The girl smiled prettily, then started slightly and stared at him.

"Aren't you Mr. Martin?" she asked, in a voice which had a decided American accent. "Detective Sergeant Martin of Scotland Yard, I mean?"

Peter nodded and looked at her curiously. She clutched his arm eagerly.

"Someone pointed you out to me when I called at Scotland Yard the other morning to report to the Commissioner," she said quickly. "My name is Madge Evans, of the United States Secret Service. I'm over here on the track of a diamond thief."

She opened her handbag and produced an envelope in which were her warrant card and passport. Peter examined them and handed them back satisfied that they were in order.

"The diamond stolen was the famous Lavery diamond," she continued. "And it's up to me to get it back for—oh, all sorts of reasons. There's the reward, of course, but it counts less than showing what I can do. You know how it is."

Peter nodded vaguely. He was unconsciously comparing this girl with the other, and the comparison was all in favour of the girl he had found in the flat. It was funny to think that this girl was a detective, the other a crook.

"I've located the thief," the girl continued. "He's hiding in a house a few blocks away, but I'm afraid I'll bungle the arrest if I go after him myself. Will you help me?"

"Like a shot!" Peter agreed promptly. "Where is this house?"

"I'll show you," the girl replied. "Come along. Gee, I'm glad I met you!"

Peter hesitated. "Perhaps I'd better call up the Yard and have the place surrounded," he suggested.

The girl shook her head decisively. "There isn't time," she replied. "He may make a break any moment. Our only chance is to grab him now."

Without further parlay they set off down the road at a brisk pace. Before they had gone far, they turned down a side street and halted in front of a house.

"This is the place," the girl murmured.

Peter recognised it. "Why, it's Mother Dawson's!" he declared.

The girl nodded. "A famous hang out for crooks, I understand," she agreed. "He's got a room on the top floor."

Mother Dawson was an ancient hag who ran a disreputable boarding house. On various occasions a police raid on Mother Dawson's house had resulted in the arrest of several 'wanted' men. The landlady herself had never been charged with any crime, although she was suspected of being a receiver of stolen articles.

The girl ran up the steps of the house with a piece of wire in her hand. She bent over the lock for a few moments, then there was a click, and the door swung open. She turned with a smile to Peter who was standing behind her.

"An unofficial entrance is justified," she said. "If we tried to get in by orthodox methods the bird would get the alarm and fly the nest before we were over the threshold."

She put a warning finger to her lips, and taking the hint, Peter followed her on tiptoe as noiselessly as possible. They went silently through the hall and up the stairs. They passed three landing without raising the alarm. On the top floor the girl halted and pointed to a door.

"He's in there," she whispered.

There were three doors in a row and the girl had pointed to the one in the middle. Peter felt for his revolver. At that moment the doors to the left and right opened. At one door appeared Pete Carponi and at the other 'Shorty' Manusco. Each of them was holding a vicious looking automatic.

"Well! Well!" said Carponi genially. "Visitors, eh? Just dropped in for tea, I suppose? How nice!"

Peter's hand moved in the direction of his revolver pocket. Carponi's hand tightened on the trigger.

"I wouldn't, if I were you," he rasped, "not unless you want your carcass perforated like a sieve. Just move back a bit, please."

Peter obeyed.

"A little more—"

Peter edged back still further.

"That's right. Now, 'Shorty'!"

'Shorty' clubbed his gun. Peter felt a stunning blow on the back of his head, then all went black and he knew no more.

Peter returned to consciousness with a severe throbbing in his head. He felt as though a score of boilermakers, all armed with sledgehammers, were pounding on the wall of his skull.

His eyes were like lumps of red-hot lead. It was like tearing his eyelids apart to open them.

Much of the pain in his head was centred on one spot, which felt as though it were pillowed on a nest of wasps. When he realised what had happened, he vowed that he had an account to square with 'Shorty' Manusco—and Carponi—but especially Manusco, whose clubbed automatic had made Peter's head feel at least three times its normal size, and red-hot into the bargain.

He tried to stretch his legs, but found that he was bound hand and foot. He was lying on something soft, and yet hard in places, like a mattress with bricks in it. He could see nothing. It was either late or night or the blinds were drawn, for the room was in darkness.

He suddenly thought of Madge Evans, the American girl detective, and wondered whether the gangsters had been gentlemen enough to treat her less harshly. He sincerely hoped that she had been spared the thud on the head that had fallen to his lot, and that she was not being cut into little pieces by ropes.

It was too much to hope that she had escaped while the gangsters' attention was concentrated on him, but at least it was comforting to reflect that even Chicago thugs could not deal as drastically with a girl as they had with him.

"What you guys lack is finesse," she was saying scornfully. "There ain't twenty-five cents worth of savvy between you. You just had to take your guns along last night, instead of doing the job in a gentlemanly way, and what's the result? Every cop in

London is looking for us. Gunplay don't go in London. How long d'you guys think it will be before the cops take a notion to search this place?"

"Aw, draw it mild, Sadie," retorted 'Shorty's' grumbling voice. "Didn't 'Squiffy' and me go without our guns de first time we searched 'The Dude's' flat, and what did it get us? I had to beat it quick down the fire-escape and 'The Dude' got 'Squiffy.' I tell you, a guy that ain't got a gun can't argue with a guy that has."

Sadie laughed jeeringly. "Get wise to yourself," she snapped. "The cops over here don't carry guns, but you don't get far when you argue with *them*."

"If I only had a machine-gun," snarled 'Shorty' viciously, "I could stand off every cop in London."

"*And* the Army *and* the Navy," sneered Sadie. "Gee, you're a great little feller, ain't cha?"

"Cut it out, Sadie," snapped Pete Carponi suddenly. "We did our best last night. If we'd managed to plug 'The Dude' we'd have got the diamond. I'll bet he carries it on him. I can't figure out yet how he got away. I was sure we hit him several times—once right in the back."

"He ain't human," put in 'Shorty' morosely.

"He's human alright," retorted Sadie, and added viciously: "the yellow, double-crossing, two-faced rat!"

"Let's cut out the snappy conversation," said Carponi, "and get down to brass tacks. What's the next move? Any suggestions?"

"I've got a bagful," replied Sadie. "But the first thing to do is to get away from this dump. The police know it too well for our safety. They'll be raiding the joint any time now and we've got be clear before they do."

"Can we trust 'Nippy'?" demanded Carponi.

"Sure, 'Nippy's' alright," responded Sadie. "Didn't he tip us off about that smart cop, Peter Martin, that was trailin' him?

If he had wanted to see us, that was his chance; but he didn't, did he? He's alright. He thinks he can get enough dough by sticking with us to take him to Australia afterwards with his pockets lined with greenbacks."

Just then there was noisy clatter on the stairs.

Then Peter heard three long raps, followed by two short ones, and the sound of the door of the next room opening. He heard 'Nippy's' breathless voice next, charged with excitement.

"I've seen 'The Dude' boss," he cried. "Drivin' a sports car down Piccadilly, as bold as brass, 'e was! 'Is car was full of luggage, too!"

"Didya follow him?" demanded Carponi, roughly.

"Did I? What d'you fink?" retorted 'Nippy' sarcastically. "'Course I followed him—clear to Staines. It was a bit of luck that the roads were full of traffic and me taxi was able to keep up wiv 'is car. We lost him at Staines, but by nosin' round a bit, I found the cottage 'e's rented for a month in a quiet place about a mile and a half out!"

"So, you took a taxi, didya?" snarled Carponi. "You poor fish! You might have lost him. Why didn't you pinch a fast car?"

"I can't drive," whined 'Nippy.' "'Sides, a fat lot of good it would do to be had up fer pinchin' cars. The cops is fly in London."

"You little rat," sneered Carponi. "Why, Sadie uses a stolen car when she goes shopping—and a different one every time. Don't you Sadie?"

"Sure," answered the girl cheerfully. "And never less than a Bentley or a Rolls. But let's get to business, Pete. We're going after 'The Dude' at once?"

"On the jump," was Carponi's emphatic reply. "Just as soon as we can rustle up a car."

"I'll see to that," replied the girl. "Just leave it to me."

"O.K.!" responded the gang leader. "Get a powerful car, Sadie. We don't want to be all night on the job. A big, roomy saloon will do."

The door of the next room was slammed, and Peter heard the girl's footsteps go lightly down the stairs.

"Wot abaht the cop in the next room?" asked 'Nippy' suddenly.

Peter heard 'Shorty's' low, ugly laugh.

"We'll croak him before we go," he replied.

"No, we won't!" retorted Carponi. "It's too dangerous."

"Afraid?" sneered 'Shorty.'

Peter heard a chair go over, then a choking gasp as Carponi's hands grasped 'Shorty's' throat.

"You rat," he snarled, shaking the diminutive gangster viciously. "I'm afraid of nothing—and no one. Get that into your brain."

There was a crash, as 'Shorty' was thrown into a corner. Then the little gangster spoke with an effort.

"Sorry, boss," he wheezed. "I didn't mean to rile you."

"Then talk sense," snapped Carponi. "We can't leave the cop here, or he'll have all Scotland Yard after us when we get free. We'll take him with us."

Just then the door of the room in which Peter was lying was opened gently. In a moment or two he felt soft hands going over his body, fumbling with the ropes that bound him.

'Madge Evans, the girl 'tec', he thought—and wondered how the girl had got free.

"Lie still," she whispered. "I'm going to get you free, then go for help!"

Then he heard a hacking sound as a knife sawed through his bonds. When he was free the girl slipped an automatic pistol into his hand, then went noiselessly out of the room.

It was several minutes before Peter managed by rubbing to coax the circulation back to his legs sufficiently to stand up. He was still groggy and his limbs ached, but there was a fierce exultation in his heart. Grasping the automatic tightly, he tiptoed out of the room and along the landing to the door of the next room. He threw it open suddenly and stepped in.

"What the—" began 'Shorty', then broke off suddenly as he saw the menacing automatic in Peter's hand.

"Up with your hands—all of you," commanded Peter.

Peter marshalled the gangsters against the wall and surveyed each of them grimly in turn.

"I've got that rap on the head to repay you 'Shorty'," he remarked. "But it will have to wait."

There was a swift patter of footsteps on the stairs and the girl Peter knew as 'Madge Evans of the U.S. Secret Service' entered the room. She stopped short when she saw the gangsters lined up against the wall, with Peter seated on the table. Peter rose as she came in.

"Did you 'phone for help?" he asked.

She nodded.

"That's fine. I say, can you handle an automatic?"

She nodded again. "I certainly can," she replied. "That was part of my early training."

He slipped the automatic into her hand. "Here, keep this trained on the boys while I search them for arms."

The girl obligingly pointed the automatic at the gangsters. Peter advanced to search them, but stopped short when they all dropped their hands and burst out laughing.

He wheeled round sharply. The girl still held the automatic but she was aiming it unswervingly at him! "What on earth are you up to?" he demanded.

Carponi came forward, shaking with laughter. "Allow me

to present to you 'Cincinnati Sadie', the cleverest con-woman in the world," he said, indicating the girl. "You poor boob! This is too good for words!"

Peter stared at 'Madge Evans', scarcely comprehending.

"But—but the warrant-card and the passport you showed me—" he began.

The girl smiled triumphantly. "I pinched these from the real Madge Evans, coming over on the boat," she replied. "When 'Nippy' came and told us that you were snooping about the neighbourhood, I went down and pulled you in to keep you out of mischief. Gee! You fell for that yarn easily. If all the cops in London are boobs like you, we ought to be safe enough!"

Peter still stared. If this was 'Cincinnati Sadie', who was the girl who had held him up in 'The Dude's' flat, he wondered, and who was the girl who had just set him free?

Carponi grabbed Peter by the arm. At the same time 'Shorty' jabbed him in the ribs with a huge automatic.

"You're coming with us, and watch your step," the gang leader announced menacingly. "Make one false move while you're in the car and it'll be the last you'll ever make!"

'Cincinnati Sadie' had made no mistake in her choice of a car. The Hispano-Suiza which she had appropriated was large, roomy and fast. The former qualities showed themselves when Peter, Carponi and 'Shorty' were accommodated in the rear seat, the detective between two gangsters, who each had an automatic pressed to his side.

That the Hispano was speedy was proved when they were beyond the surging traffic. Sadie trod upon the accelerator and the car ate up the road, her wheels spinning at sixty miles an hour. Even over that speed the car was a steady as a rock. It held snugly to the road and its engine was almost noiseless.

"Gee!" said Sadie. "Wouldn't it be swell if there was always a classy boat like this, hanging round to be had for the taking?"

'Nippy' shivered. "They'll be a 'ue an' cry after it," he complained. "It won't be 'ard for the police to spot a posh car like this, neither, an' then where'll we be?"

"In a Rolls or a Sunbeam," retorted Sadie cheerfully.

"You don't think we're going to play about this buggy for long, do you? We'll ditch it at Staines and pinch another for the return journey."

"An' what'll we do if we're caught?" whined 'Nippy'.

"Ask Carponi!" suggested Sadie.

'Nippy' shivered again. He knew only too well the reply that Carponi's huge, blue-nosed automatic would give to the policeman who asked awkward questions. Fervently, he wished himself the luck to get out of this affair without being hanged, and just as fervently he prayed that no policeman would provoke the gang leader to murder.

Sadie drove to 'Nippy's' directions until they were a mile or two beyond the boundaries of Staines, then turning on a quiet road the proceeded for a further half-mile. Here Sadie stopped the car and got out, with the little informer.

He pointed to lights which shone about two hundred yards away. "That's 'The Dude's' bungalow," he explained.

Sadie poked her head in the rear window of the car and had a whispered conversation with Carponi. It was decided that they should drive as near as possible to the bungalow, and trust to luck that their quarry would not be alarmed by the noise of the engine.

Putting the lights out, Sadie drove at a crawl in top gear. There was nothing to betray the approach of the car to the man in the bungalow. Its progress was entirely noiseless.

Just short of the path that led to the door of the bungalow, Sadie stopped the car. Carponi and Manusco climbed out, and Sadie took their place. She held an automatic in her hand, the barrel of which she pressed tightly against Peter's neck.

"I'd hate to bump you off," she said softly. "So please sit as quietly as possible."

"Certainly," Peter whispered. "Anything to spare you mental anguish. I wouldn't like to add to the things you have on your conscience already."

"That's sweet of you," she murmured. "But please stow the chatter. I hate talkative men."

On tiptoe, 'Shorty' and Carponi proceeded up the path towards the house. Their plan was to take up positions at the front and rear respectively, and make a simultaneous attack. This intention was frustrated. Before they were half-way up the path, they were suddenly bathed in the beam of a powerful flashlamp. At the same time there was a muffled 'pop' like the sound of a cork being drawn, which is roughly the sound made by an automatic to which a silencer is attached, and a bullet whizzed over Carponi's head and embedded itself in a tree across the road.

The gangsters hastily retreated to the car. They delegated to 'Nippy' the task of guarding Peter, while they held a whispered consultation with Sadie. 'Nippy' was trembling so much that Peter was afraid the automatic which the police informer held against his neck would go off accidentally at any minute. It mattered little to the detective that the bullet that would end his career would be fired intentionally; it was the bullet itself which mattered. 'Nippy' himself seemed to be in mortal terror that the automatic would blow up, or something of the sort, and his terror made the danger greater, for his fingers were twitching with anxiety.

The girl and the gangsters came at last to an arrangement. Sadie produced a white silk handkerchief and, holding it above her head, advanced gingerly up the path to the bungalow. The ray of light illuminated her figure, but there was no sound from the bungalow until she actually rang the doorbell, then the door opened and 'The Dude' appeared.

They could just make out his face in the darkened doorway. He made Sadie stand between him and the car and the two talked together for some minutes. Suddenly, with a lightning movement, Sadie leapt to one side.

"Now!" snapped Carponi tensely.

'Shorty' had been standing, hidden by the bonnet of the car, his automatic levelled and his hand upon the trigger. At the word of command, he fired rapidly three times at the man in the doorway.

'The Dude' staggered as all three missiles hit him. He stepped back, however, and slammed the door.

"Good work 'Shorty'!" exulted the gang-leader, pounding the little gunman on the back. "That was a neat as anything I ever saw. You got him right in the chest with every bullet!"

Sadie came racing down the pathway. "Gee, that was rotten!" she declared, and her face was white. "I ain't got no stomach for a lousy trick like that. Betraying a guy under the white flag is as low as anyone can get. I feel sick."

"Aw, pipe down," snarled 'Shorty.' "You know we was going to do it."

The girl passed a weary hand over her forehead, brushing back her hair, which was limp and moist. "Yeah, I knew alright!" she replied bitterly. "It ain't you guys I'm mad with, it's myself. I never thought I'd stoop to a dirty trick like that."

Carponi turned on her angrily. "Quit your grousing," he retorted. "Didn't he double-cross you?"

The girl shrugged her shoulders. "Yeah, I suppose so," she assented wearily. "Well, go on—go on and finish the trick."

Without any attempt at concealment the gangsters and the girl proceeded up the path. They anticipated no trouble, for had not 'Shorty' put three bullets into 'The Dude's' chest? A man with so much lead in so vital a part would be beyond arguing about a diamond. All that remained for them to do was to enter the house and take the diamond from 'The Dude's' dead body.

They did not glance into the dark interior of the car. Had they done so, they would have been intensely surprised. Peter was kneeling on the floor with an automatic in his hand awaiting his opportunity to take a hand in the game.

When 'Shorty' had fired three shots, 'Nippy' had fallen back on the cushion at the sudden shock. Seizing the opportunity, Peter had kicked the automatic from the police informer's hand, and proceeded to strangle him with enthusiasm. Not until 'Nippy' was unconscious, and practically asphyxiated, did Peter release him and let his senseless body slip down onto the floorboards. Then Peter grabbed the automatic, and squatted down, awaiting his chance. It would have been suicide to try the issue with two armed gunmen, who were expert at gunplay, but he hoped that an opportunity would present itself which would enable him to gain the upper hand.

He had little doubt that 'The Dude' was dead, so it was useless to interfere until the crooks had found the diamond. Then he would count himself in on the game.

Secure in the belief that 'The Dude' was dead, the gangsters went serenely up the pathway. Their confidence was turned into consternation when a bullet whizzed over their heads. Then 'Shorty' cursed as another piece of flying lead took a piece out of his ear. A third shot grazed Carponi's skull.

Without waiting for more, the girl turned and ran, and the gangsters followed her with equal speed. Another bullet, which kicked up the dust at their heels, accelerated their progress. None of them stopped until they were on the side of the car farthest from the stream of flying death.

'Shorty' swore lustily. "Gee, chief," he snarled. "I told you that guy wasn't human. Three times I hit him, and each bullet was enough in itself to put paid to his career and yet he's alive and kicking."

Carponi was visibly impressed. "You're right, 'Shorty'," he agreed. "And the other night you plugged him square in the back. That was enough to do in any ordinary guy."

"Do you suppose there was someone else in the bungalow with him?" put in Sadie thoughtfully.

Carponi shook his head. "No, that ain't likely," he replied with conviction. "He wouldn't trust anyone. Gosh! He must be armour-plated or sumfin'."

Sadie turned to the little gangster. "Put that flashlamp out of action," she directed.

Taking aim carefully 'Shorty' fired a single shot at the circle of light. There was a pop, a crash, a tinkling of glass and the light disappeared. The reply from 'The Dude' in the bungalow was a bullet which smashed one of the windows of the car and buried itself in the clock on the dashboard.

Sadie turned to Carponi. "What now?" she demanded.

At that moment Peter stepped from behind a tree where he had hidden himself, while the crooks were proceeding up the pathway. The automatic gleamed darkly in his hand.

"Put 'em up!" he commanded brusquely.

The girl and the gunmen wheeled round and stared at him. The automatic in his hand travelled in a half-circle, menacing each of them in turn. It barked suddenly as 'Shorty' swung his automatic up. The little gangster cursed as the weapon dropped from his shattered fingers. His face wore an expression of intense agony. His hand dripped blood.

"Sorry 'Shorty'," said Peter. "But if you *will* play with guns accidents are likely to happen. Next time you feel an itching to 'plug' someone, remember what it's like and don't!"

The gangster moaned and swayed on his feet.

"Sit down 'Shorty'!" directed Peter, and the little gangster dropped onto the running-board of the car.

At that moment the moon came through the clouds and for a moment showed the gangster's shattered hand in all its horror. With a scream Sadie fainted. Carponi caught her as she fell.

Peter stood still, uncertain what course to take. As he hesitated Carponi slung Sadie at him. The girl's body struck the detective and caused him to stagger. At the same time, the girl twined her arms and legs about him and they fell struggling to the ground. Peter got his hand free which held his automatic, but as he did so, Carponi's foot came down on his wrist with agonising force and the gang leader possessed himself of the weapon.

Then the girl rose to her feet with a mocking smile.

Peter slowly followed suit.

Carponi burst in raucous laughter. "You boob!" he cried. "You poor boob! Why, Sadie ain't got twenty-five cents worth of nerves in her whole body. Gee, I've seen her look at a guy that was just croaked without changing colour!"

Sadie laughed mockingly. "And I thought that the Scotland Yard cops were hot stuff!" she exclaimed. "Gee, how I've been misled. Are they all as dense as you, big boy? Or are you the baby of the force?"

Peter reddened a little but did not reply. He felt deeply the humiliation of having been effectively tricked for the fourth time that day. He felt that he deserved all the scorn that could be heaped upon him.

Carponi jerked his thumb towards 'Shorty.' "See if you can help the little feller, Sadie," he suggested. "He's got a bad hand there."

An angry curse was 'Shorty' Manusco's reply. "What d'ya think I am?" he demanded, rising to his feet and swaying a little. "I'm no baby to be mothered and fussed over. Gimme a gun, and let me blow hell outta this fly cop!"

Despite himself, Peter felt a sneaking admiration for the diminutive gunman. Callous, cold-blooded murderer he certainly was, but there was a wide streak of gameness in his composition. There was nothing of the quitter about 'Shorty'.

"Take it easy now," directed Carponi. "Just take it easy. There's no use getting all worked up, 'Shorty'. Remember, we've got 'The Dude' to deal with and that diamond to find."

'Shorty' nodded brusquely. "Yeah, and after we've dealt with 'The Dude', I'll deal with the cop," he snarled. "We'll croak them both in the bungalow and set fire to the dump."

"Alright!" agreed Carponi soothingly. "Now we gotta work out a plan of campaign. Wha'd'ya say, Sadie? How're we gonna get inside that bungalow?"

Despite 'shorty's' surly grumbling, Sadie tied up his hand as neatly as she could with handkerchiefs torn into strips. Over the bandage, which quickly became soaked with blood, she tied a large piece of 'Shorty's' shirt, which she had cut out with nail-scissors. It was rough work, but the best that could be done in the circumstance.

Then the gang held a council of war. It was a desperate conference. The three realised that whatever was done must be accomplished hurriedly, for police interference might be expected at any moment. It was certain that the firing had been heard and that some of the residents nearby would have been interested enough to communicate with the police.

At last, a course was decided upon.

Sadie guarded Peter Martin with an automatic in her hand. The two gunmen crouched behind a low stone wall that bordered the garden of the bungalow, where it joined the road. They had two loaded automatics each, and several additional clips of ammunition.

Shooting with his left hand, 'Shorty' started the hostilities by smashing every window in the front of the house. Carponi had a powerful flashlamp, which he turned on the door for long enough to make out the lock and send four bullets crashing into it, one after another.

The onslaught was replied to from the bungalow by several muffled reports. Carponi hurriedly extinguished the flashlamp, but a well-directed bullet clipped it from his hand and left him blowing on his stinging fingers. Other bullets spatted on the wall behind which the gunmen were crouched.

Taking the flashes of 'The Dude's' automatic in the darkened house as a target, Carponi fired a little to the left of them, and 'Shorty' a little to the right. They emptied the contents of the four automatics and two of the spare clips at the bungalow. 'The Dude' fired half-a-dozen shots in reply.

When the lull came in the firing the two gunmen crawled along beside the wall to the path. Their plan had been to keep 'The Dude' busy dodging bullets then to dash for the bungalow at a strategic moment. If one of the bullets happened to find the target it was seeking, so much the better.

Their plan succeeded; they gained to the door of the bungalow without obstruction. Setting his shoulder to it, Carponi sent it crashing back. The bullets he had pumped into the lock had done their work well.

'Shorty' cautiously fired a couple of shots into the hall before they entered. The bungalow was ominously silent. They stood still in the hall for a few minutes, listening for a step, a creaking floorboard, or anything which would give a clue to the whereabouts of the man they were seeking. Apart from their own breathing, they could hear nothing. It appeared for a moment that their quarry had escaped.

Carponi threw open the door of a room opening off the hall, then sprang to one side, expecting a volley. Nothing happened. His groping fingers found the electric light switch in the room and depressed it. The two gangsters peered through the doorway, then confidently entered the room.

'The Dude' lay face downwards and motionless upon the floor. Blood was coming from the side of his head. He was breathing fitfully.

'Shorty' sneered disgustedly. "Gee, chief," he snarled. "The guy laughs at lead when you hit him in the body, an' heels right over when you hit him a slight clip on the head."

Carponi knelt down beside the man. He ran his fingers over

'The Dude's' body. "As I thought," he declared rising to his feet. "The guy's wearing a bulletproof waistcoat. No wonder you couldn't croak him, 'Shorty'."

'Shorty' stared incredulously. 'The Dude's' jacket was torn to ribbons, and underneath the bulletproof waistcoat showed through.

"Well, I'll be danged," was 'Shorty's' comment. "Can you beat that? I didn't know there was such things."

"You should read the papers," replied his chief. "There was some talk of getting the Chicago cops a bulletproof waistcoat apiece, but they cost so much that the Commissioner decided it was cheaper to get new cops!"

They carried 'The Dude' to a bed that lay against the wall and threw him on it. This was out of no consideration for the unconscious man, but merely to make their own task easier.

They stripped every stitch of clothing from him except his underwear, and cut and tore it to shreds in an effort to find the diamond. They looked between his toes, in his mouth, in his hair.

'The Dude's' monocle still dangled on a cord round his neck. 'Shorty' seized it and jabbed into place with a laugh. It looked funny to see it with the half-open, vacant-looking, eye staring unseeingly through it.

When they ceased their investigation, they were convinced that the diamond was nowhere upon 'The Dude's' person. It must be hidden somewhere about the house.

Carponi called Sadie. She came, marshalling the detective in front of her. When her eyes fell upon the unconscious man they lit up with joy.

"Did you get the diamond?" she demanded.

Carponi shook his head. "He hadn't got it on him," he replied. "But we'll get it alright, when he comes too."

She crossed the room to the bed and looked down at the

279 The Monocled Man

unconscious man. "I always said you'd get it in the end you double-crossing rat," she hissed between her teeth.

'Shorty' laughed raucously. "The guy can't hear you!" he reminded her. "He's dead to the world."

Sadie's dark eyes were bitter. "He'll hear me alright before he's through," she retorted. "There's bound to be some water in the kitchen. Get a bucketful and throw it over him!"

Carponi hurried away, and returned shortly with a large jug of water which he emptied over 'The Dude's' head and shoulders.

'The Dude' stirred feebly and moaned.

Sadie nodded in a satisfied way. "He'll come round directly," she said, "and when he does, we'll give him the works."

Carponi glanced at Peter. "We can't waste time standing over this cop to see he doesn't escape," he declared. "There's a length of rope in the car. I'll go and get it. It won't be a bad idea to tie up 'The Dude' too. |He might make a fuss when he comes round."

Sadie laughed harshly. "He'll do that alright when he sees me," she replied.

Carponi left the room.

There was tiny fire burning in the grate and Sadie gazed at it reflectively. Then she went to the kitchen and found wood and coals.

When Carponi returned with the rope, there was considerable blaze in the grate, with the poker in the heart of it. He glanced at it curiously. "Feeling cold?" he asked.

"Not me. I'm just warming up my little persuader," retorted Sadie. "I'm going to make that guy open his mouth."

Carponi glanced at the girl's stern features, but said nothing. He motioned Peter into a chair.

"Pity my hand is smashed up, boss," commented 'Shorty.' "I could do that job better than you."

Peter glanced at him. "So, it was you who tied me up last time?" he asked.

'Shorty' leered at him. "It was me alright," he snarled. "And when we find that diamond and beat it away from here, it'll be me who'll plant a slug right through you."

Under 'Shorty's' directions Carponi lashed Peter to the chair. Peter set his muscles in the hope that he would thereby be able to ease his bonds a little later, but Carponi's workmanship destroyed that slender hope.

In a few minutes the detective found himself trussed up so tightly that he could scarcely breath. Then Carponi turned his attention to 'The Dude', who was stirring spasmodically, and showing other signs of coming round.

By the time 'The Dude' opened his eyes wearily, his hands and feet were securely tied. He blinked about him for a moment, then started violently when Sadie walked to the bed and stared at him. He closed one of his eyes—the one that was not propped open by the monocle—and when he opened it again his expression was inscrutable.

"Well, Sadie," he murmured.

Sadie's expression was hard. "I want that diamond 'Dude'," she rasped. "Do you get me? I want it and I mean to have it."

'The Dude' grinned wearily. "You used to be more subtle Sadie," he replied. "Haven't lost your finesse, have you?"

The girl made an impatient gesture. "Don't beat about the bush," she retorted. "We've got not time to waste."

'The Dude's' expression brightened. "The police I suppose?" he suggested.

"Never you mind," she snapped. "We want that diamond and we're going to get it, police or no police. Before we pinched it you told me you had a hiding-place that no one would ever find. Where is that hiding-place?"

"I'm telling you the same still," replied 'The Dude' evenly. "You'll never find it!"

Carponi took a step forward. "Look here 'Dude'," he said placatingly. "We only want what's Sadie's by right. Give up that diamond and you'll get your share. Honest."

The other laughed. "I know you, Carponi," was his only reply.

'Shorty' drew his automatic. "Let me crack him and be done with it, boss."

Carponi glared at the man on the bed. "You hear?" he demanded. "You can give up that diamond or I'll let 'Shorty' plug you."

"And lose the diamond altogether?" retorted the man on the bed. "If I was dead, you'd never find it."

Sadie shook her head impatiently. "It's no use, Carponi," she declared. "Let me deal with him."

Carponi shrugged his shoulders. "Alright."

The girl looked straight into the eyes of the man on the bed. "You know what I think of you," she said viciously. "I wouldn't give you a drink of water in the Sahara Desert. If you were drowning, I'd push you under. I hate you; you rat!"

"So I gather," responded 'The Dude' cheerfully.

She leaned over and slapped his face. Her rage was so great that it was some moments before she could continue.

"I'd like to see you boiled in oil," she continued fiercely. "Why, you yellow-livered, double-crossing skunk, there isn't anything I wouldn't do to get my own back on you. Don't think I'm talking just to hear my own voice. I mean it—and I'm going to show you just how far I'm willing to go."

She darted to the fireplace and was back in a moment with the white-hot poker in her hand. "Look at that!" she cried, brandishing it in front of his eyes. "What good will the diamond be to you when I've got that pressed against your cheek, scarring the skin, cooking your flesh! How long will you hold out when you can feel the pain?"

The man on the bed turned white. His terror was rendered almost ludicrous by the monocle that gleamed in his eye.

The girl sneered triumphantly. "*Now* do you get me!" she cried. "I want that diamond, 'Dude' and I don't care how I get it. Will you come across or do you want to hear your flesh sizzling?"

'The Dude' trembled. "You wouldn't do it!" he whispered. "You wouldn't do it!"

He was desperately staring at the girl's eyes as he spoke, and her malignant expression left him little room for doubt.

"Oh, wouldn't I?" she retorted. "Try me then! See how long you can stand it. Why, you poor boob, I'll enjoy it!"

She brought the white-hot poker closer and closer to him until it actually rested for a moment on his cheek. 'The Dude' fainted.

The girl stepped back a pace with frustrated venom on her eyes.

"Tickle him up a bit more," suggested 'Shorty.' "He's only shamming!"

Sadie jammed the poker back into the fire.

"What's the use?" she demanded. "He wouldn't feel it! He's unconscious alright."

SADIE GLARED at Carponi. It was evident that she was in an advanced stage of fury. The collapse of her victim had frustrated her intention to torture him. "Did you go over him thoroughly?" she demanded.

Carponi pointed to the unconscious man on the bed, who was clad in his underwear. "You can see for yourself," he snapped in reply. "We stripped him down to that, and examined every inch of him."

Sadie snatched up the unconscious man's clothes which lay tattered on the floor. Already in shreds, she tore them still more, until they were in tiny pieces. Then she threw them aside and her eyes travelled round the room looking for likely hiding-places. There was little enough in the way of furniture in the room. Except for the bed on which 'The Dude' lay, there was only a plain, varnished kitchen chair to which Peter was tied, and a cheap kitchen table on which some ammunition and an automatic pistol lay.

An idea occurred to her, and she set Carponi the task of opening each cartridge with his pocket knife, but inspiration had led her on a false scent. She had hopes that a dummy cartridge might contain the diamond, but the ammunition was all genuine. She examined the kitchen chair to which Peter was roped and satisfied herself that it held no hiding-place. With an axe Carponi split up the table but his efforts were fruitless.

They sounded every corner of the room for a faulty floorboard but did not even find a crevice which would hide as much as a matchstick. They lifted the unconscious man from his bed and dumped him in a corner, while they tore his mattress to pieces and broke up the iron bedstead. At last, they admitted ruefully that further search in that room was useless. If the diamond was actually hidden in the room only 'The Dude' could find it.

"He's bound to have it with him, I suppose?" asked Carponi at last.

"Of course," snapped the girl. "You don't suppose he'd trust it to anyone, do you? Or leave it where he couldn't get his hands on it in a hurry?"

Carponi grunted. "It's a pretty hopeless business, this searching," he retorted. "He may have planted it anywhere—in the garden, for instance, and we can't plough up every inch of the lawn looking for it."

The girl faced him scornfully. "Use your brains!" she responded. "The diamond's in the house, alright. 'The Dude's' planted it somewhere where it wouldn't be found in a hurry if he was caught and sent to prison for a stretch. He wouldn't hide it in the garden where it would be at the mercy of any doddering fool who pottered about with a rake and a trowel."

"Why not wait until he comes to and try the poker again?" suggested 'Shorty.'

The girl laughed mirthlessly. "You poor fish!" she rasped. "How long do you think it will be before the police come along to investigate the fireworks? Someone's bound to have heard the shooting. We've got to work fast."

'Shorty' grunted imperturbably. "Dontcher worry about the cops," he responded. "They don't carry guns. We can shoot our way through a regiment of them easily. Say, if I had a machine gun—"

"Forget it," she retorted. "We've got away with the gun stuff so far, but that luck ain't gonna last. Say, if you did shoot your way through a regiment of them where would it getcha? You'd find your way blocked by another regiment, an' another. You can't scare these British cops and you can't buy 'em. If we hang around long enough, we'll get it in the neck. Our only chance is to find that diamond and find it quick, then beat it fast for Liverpool without being pinched, we'll be in the clear."

The gangsters were silent. Her flow of words had evidently impressed them. She seized the opportunity to rouse them to action.

"Besides this room, there's only three others in the shack, and a kitchen," she said. "You and 'Shorty' search the rooms. Carponi and I'll search the kitchen. Make it snappy now, but don't overlook anything."

"Where's 'Nippy'?" asked Carponi suddenly.

Sadie laughed sarcastically. "Standing in the road with his knees knocking together," she explained. "I found him in the car, scared to death, and with huge bruises on his neck where the cop there nearly choked the life outa him. He's watching for the cops, and he'll sound the horn of the car at the first sign of danger."

The gangsters left the room and went about the business of ransacking the other rooms of the bungalow. Of the three, Sadie was the most thorough. She emptied the flour-bin upon the kitchen floor, and raked over the flour with a fork. She crumpled the soap to little bits and cut up every loaf in the place. There was not a single hiding-place in the kitchen which ingenuity might contrive that she did not investigate.

From the sounds of smashing and crashing that came from one of the other rooms it was evident that the two gunmen were busy in their own way.

In the front room Peter Martin was struggling desperately with his bonds. All his efforts were futile, however. Carponi had trussed him so cunningly that the ropes merely tightened as he struggled.

The situation seemed desperate. If Peter could turn the tables on the gangsters and arrest them before they made a getaway, he could redeem himself for falling so innocently into the various traps which had been set for him.

On the other hand, if the police arrived at the bungalow—if they ever did arrive—to find the birds flown, and Peter Martin trussed to a chair, he could never face Inspector Grief again. It was little consolation to reflect that if he was found with a bullet wound in his forehead, facing Inspector Greig again wouldn't be necessary!

He ceased struggling and set his mind to work on the problem of getting free. It was useless to think of pocket-knives, for his knife had been taken from him, and even if it hadn't, he was too tightly trussed to get at it. Or burning through the rope with a candle, for the room was lit by electricity. Nor could he get his teeth within a foot of the knots, even if there had been time for chewing, which there wasn't.

Concentration brought its reward... He suddenly thought of the fire and red-hot poker.

It was a ticklish job, but by manoeuvring until the ropes nearly cut him in two at the middle, he managed to get his feet under the knob at the end of the poker. It seemed to take hours of tapping at it—futile little taps, for his legs were too tightly tied to permit of much movement—before the poker slid out of the fire slowly onto the fender.

Then the problem arose of getting the ropes into contact with the red-hot end of the poker. Hard as it had been to get the poker out of the fire, this was even harder. It occurred to him that by swaying sideways he might be able to upset the chair. On the other hand, it was practically certain that the crooks would hear it fall and put a stop to his scheme.

He decided to take the chance, and to so contrive it, if possible, that he deadened the noise by twisting his body to act as a cushion. Then for some minutes he rocked and swayed in agony as the motion made the ropes bite deeper into his flesh. Moments passed and the chair began to sway. More moments and it tottered. He was just in time to relax himself and twist as it fell, so that he landed on the floor with the chair on top of him. Even so, the manoeuvre made a slight sound, which the gangsters would certainly have heard had they not been making more noise themselves.

In the position in which he found himself, doubled up on the floor with the chair on top of him, and the ropes tightened by the strain, Peter suffered agony. He half expected his legs to be cut from his body and his trunk to be severed. That would solve the problem of getting free, but it was not much use getting free in several pieces. In spite of the pain he was undergoing, he contrived to wriggle nearer the fireplace and rest his arms on the fender. In that position the ropes that bound his wrists were placed on the red-hot end of the poker.

There was an odour of burning rope mingled with the smell of scorching flesh. Peter felt sick as his wrists suffered from the intense heat which was eating through the rope. As the ropes parted, one wrist came into contact with the poker, and he almost screamed in pain. By a tremendous effort of willpower, he controlled himself. He pulled his wrists apart and the rope uncoiled up his arms.

He was free!

There were still his legs to release, but holding the poker in his hands, that part of the problem was child's play. As the last coil of rope fell from him, he heard footsteps in the hall. It was 'Shorty', who had smelled the burning rope, coming to investigate.

Swiftly and silently, Peter slipped across the room and hid behind the door. As 'Shorty' cautiously looked into the room, with his automatic levelled ready to shoot, Peter thrust the hot poker into the crook's face.

With a howl, 'Shorty' sprang in the air, dropping his pistol, which went off as it fell.

Peter dived for the automatic, and jumped to his feet with it in his hand. With his finger on the trigger, he brought the barrel down *smack*.

WITHOUT A SOUND 'Shorty' crumpled to the floor. Peter had no time to feel sorry for the gunman, for Carponi was feeling his way cautiously down the hall attracted by the noise, and Carponi had a pistol in each hand—

Peter felt it was best to commence the hostilities. Picking up the chair he threw it into the hall. As the crash echoed, it was followed by three successive reports from Carponi's gun. Aiming 'Shorty's' automatic round the corner, Peter fired. The shot was followed by a woman's scream.

"Has he got you, Sadie?" cried Carponi.

The girl moaned in the darkness. "My arm, I think," she muttered. Then there was thud as she fell to the floor.

"I'll get the cop for that!" snarled Carponi.

His automatic rained death into the doorway of the room where Peter was hidden. The detective's pistol was silent. Emboldened, the big gang-leader stepped from the shelter of the hall to the lighted doorway to fire another shot.

Like a flash, Peter's automatic spoke, and Carponi went down with a wound in the leg. Raising himself on one arm, however, Carponi levelled his weapon again. Peter threw himself to one side and the shot thudded harmlessly into the wall.

"It's no use, Carponi," cried Peter. "I can kill you where you lie with the greatest of ease, but what's the use of doing that? Give yourself up, man. The girl is wounded, and 'Shorty' is dead to the world. You haven't a chance!"

Taking the course of discretion, Carponi threw his automatic into the room.

When the four prisoners were arrayed against one wall, they presented a ludicrous or pathetic picture, according to the way one looked at them. Peter considerately cut the ropes that bound 'The Dude' who had not yet regained consciousness. There was something irritably funny about the unconscious man, clad in tattered woollen underwear and with a monocle glistening in his eye.

Peter placed the chair in the middle of the room and sat facing the row of battered crooks, with two automatics conveniently placed on his lap. He was scarcely settled comfortably before there was a shrill whistle followed by the sound of footsteps running up the pathway. Then 'Nippy' burst into the room panting breathlessly.

"There's a whole string of cars coming along the road, boss," he cried.

He stopped short suddenly when he saw the detective, who levelled one of the automatics at him. Then he turned his head slowly and gazed with consternation at Carponi.

"Thanks for the tip 'Nippy'," said Peter cheerfully. "Now be a good boy and join your pals on the floor until the police come."

Keeping an eye on the menacing automatic, 'Nippy' eased himself onto the floor beside Carponi. His face looked as long as his arm.

There was a grinding of brakes on the roadway outside, then a police whistle sounded.

The Flying Squad had arrived, and they went efficiently about the business of surrounding the bungalow. When there was no loophole for escape open, Inspector Greig and three other detectives entered the bungalow. At their heels was a pretty girl.

They moved cautiously down the hall, until Peter cheerfully urged them to "Come right in."

"All ready to pop on the bracelets and wheel 'em away, sir," he reported crisply.

The inspector's eyes kindled warmly.

As briefly as possible Peter recounted the events which had led to the capture. Inspector Greig nodded approvingly as he finished.

"By the way," the Inspector murmured, indicating the pretty girl, "this is Miss Evans of the United States Secret Service! Her papers were stolen by 'Cincinnati Sadie', but we've been able to establish her identity."

Peter nodded, with just a trace of aloofness. He had not yet forgiven this girl for locking him in a cupboard at 'The Dude's' flat.

The girl smiled sweetly and all but dissipated his sulkiness.

At Scotland Yard Greig had 'The Dude' taken directly to his own room, while the gangsters were bundled into the cells. Peter Martin and Madge Evans were present at the interview.

"There are two questions I'm going to ask you," said Greig smoothly. "Where is the Lavery diamond, and what have you done with 'Squiffy' Fields, whom you found searching your flat?"

'The Dude' smiled and adjusted his monocle. "I happened to be bored by the play I saw that night," he replied suavely. "So, I came home early. I fancied I heard a rustling when I opened the door, and when I entered the drawing room, that little beast 'Squiffy' tried to slug me. I ducked, and returned the compliment by bashing him with a brass candlestick. It cracked his skull and made a fearful mess—"

"Where is he now?" Greig interrupted.

The other smilingly reproved him. "Don't be impatient. I'm coming to that," he replied serenely. "I took him to the West London Infirmary. I told them that I'd seen him knocked down by a car and that the driver had got away."

"And they believed that story?" demanded Greig.

'The Dude' shrugged. "They looked a bit odd," he admitted; "but I gave them a false name and address and left quickly before they could become nosey."

Inspector Greig drummed his fingers on his desk. "Where is the Lavery diamond?" he asked pointedly.

"Oh, as to that," replied 'The Dude' smilingly, "I can tell you nothing."

"You stole it!"

'The Dude' shrugged his shoulders. "That will have to be proved, won't it?" he pointed out. "I know the New York police suspect me; but then they are a very suspicious lot."

"They have 'Cincinnati Sadie' Levinsky's evidence to back them up," replied Greig evenly. "She admits that you and she stole it in partnership."

The other's expression was unperturbed. "Then let *her* tell you where it is now," he retorted.

His eye was fixed on the Inspector's desk as he spoke and his brain was working rapidly. There was an automatic on the desk, part of the evidence in the case, and it lay quite close to 'The Dude's' hand. If he could secure it there might be a chance to hold up Greig and Peter Martin and escape from the office.

His hand moved swiftly and, in a moment, he was on his feet, and backing towards the door with the automatic levelled at the detective. Inspector Greig merely smiled, for the weapon was not loaded. Peter did not know this. Ignoring danger, he sprang at 'The Dude.' His right fist made contact with stunning force with the crook's right eye.

'The Dude' pulled the trigger of the automatic, but no report sounded. He went staggering about the room, blundering into the desk, and bumping his head against the Inspector's hat rack. His right eye was closed and rapidly swelling. His left eye was wide open, and the monocle was still in it, but despite of that he did not seem able to see at all. To all appearances he was blind.

Peter was the first to sense the truth. "Good Lord, Chief," he exclaimed. "That monocle is only a fake! He's got a—"

Without the camouflage of the monocle the truth was obvious. 'The Dude' had a glass eye in his left socket! He had worn the monocle to disguise the difference between his two eyes, genuine and false.

'The Dude' shrugged his shoulders philosophically. He saw that the game was up. He put up his hands, lifted his eyelid and slipped out the glass eye. Behind in the socket gleamed the Lavery diamond!

Later Peter Martin and Madge Evans were left alone in Inspector Greig's office while the Inspector made his report to the Chief Commissioner.

"I can't quite understand," said Peter, after a while, "why you held me up and locked me in that cupboard. Why on earth didn't you explain who you were and save all that trouble?"

Madge smiled gently. "You wouldn't have believed me," she replied. "Remember, I had nothing to prove my identity. You would have taken me to Scotland Yard for investigation, and they might not have believed my story at the Yard either. I had my eye on the reward for the recovery of the diamond and I simply hadn't any time to waste, so I put you in the cupboard and hoped that I'd get the chance to apologise and explain afterwards."

Peter was thoughtful. "It was you, of course, who released me at Mother Dawson's and gave me the revolver?" he said.

The girl nodded. "Yes; then I beat it for help as quickly as I could," she replied. "When I came back with Inspector Greig and a squad of detectives you were gone. It took us hours to trace the big Hispano you had gone in. Somebody in the neighbourhood of the bungalow heard the shots and 'phoned Scotland Yard direct, so we came right out, to be in at the death."

Peter sighed. "I think you're wonderful," he murmured.

THE END

THE SECOND BOTTLE

THAT WAS A COLD hard winter and I'm the boy that knew it. The river was frozen solid; you looked down from the bridges and saw the ore barges, gripped tight by the ice and stuck fast there, waiting for the first spring thaw. That year they had a long wait. The wind went through you like a knife and so did the looks they gave you, the people of the town, when they saw you were a stranger. They didn't have jobs enough for their own and it was a cinch they didn't have a job for you. You can't write home for money when the only home you can remember is an orphanage. When you graduate from one of those places, boy, you're on your own. When I got real hungry, I pawned my overcoat for two bucks. That was asking for pneumonia, a cold hard winter like that, but I was a kid at the time, and when you're a kid and you're hungry you gotta eat, that's all there is to it, you gotta eat.

I went into this diner. It wasn't much, a hole in the wall. And ain't this a laugh: I had two bucks in my pocket, but I was cold, so hungry, I couldn't get the words out when the Greek asked what I wanted to eat. I just sat there, shaking all over, opening and shutting my mouth and not a word coming out.

The Greek gave me a hard look and I figured he was going to bounce me out on my ear. I tried to tell him, "It's okay, I've got money," but the words wouldn't come. He kept looking at me, and after a while, I saw he wasn't sore anymore.

"Hungry?" he said; and I couldn't even answer that. All I could do was nod.

"I been hungry, too," he said.

Believe it or not, he set me up a hamburger and a cup of java. While I ate, he kept looking at me, and soon he said maybe he had a job for me. Did I ever work in a restaurant? He asked. I said I had been a dishwasher for a spell and a busboy for another spell. He said his night counterman had quit on him. Not much of a job, they didn't do much business at night, but at least a guy could eat.

"A buck a night and meals," he said, "and you work from ten until three in the morning. How's about it?"

I didn't kiss him but I sure did feel like it. So, then he gave me another hamburger and more java and told me the other side of the picture. The catch was that the night chef was a sonuvagun to work with. He didn't like nobody and he made no bones about it.

"You gotta keep out of his kitchen," said the Greek. "You gotta keep out of his way if you don't want no trouble."

"I don't want no trouble," I said.

"Then don't bother him," said the Greek. "Keep away from him. Shout your orders through the hatch and don't get in his way."

I said, "I won't get in his way," and, believe me, I meant it. Well, it wasn't ten yet, but I went behind the counter and started working, figuring the sooner I learned the ropes, the better. The Greek stuck around until midnight, until he saw I'd got the hang of things, and then he told me goodnight and went home.

There wasn't nothing to it. Only, you got lonely. Some of the time you'd have two or three guys sitting on the stools, reading papers and smoking cigarettes and drinking java and eating hamburgers or scrambled eggs; and some of the time you'd have one lone cabdriver killing time, waiting for a call; but most of the time you had the place to yourself. Just you behind the counter and the sonuvagun of a night chef out there in the kitchen. And, I'm telling you, it got lonely.

*

Along about two-thirty the place was empty, then in came this old man and humped himself up on a stool at the back. He was pretty shabby, but he wasn't a bum. There was a kinda funny look about him, but I couldn't figure out what was wrong. He kept touching his coat, high up, on the left side, as if he had something hidden there and wanted to be sure it was still there.

He said, "Coffee," and I brought it to him. I noticed his hands. They kept shaking, and when he picked up the spoon it tinkled on the side of the cup. And then I got a whiff of his breath and it was enough to knock you down. So, I thought to myself, that's what it is, that's why he looks so funny, that's why he's got the shakes; he's plastered, he's cockeyed.

I walked down to the window to see if it was raining. Ten times in an hour I'd walked over to the window to see if it was raining; it helped to pass the time. This time it *was* raining, and I thought to myself, I'm going to get wet as hell if it don't stop before we close up. When I walked back along the counter, I saw that the old man was all hunched up over his java and he was crying as if his heart would break.

The way I am now, if I see someone crying, I look the other way. I leave them cry. It don't matter who, a little child, an old woman, even my own mother—if I'd know her if I saw her. I leave them to cry. But this is before I learned my lesson. I was young. I was soft. I saw this old man crying into his java and it made me feel like crying too. I went over to him to see if maybe I could help.

Do you know what hell looks like? It's black and cold and a long way down with no bottom to it. I know, because I've seen it. I saw it in that old man's eyes. He looked at me like he didn't even see me. There was hell staring out of his eyes and I felt the flesh crawling all the way up my back.

"She had it coming," he said. "She asked for it. A man's got a right to take a drink once in a while. She'd got no call to nag at me the way she did."

He was staring at me, and I had to say something, but I didn't know what to say.

"She'll get over it," I mumbled. "Maybe by the time you go back she'll be over it already."

"She won't ever get over it," he said. "This time I fixed her good."

I looked back over my shoulder, to see if someone had opened the door. All of a sudden there was a draft of cold air in the place. But the door was shut.

"She's lying back there, on the floor, with half her head blown off," said the old man. "You could go and holler in her ear, but she wouldn't stir. I know. I tried. I hollered in her ear, but she never moved a muscle."

He looked at me again and I got another glimpse of hell. He was in agony, he was on fire, he was burning up inside. The tears were running down his cheeks, but his eyes were black and cold, like ice. And I knew he wasn't kidding. I could tell this wasn't a pipedream. She had kept nagging at him, and this time he had fixed her good.

And then I noticed this bulge, like there was something in his breast pocket. He kept touching it to make sure it was still there. All of a sudden, I knew what it was. It was a gun. It was the gun he had killed her with.

"I don't want to go back there," he said in a whimpering

voice. "She's lying there, on the floor. I don't want to go back. I don't want to look at her."

*

I took two steps back and that brought me to the kitchen door. I took another step back and I was inside. I heard a sound like a snarl and looked round—and there was the sonuvagun of a chef glaring at me. He looked sore enough to stick me with the long knife he had in his hand.

"Get the hell out of my kitchen," he said; and he meant right now.

"Look," I said. "There's a crazy guy out there. He's got a gun."

"Don't give me no lip," said the chef, scowling and taking a step forward. "Get the hell out."

I went back where I came from, and the old man was still there, crying. He looked at me as if he didn't like me, as if he was sorry for what he'd told me. And I thought to myself, He's got a gun. Maybe he'll fix me so I can't tell anyone else. It was so cold I was shivering, and yet the sweat was bursting out on my face and hands.

And then the door opened and a cop came in. I was never so glad to see anyone in my life. His uniform was glistening with rain. He didn't look at the old man. He humped himself onto a stool and clapped his arms together to warm himself.

"Java and sinkers," he said.

When I brought them, half the java was in the saucer.

"Clumsy," he said. "New man?" he said. "Ain't seen you around before."

I wanted to tell him, "This is my first night here, and if I get out alive it'll be my last," but I didn't know what the old man would do if I opened my mouth. I didn't want the old man to get nervous and start shooting. I brought the cop a clean saucer and when I put it down, I winked at him out of the eye that was farthest from the old man. He stared at me and then he winked back. He poured the java into the clean saucer and blew on it to cool it.

"Dirty night," he said, and put the saucer to his mouth.

I looked at the old man and his heads turned the other way. I looked at the cop and jerked my head toward where the old man was sitting. I tried to make signs to show him that the old man was dangerous. But this was a dumb cop. He stared at the old man and shrugged his shoulders. He looked at me like he didn't get it, like I was crazy. He emptied the saucer into his big mouth and poured more java into it.

"What's the matter?" he asked. "You got the jumps?"

And then the old man got up and walked along the counter. He'd got those cold black empty eyes fixed on the both of us, and they were still running with tears. I shut my own eyes tight. If the old man pulled his gun, I didn't want to see it. If I had to take it, I'd take it with my eyes shut. And then I heard the tinkle of a coin on the counter and the door opening and shutting.

I opened my eyes and the old man was gone. From the window I could see him lurching through the rain. I grabbed the cop's arm, spilling java all down his front.

"The old guy," I said breathlessly.

"Old Man Kelly," said the cop. And now he was sore. He was mopping up the java with a paper napkin and glaring at me. He thought I was a screwball. "Old Man Kelly," he said again. "What about him?"

"He—he killed a woman."

"Sure," said the cop. "His wife." He said it as if that made it alright. "He shot her through the head."

"You know?" I shouted, and my eyes popped out. "You know—and you let him walk out of here like nothing happened?"

"He killed her twenty years ago," said the cop, "and did fifteen years in the state pen for it."

"The way he talked—" I said, still trembling all over.

"Old Man Kelly is a two-bottle man," said the cop. "With the first bottle, he gets a crying jag on and thinks she's lying back there with her head blown away, waiting for him to come home. When he finishes the second bottle, he don't give a damn."

"But he's got a gun. I saw the bulge."

"That was no gun," said the cop. He pushed his cup over for me to fill it again. "That was the second bottle."

THE END

Coming Soon from Moonstone Press

Printed in Great Britain
by Amazon

51477818R00169